A Fine Day for a Drive

RICK COGBILL

To Paul & Jackie!

[signature]

SlimCookie Productions

A Division of Cogbill Management Services Ltd.

Summerland, British Columbia

This book is a work of fiction. References to real people, events, establishments, organizations, or locales are intended only to provide a sense of authenticity and are used fictitiously. All other characters, and all incidents and dialogue, are drawn from the author's imagination and are not to be construed as real.

A FINE DAY FOR A DRIVE

Copyright © 2009 by Rick Cogbill
Published by SlimCookie Productions
Box 1153, Summerland, BC V0H 1Z0 Canada
www.thecarside.com

Cover Illustration by Ben Crane
www.bencrane.com

Book Design by Lorraine LaPham
The Peach Workshop
lorrainelapham@gmail.com

Library and Archives Canada Cataloguing in Publication

Cogbill, Rick, 1956-
A fine day for a drive / Rick Cogbill.

Includes index.
ISBN 978-0-9813430-0-6

I. Title.

PS8605.O3395F56 2009   C813'.6   C2009-906038-8

ISBN 978-0-9813430-0-6

Printed in Canada

*In memory of Clara May Cogbill
– one of "God's special angels sent down to earth."
Your life of patience, love, and graciousness still continues to
inspire, especially those who had the privilege of calling you
"Mom."*

A NOTE OF THANKS...

To my wife Nan, and our children Sarah, Laura, and Steven – together you have made my life unbelievably "Fine." These stories live because of you.

To Will Enns, who took a creative writing class in night school and then craftily used it to get me hooked on writing. Buck Pincher could not have a better role model...

To Allan Janssen, the courageous editor who took on The Car Side column when I first suggested it over a decade ago...it's been a true pleasure working with you all these years.

To Pat Massey, Erna Schram, Nan Cogbill, Will Enns, and Sarah Hawkes for providing excellent feedback and editing advice. Thanks for taking the time to read this manuscript over and over and over again!

To the late Len Rich who, along with other members of WACO (Writers Across Canada Online), encouraged me to pursue my writing in those early years. I hope the fishing's good on the other side, my friend.

To the folks at Newcom Business Media, especially Jim Glionna (President), Martyn Johns (Publisher), and David Menzies (Editor) for not only hosting my column, but for supporting and promoting this book as well.

Chapters at a glance

FOREWORD

Rick Cogbill makes me laugh.

That might sound obvious, given that he's a humour columnist. But I've come to learn in almost 20 years of editing that few humour columnists are consistently funny. And when they are, they're not laugh-out-loud funny. They're just knowing-smile kind of funny. A select few are nod-and-chuckle kind of funny. Only the very best are spit-out-your-coffee kind of funny. That's Rick.

When he proposed a humour column for Canadian Technician magazine, promising that it would be both entertaining and informative, I was skeptical. People told me it couldn't be done. And even if it could be done, it couldn't last. But Rick and his whacky band of characters have been making me spit out my morning coffee since 1998. You should see my office!

Yes, the situations he describes are ridiculous…but they're also rooted in a strange kind of reality and are populated with a cast of characters that people can truly relate to. The well-meaning apprentice who has to learn everything the hard way. The grizzled old mechanic who's seen it all. The blue-collar philosopher who surprises you with a fresh perspective on things.

There are no villains in Slumberland. Everyone has redeeming qualities. Even the customer who twists the truth to earn a discount, and the supplier who feigns ignorance about a duplicate bill. Slim Shambles – Rick's alter ego – faces them all with weary grace.

The humour comes from a good place. Like most writers, Rick has genuine affection for his characters. He knows them. He's had coffee with them – many, many coffees – and he tells their stories with a mixture of frankness and fancy. That his columns have been so well received is no surprise to me. He speaks lovingly of a profession that does not always get its due. Rick casts a warm light on the shadowy corners of the auto repair industry to reveal the heroic characters who are meeting life one broken car at a time.

Now I learn that his columns were just a taste of his unique imagination. The full meal – a veritable smorgasbord of fun and adventure – is here, in *A Fine Day for a Drive*. There is a bigger cast of characters and their playground has expanded beyond the walls of Slim Shambles Auto Repair. Those of us who have been waiting patiently to learn more about Slim's back story, and about life in Slumberland, have already tucked our napkins and are ready to dig in.

This is a laugh-out-loud book that celebrates the believably absurd. Slim Shambles rides the lead car as grand marshal in life's giant parade of fools. And I, for one, will gladly take my spot on the sidewalk to watch Basil, Tooner, Beanie, and the rest of the gang pratfall past.

— *Allan Janssen*
  Editorial Director, Canadian Technician *magazine*

PREFACE

This book began a long, long time ago...I just didn't know it.

Who would have thought that my childhood, my years spent as a mechanic and shop owner, my experiences in Africa, or even my courtship with my wife would all combine into a collection of humorous stories that would bring about a few moments of comic relief to our sometimes cumbersome existence.

It's a good reminder that a lot of the "stuff" we find ourselves going through at the present will one day (hopefully) become the memories we can laugh at. It kind of puts it all back into perspective – as the Good Book says, "*A merry heart doeth good like a medicine...*"

That being said, let me get one thing straight – this is a work of fiction. The stories you are about to read take place in Slumberland, a fictitious town on the western shores of the equally fictitious Hollownoggin Lake, located in the *obviously* fictitious Hollownoggin Valley, in southern British Columbia, Canada (okay, Canada is a real place...I'll give you that much).

However...there is a pervasive rumour that *A Fine Day for a Drive* is really about life in the town of *Summerland*, which is by purest coincidence located on the western shores of *Okanagan Lake*, in the *Okanagan Valley*, and also in southern British Columbia, Canada.

How preposterous.

As a resident of Summerland myself for almost 28 years, *and* as the author of this book, I should think I'd be among the first to notice any similarities. Still, the rumour persists.

So much so, that certain residents (I will call them loyal readers) have informed me that they can pick themselves out in the stories. Can you imagine? Personally, I think there's a bit of egotism involved here. What rational person would read the story of, say, David and Goliath, and then stop you on the street and exclaim, "Hey, that's me; I'm the big guy with the sword!"

As a result of this rumour, it's possible that Summerland might begin to experience an influx of the curious and the gullible, eager to see if such landmarks as Rolph's Diner, Baldy's Barber Shop, or even Hunchback Mountain really do exist. Well, these are things far beyond my control.

On the other hand, if you do happen to pay Summerland a visit, be sure to say Slim Shambles sent you – it might get you a free coffee at The Bean Dust Café.

What I will admit to is that *most* of stories you are about to read are based on actual events, either from my career as a mechanic or from my life experience as a husband and father. As to *which* events really happened…well, I'll give you a hint: real life is often more bizarre than anything we can come up with in our imagination.

I don't know of any books written about small town life from a mechanic's point of view – maybe this is the first. Mechanics like to fix things; that's why they do what they do. And if they had their way, there would be a parts store selling overhaul repair kits for whatever ails us as a society.

What my fellow technicians (and I suspect the rest of the population) need to remember is that, unfortunately, not everything in life can be fixed. Sometimes the best you can do is look for the humour in a situation, and then hang on and enjoy the ride. If singer Tom Cochrane is correct and 'Life is a highway', then having a good sense of humour will go a long way in smoothing over the bumps in anyone's road.

So here's hoping that *A Fine Day for a Drive* will brighten your day as you set out on another round of daily adventures. Happy motoring!

Rick Cogbill
Summerland, British Columbia
Canada

CHAPTER 1

∞ DON'T BANK ON IT ∞

The wall phone rang violently, knocking the receiver right out of its cradle. That's usually a bad sign.

After wiping some grease off my hands, I grabbed the swinging device and held it gingerly up to my ear. "Hello, Slim Shambles Auto Rep…"

"Slim!" bellowed a thundering voice. "My timing belt broke and my car's being towed to your shop as we speak!"

I flinched as I recognized the caller. "Okay, Henry. I'll see if I can find time…"

"You'd better find the time – I need that car!" A hard-driving businessman, Henry Crankle didn't know the meaning of waiting in line. "And don't say you warned me six months ago that the belt was due for changing."

"But…"

"And don't even *think* of suggesting that I might have caused further engine damage."

"But…"

"JUST CHANGE THAT BELT AND MAKE IT RUN!"

"Okay, but…"

"Oh yes." He lowered his voice. "I can't pay you until next month." The line went dead, leaving me little recourse except to jot Henry's name down on the already crowded appointment pad. His car was showing up whether I wanted it or not.

It's happened again, I thought glumly. *Arrested, tried, and convicted in under 30 seconds. If only Canada's criminal justice system could work this smoothly.*

Suddenly a loud crash from the front office caught my attention. Rushing in from the shop, I discovered Buck Pincher frozen in time like a deer caught in the headlights. The remains of a full pot of coffee flowed around him on the floor, mingling with shards of glass from the broken carafe. "Buck," I cried. "What's going on in here?!"

He shrugged. "Dunno. I was just pouring myself another cup of your tasteless brew when the whole pot fell to the ground. It must've had a defective handle."

I looked at his vibrating hands. "There was nothing wrong with that handle, Buck. I'd say you're in caffeine shock. That's got to be your fifth cup in the past hour."

Buck Pincher is an old friend – I use the term lightly – and that's the only reason I put up with him as a customer. Whether he's stealing my sugar cubes or breaking my equipment, he always drives away from my shop with more than he paid for. I handed him a mop from the closet. "Here, clean up your mess. I think Basil has your car ready."

Buck sniffed indignantly. "Well, it's taken long enough. As a matter of fact, it's your own fault I drank so much coffee. There's nothing else to do around this drafty hovel you call a shop."

I felt a major headache coming on as I realized once again that the hardest part of being a mechanic was not fixing the cars – it was dealing with the customers. Somewhere within that four-year stint of perdition called *Trade School* there should have been a course on conflict resolution, or in Buck's case, crisis management. But my schooling in the trade occurred during the 'Unenlightened Era,' where we were taught how to rebuild cylinder heads, not get inside the customer's head.

At that moment, the delivery truck from Herkle's Auto Parts careened into the parking lot, throwing up a cloud of dust and gravel in its wake. Herk's driver, young Rodney, threw open his door and extracted his lanky body from behind the wheel. "Hey Slim!" he hollered with a wave. "Got yer thirty cases of antifreeze here. Where d'ya want 'em?"

The hair on the back of my neck stood up as my temples began to pound. "Thirty cases! Who ordered that?" But I already knew the answer: it was month end, and Herk's sales numbers were low again. Somehow, he had the mistaken impression that I was committed to helping his parts store stay profitable. I went over to the truck. "Look, I'm only taking ten cases. Stack them in the compressor room. Then take the rest back and tell your boss to smarten up."

Basil, my technician and sole employee, came out of the shop, wiping his hands on a rag. "Are we having a difficult day?"

I sighed. "You could say that. Is Buck's car done yet? I need him out of here before he breaks something else."

Basil chuckled. "He just drove off. Apparently, we're supposed to send him the bill. He wants a discount – something about compensation for the health-damaging effects of our coffee."

I closed my eyes in defeat. "Great…just great." By now the headache had not only arrived, it had moved into the guest room and unpacked its bags. I think it planned to stay awhile.

Basil took the hint and left quietly for lunch. I didn't feel like eating so I drove a Ford pickup inside and put it up on the hoist. It needed an oil change, a nice mindless job that I could putter with in peace.

But even that turned into a chore. The truck rocked back and forth in the air above me as I wrestled with a stubborn oil filter that refused to budge. I should have been paying closer attention to what I was doing, but my mind was rehashing the furious activity of the past three months. And suddenly it hit me: what had I been thinking?

On less than a moment's notice I'd quit my job as a mechanic for a local gas station and started up my own repair shop. It had taken all of two days. On Saturday, I was a mechanic who repaired broken down cars. But by Monday morning I'd become a shop owner who repaired broken down cars *and* who'd spent his life savings to put his name above the door for all litigating lawyers to see and file for future reference.

Suddenly the filter came loose and hot oil gushed over my arm and onto the floor. I danced around the service bay, hollering my disapproval for all to hear. But I didn't get a lick of sympathy – just the sound of my own voice echoing back at me.

"Time for a break," I muttered, wiping my arm with a rag. A cup of coffee would have been nice right about then, but thanks to Buck Pincher that wasn't going to happen. I went to the small fridge we kept in the corner and took out a soft drink. It was a good thing we didn't keep anything stronger on the premises.

I sank into a squeaky office chair that'd been welded back together four times, and took stock of my new surroundings. The rented steel frame building was clad with sheets of corrugated metal. It wasn't the classiest structure, but it held three cars inside and kept most of the rain out. In one corner, a four-post above-ground hoist supported the truck I was servicing. Around the walls stood the typical array of battered equipment you'd find in any automotive repair shop, including a floor jack, some safety stands, a battery charger, and an antique bench grinder.

My landlord, Dutchy Smits, ran a towing company across the street in a similar steel building – he seemed to have a penchant for them. Dutchy gave me the royal tour the day I moved in. "Ja, and in here is the compressor," he declared, opening a side door into a small room dimly illuminated by a low wattage light bulb. "You will take good care of this, ja? It came from Europe."

I stared at the strange looking contraption. With its gaggle of pipes and cooling fins projecting in every direction, it looked like something out of a Jules Verne fantasy novel. But I held my tongue. For all his gruffness, Dutchy offended easily.

Surrounded by cases of engine oil (and now antifreeze), the ancient compressor rattled away as it supplied moist air to my air guns and ratchets, ensuring an early demise to their usefulness as tools. I made a mental note to stock up on more air tool oil.

In the middle of the shop stood my pride and joy – a rolling red tool cabinet brimming with tools of every size and description. Foundational to my existence as a professional mechanic, it represented years of careful and deliberate purchasing decisions based on the multi-faceted demands of my chosen profession. My wife blames it more on the multi-faceted talents of the tool salesman. To me, my tool cab was indispensable. To Cookie, it was just a money pit.

My office consisted of a small wooden addition off to one side of the larger shop, with enough room for a battered desk, a few chairs, and a coffee table. The dusty front window revealed a glorious view of Slumberland's industrial area.

I leaned back in my chair as the welds groaned in protest. Yes sir, this was to be my kingdom and I the supreme ruler. Self-employment meant that I could be the proverbial master of my own destiny, the undisputed captain of my ship. My repair facility would become second to none, where motorists from far and wide would flock to have their vehicles serviced under my expert care. No one would question my judgments; none would balk at my modest fees. But today that dream was starting to unravel. Like I said, what had I been thinking?

Just then the jangling of the telephone pierced the air. The throbbing behind my eyeballs sent out warning signals in Morse code, but thankfully it wasn't another demanding customer: it was the voice of my wife. "Hi honey," Cookie said cheerfully. "How's it going?"

I glanced down at my scalded right arm. "Oh, same as always," I replied. "What's up?"

"Just calling to remind you that you have an appointment with the bank in five minutes."

I jumped up from my chair, promptly breaking one of the welds. "Yikes, I forgot! Thanks for reminding me." Slamming the phone into its cradle, I wrestled out of my coveralls and then ran for the steel sink in the corner of the shop. The various cuts and scraped knuckles screamed in protest as I attacked my hands with a gritty hand-cleaner, but I needed to look presentable. It was time to see my banker about an equipment loan.

Fortunately, Basil had just returned from his lunch break. "Watch the shop until I get back!" I yelled, running out the door. "I'm late for the bank!"

Basil waved nonchalantly. He rarely got excited over things the way I did.

I jumped into my rusty GMC pickup and headed for town. Like most guys starting out in business, I was using my own hand tools and some second-hand shop equipment bought with my meager savings. But it was the early 1990's, and the new vehicles coming out of Detroit at that time were making the changeover to computerized fuel injection. It was the beginning of the end for the carburetor, and as cantankerous as those gas-guzzling devices could be at times, it was a little unsettling to see them being phased out so quickly.

It was bad enough when the Big Three began introducing electronic ignition systems in the mid 1970's. Now we mechanics were hearing strange words like *On-board Computers* and *Mass Air Flow Sensors*, exotic new creations dreamed up in the name of progress by nerdy engineering types who lived in little cubicles above the factory floors.

As a result, every mechanic I knew was slogging through extra training courses at night and on weekends, just to keep up with the changes. On top of that, we needed new diagnostic equipment, and that meant one thing – bring money and lots of it. Hence my trip to the bank.

A quick glance at my reflection in the glass doors of the bank lobby revealed nothing seriously out of place. On the surface I didn't look too bad, but there's a problem with working on cars for a living: your clothing, if not your very skin, often reeks of dirty oil fumes and raw gasoline. No doubt the bank secretary smelled me coming long before I arrived at her desk. She wrinkled her nose and looked up. "May I help you?"

Swallowing hard, I hid my work-stained hands behind my back. "Yes, I'm Slim Shambles and I'm here to see the bank manager about a business loan. I have an appointment."

The secretary scanned her book and grimaced. "Oh yes, here it is. Mr. Shambles...the mechanic." She got up briskly. "Please follow me." At that moment, my work boots caught her attention. She dropped her voice to a whisper. "Ah, we'll be going upstairs."

I glanced around in confusion, wondering at the secrecy. I whispered back, "Uh, yeah?"

She leaned closer. "There's carpet upstairs."

"Uh…okay."

She glanced significantly down at my feet again, and I finally got the message. It's a curse of the trade; we are judged by the stains we leave behind.

In the end, the secretary and I came to a mutual understanding, and I suddenly found myself within an expansive office, standing on the subordinate side of an antique oak desk. A black ebony nameplate on one corner spelled out the words *Lewis Change, Bank Manager*. The gold lettering was impressive, and so was Lewis.

"Mr. Shambles, how good to meet you!" Well-dressed and portly, Lewis stood and reached across his desk to shake my hand. Then he paused. "Excuse me, but why are you holding your shoes?"

"It's a long story," I replied. "Would you like me to set them down somewhere? You know, in case I have to sign some important papers or something?"

Lewis took a couple of tentative sniffs and shook his head. "No, no, on your lap will be fine." We both took our seats. "Now, what can I do for you?"

I explained the whole situation, sticking to the basic facts as much as possible. If there's one thing I can't stand in my own business, it's when a client tries to coerce me into giving them what they want. "And did I mention that I've been a client here for ten years?" I asked.

"Three times," said Lewis, frown lines creasing his expansive forehead as he scanned my file. "It says here you have never missed a loan payment."

I brightened hopefully. "Yes sir! I'm glad to see we're on the same page."

Lewis tapped the file folder with his finger. "We're not, really. From what you are telling me, some significant changes have recently occurred in your financial situation." He made a notation on my file and peered at me over his glasses. "As of this minute, even your personal line of credit has been revoked."

My mouth dropped open. "Revoked? But...but why?! What's changed?"

Lewis folded his hands and settled back into his black leather chair. "Allow me to explain. Three months ago, you were an employee of another company. But now, you are self-employed." He clucked his tongue and shook his head in mock sadness. "That makes you a serious credit risk."

Like clouds parting on an overcast winter's day, my financial outlook became amazingly clear – it had sunk to cold and bleak. "But what difference should that make?" I protested. "It'll be the same *me* making the payments!" I sank back in my own chair. Without that new equipment, my ability to service newer vehicles was doubtful. I needed this loan badly. "If my personal credit is no good, then what do you want?"

Lewis cleared his throat as he inspected the cuticles of his left hand. "The bank requires three years of financial statements showing the viability of your business before we can lend you any funds." He paused. "Oh yes, and don't forget the co-signers and your first-born child."

My mouth dropped open, and my headache, which had been taking a short nap, now woke up screaming for attention. Perhaps that's why I responded the way I did.

Leaping to my feet, I dropped my boots and hollered, "You want me to produce three years of statements when I've only been in business for three months? I thought fraud was a crime!"

Lewis was not used to dealing with irate customers, an obvious indication that he'd never repaired cars for a living. The appointment was over and he showed me the door without so much as a friendly handshake. My only consolation was in knowing that two greasy black boot marks awaited him, should he ever decide to inspect the white carpet on the other side of his desk.

Back at the shop, Basil could read the results on my face. "Hmm," he said. "No luck at the bank, I presume?"

"Not a penny's worth," I fumed.

He picked up a sticky note from my desk and handed it to me. "Dutchy towed in Henry's car while you were out – something about a broken timing belt."

I scanned Dutchy's messy penmanship. 'Slim – Henry needs a new timing belt, ja? I told him it wouldn't be more than a hundred bucks, so don't get greedy. P.S. Remember – the rent is due on Friday.'

I don't mind it when Dutchy pre-diagnoses the vehicles he tows in. What drives me nuts, though, is the price quote he gives the customer before I've even see the car.

Basil took pity on me. "Look, have a coffee," he suggested. "I picked up a new carafe at the store during my lunch hour, and I've just brewed a new pot." He reached for his jacket. "I'll be back in a few minutes." Without another word, he climbed into his old Fiat and headed downtown. Knowing Basil, I figured he was making a donut run. Comfort food wasn't a bad idea at a time like this.

I glanced at the coffeepot. Repair shop java can be potent stuff, often strong enough to peel paint. But fresh, deep-fried, sugar-saturated donuts go a long way in detoxifying the brew, so I decided to wait until Basil returned.

Sitting back gingerly in my chair, hoping the remaining welds would hold up, I wondered if I could still get my old job back down at the gas station. I could picture the phone call now…

"Oh hi, Barry, Slim Shambles here…Yes, I'm sure it's a surprise to hear from me…Say, I was wondering if I could get my old job back… Ah, what's that?…Yeah, I realize I left because you were turning the shop into a convenience store…Well, no, it's not that I'm desperate… well, maybe a little desperate…yes, I could work for half my former wages…sure, I can stock shelves…yes, I know I sound like an idiot…"

I shuddered. Would it really come to that? Rummaging through my desk drawer, I found a bottle of aspirin. My headache recoiled in fear, aghast that I would even think of chasing an old friend out the door without so much as a 'see you later.' But I was past caring.

Across the road, Dutchy was peering down at me from his office window. No doubt he was wondering why I hadn't started on Henry's car yet. I groaned in despair. So much for my vision of the perfect automotive repair shop. Far from being the captain of my ship, I felt like a galley slave on somebody else's barge.

I was still sitting there feeling sorry for myself when Basil returned, whistling cheerfully as he came through the door. "I see you found the bakery," I said, referring to the brown paper bag clutched under one arm.

"I did indeed," he replied. "But I've got something else for you first."

I took the envelope he held out and opened it. It was a bank draft for $15,000 – the exact amount of the loan I'd been after. "What's this?" I gasped. "Did you rob the bank?"

"Not exactly," he chuckled. "I simply arranged a little creative financing." He rummaged through the bag for a cream-filled long john. "On the way back from the bakery," he mumbled between bites, "I stopped by the bank and took out a loan. You can make the payments."

I stared at the bank draft. "You got a loan that quickly? But what did you tell them?"

He shrugged. "I merely said I wanted some money to buy equipment to use in my new job at Slim Shambles Auto Repair. They handed me a pen and said, 'Sign here.'"

"Just like that?" I was astounded. "So let me get this straight – the bank knows you wanted the money to buy the same thing I wanted to buy, right?" Basil nodded cheerfully. "Then why'd they give *you* the money, but not me?"

"I'm not self-employed," replied Basil smugly. "*I* work for *you.*"

That didn't make any sense. Everybody knows that if times get tough, it's the employees who get laid off, not the owners. But then, that's bankers' logic for you.

As for me, the teeth of this gift horse had been examined long enough: it was time to ride the nag. So I stashed the bank draft in the cash box and then dialed the number for the tool salesman.

"Oh, by the way," Basil added. "Lewis says to call him when we get the new equipment. He wants his car to be the first to try it out."

Kicking my headache out the front door and tossing its bags after it, I made a mental note to order up a new adding machine as well, one with lots of zeros. I would need it to calculate my special repair rate for bankers.

Suddenly my little three-bay shop in the middle of Slumberland's industrial park didn't seem so bad. *Maybe, just maybe*, I thought, *I'll get to be the captain of this ship after all.*

CHAPTER 2

A SLIM VIEW ON GARDENING

My breath came in ragged gasps as I scaled the last one hundred torturous yards up Hunchback Mountain. Advancing one handhold at a time, I searched desperately for any crack or crevice where my bleeding fingers and scuffed hiking boots could find purchase. Experts scoff that the climb doesn't compare with Everest, or even Kilimanjaro, but it was certainly testing my own personal limits of endurance.

The limits of my patience were also under attack, as packs of bratty little kids kicked gravel in my face as they scooted past me. "Hey, you should be more careful on this treacherous goat trail," I yelled after them. "Somebody could get hurt!"

"Goat trail?" One chubby kid stopped and looked around at the well-marked and recently graded pathway. "They must be pretty big goats, mister."

And if that wasn't bad enough, their mothers were downright rude, snickering loudly as they waited for me to roll out of the way so they could amble by with their strollers and picnic baskets.

But that's Slumberlanders for you: they're made of tough stuff. I wasn't born here, and it's an excuse I'm sticking with.

Clawing my way to the flagpole that projected skyward from the very pinnacle of the ancient volcanic formation, I dragged myself upright and paused to catch my breath. It was a clear day and to the east, I could see Hollownoggin Lake sparkling like a blue jewel in the late morning sun. Twenty feet south of where I stood, the ground ended abruptly. A sheer rock face dropped nine hundred feet straight down into a patchwork quilt of orchards and vineyards that spread out around the entire base of the mountain. Squinting northward, I could make out downtown Slumberland. Only four blocks long, Main Street looked very small from way up here.

But the primary reason I'd made this perilous hike wasn't to scan the four points of the compass – rather it was to look down. Dropping to my hands and knees, I left the safety of the flagpole and inched my way over the rocky ground to where a metal handrail skirted the precipice. Gripping it tightly, I inched my way upright and peeked over the edge. Directly below me lay Slumberland's small industrial park, and more importantly, the location of my brand new business. Far, far below, the metal roof of Slim Shambles Auto Repair glinted in the morning sun. The sight of it made my chest swell with pride. It also gave me a nosebleed.

"Hey mister!" bawled a scrawny youngster swinging nonchalantly from the handrail beside me. "Whatcha looking at?"

"That's my shop," I said, pointing it out to him.

He leaned over the railing and squinted at the collection of buildings. "Which one? Can ya point to it?"

"I am," I hissed through tightly clenched teeth.

He looked at my white-knuckled fingers tenaciously gripping the handrail. "No you're not."

"Follow my left ear, kid. What's the matter, are you blind?"

He backed away and ran to find his mother. "Hey mom," he hollered. "Look at the weird man. He can wiggle his ears!"

His mother shushed him. "He's not weird, Dilbert," I heard her say. "He's probably just afraid of heights. Maybe he's not from here."

Those words sent a wave of panic through me far greater than my fear of heights. In Slumberland, any variation of the phrase 'he's not from here' could mark you as a stranger who couldn't be trusted. It could also be the death knell for any up and coming business.

It's not that newcomers aren't accepted here. Let's just say that not everyone can pass the entrance exams. New business ventures are especially vulnerable to wild speculation by the locals who hunker down inside Rolph's Diner with their morning coffees.

"Hey, Rolph, did ya see the new hardware store that just opened up on Main Street?"

"Yeah, I did, Earl. Wonder how long it'll survive?"

"Dunno. The owner ain't from here. If he makes it three years, mebbe I'll stop by and see what he's got for fishing gear."

"Three years? Don't be in such a rush, Earl – he could be one of them fly-by-nighters!"

"Hmm, guess yer right, Rolph. It was four years before I came in to try out yer coffee."

"Four and a half actually…but who's counting. Wanna refill?"

Earl looked at his cup and grimaced. "Not really…"

Not to brag, but I was smarter than most newcomers: when I moved to Slumberland I married a local girl. Not only did I find a good wife, but that act alone shortened my probationary period by decades. I know this because by our 10th wedding anniversary most folks had stopped referring to Cookie by her maiden name.

Still, having not grown up here, I was quite naïve when we bought our house. Nestled in a quiet neighborhood, it was surrounded on all sides by beautifully manicured lawns and dazzling flowerbeds. It's too bad for the neighbors that I didn't notice those obvious and glaring flaws right away.

It's a neighborhood comprised mainly of retirees with Masters Degrees in horticulture, along with a light smattering of gardening nuts. How I as a young husband and father with small children was allowed to move in still remains a mystery.

I suppose the bankruptcy sale had something to do with it. As Real Estate Eddy pointed out, the damage inflicted upon the house and yard by the now-evicted tenants had reduced it to an eyesore, an obvious blight on the reputation of the neighborhood. Any change in ownership was bound to be viewed as an improvement. Or so the neighbors thought.

The ink was barely dry on the purchase agreement when they began arriving in small groups, eagerly bearing gifts. But instead of baskets of freshly baked muffins or canned preserves, they brought lawn seed, plant cuttings, and donations of shovels and rakes. "If there's anything you need, just holler," they hinted excitedly. Billy Rose, an eighty-year-old gentleman with tears in his eyes, just kept patting me on the back and mumbling, "Bless you, son…bless you."

As soon as we moved in, I went to work on the yard. The former tenants had discovered that tossing garbage over the handrail of the sun deck was easier and cheaper than paying for weekly garbage pickup. By now the pile of rotting trash was higher than the deck itself. So the first hand tool I rented was a backhoe.

Once the final truckload of garbage, dead shrubs, and old car bodies rumbled off down the street, I turned my attention to bigger things, like retaining walls and a second deck in the backyard. Out of the corner of my eye, I could see the neighbors across the street peeking out happily from behind their living room curtains. One old couple danced a jig on their front lawn, kicking up their heels in obvious delight. I even saw a pair of gardeners two houses away toasting me with champagne over the back fence.

It really was a shame, getting their hopes up and all. Occupying myself with hammers, boards, and cement was only putting off the inevitable – sooner or later I would have to plant something.

The big things, like retaining walls, wooden decks, and barbecue pits, are right up my alley. After all, Pa Shambles had been a carpenter all his life, so I grew up around construction sites. Moreover, I'd spent all my spare hours as a kid in his workshop at home, building stuff out of scrap wood. I didn't get straight C's in Wood Shop for nothing.

No, it's the little things, the living things, like plants, grass – for that matter, full-grown trees – that give me a hard time. My thumb isn't green by any means. In fact, my friend Buck Pincher uses a different color to describe my gardening abilities.

"Slim," he observed from one of my lawn chairs, "the U.S. Army should have dropped you from a chopper in 'Nam. They would have saved a fortune on Agent Orange." He drained his glass of iced tea as he watched me massacre a flat of annuals my father-in-law had dropped off that morning. "With you on the front lines, the enemy would've had nothing to hide behind."

"It's not my fault," I growled, staring at the small plants and wondering which way was up. "These things don't come with any instructions." In fact, it is my firm belief that all plants should include a 30-day warranty. It would save me a ton of money, as the mortality rate in my garden is high to extreme. Cookie has posted a sign above the door of my garden shed that reads, "Nothing Green This Way Cometh."

She's half-right. The plants come in green; they just don't leave that way.

The other day my neighbor called me over. Mrs. Bloome was wearing a flowered print dress and sporting a large straw hat decorated with fresh daisies and dried vines. She thrust her gloved hands across the fence in my direction.

"Here you are, Slim," she declared, handing me a vibrant, thriving specimen from her prizewinning Garden of Eden. "You just put that in your flowerbed over there, next to that, er…dry stick, or whatever it is." She squinted at my petrified peach tree.

I smiled politely and took the plant from her hands. "Gee thanks, Mrs. Bloome. You've left the dirt on it and everything. That should make it safe."

She looked at me quizzically. "Safe? Land sakes, young man, with that thing you don't need to be safe. Been trying to kill it for years and I can't get rid of it!"

"Oh." The little creeper was already starting to wither. I took it over and buried it next to the other dead plants in my collection.

She tried to peer over my shoulder. "Now what did you do with those strawberry plants I gave you last fall? Did you plant them in your rockery like I suggested?"

I shifted my weight, trying to hide the shriveled runners dangling from the rocks. "Uh, we moved them to the other side of the house," I lied. It would have been heartless to tell her that under my tender care, the plants had produced berries so vile even the slugs wouldn't touch them.

To make matters worse, my own dog is against me. Buddy is a sable and white Sheltie who spends his days by the fence discussing plant husbandry with Mrs. Bloome. Then he has the gall to wander in around dinnertime and offer unwanted advice on weed control and lawn fertilization. To listen to him, you'd almost believe that having lush green grass is something he really cares about. But he doesn't fool me for a minute.

I can't prove it yet, but I suspect that the backstabbing scoundrel rounds up his neighborhood buddies during the night for the sole purpose of 'fertilizing' parts of my lawn with their own potent mixture. The placement of the burnt yellow patches is strategically planned – always in the middle of the lawn where everyone can see them.

In an effort to curtail this obnoxious behavior, I got up early one morning and followed the gang's trail of paw prints in the dew. I had words with Odie, Jake, Tina, and Biscuit, but none of them would confess. The only one who would sing was Max, two doors down. But he never stops yapping, so it's hard to believe anything he says.

In order to contribute to my neighborhood's fascination with living things, I've had to settle on the one flower type that actually flourishes under my care. I am proud to say that it exists in my yard, and in my yard alone: I give you…the dandelion.

The name *dandelion* is a variation of the old French term, *dent de lion*, a noble phrase meaning 'Lion's Tooth.' However, my neighbors don't seem to share my enthusiasm. They prefer the more modern French name *pissenlit*, which means 'urinate in bed.'

Nevertheless, to me this lowly plant has become a thing of beauty, if not a passion. In fact, I have no doubts that in Slumberland the dandelion would now be extinct were it not for my ardent efforts to ensure its survival.

The sunny yellow blooms, the deep green leaves, the majestic stalks waving in the gentle breeze – all these have combined to fill my otherwise drab yard with vibrant color and texture. And the best part is, I don't even have to water them. Better yet, after mowing off the tops I'm left with a verdant carpet of lush foliage that completely hides the arid, brown stubble of my lawn.

Last year I announced to Mrs. Bloome that I would be entering a large bouquet of dandelions in the Slumberland Fall Fair. "I think I've got a fair chance at a blue ribbon, don't you?" She was a little tongue-tied at the time, so I don't know if she agreed with me or not. But the very next morning every dandelion stalk was keeled over, deep in the throes of death. A postmortem confirmed that they'd been coated with some foreign chemical powerful enough to stunt the growth of elephants. It's hard to believe somebody in their mid-eighties could be agile enough to conduct a search and destroy mission into my yard under the cover of darkness. I've never asked her about it, and as with the local dogs, I've never been able to prove anything, either.

Buck Pincher has my whole gardening problem figured out. "Do what I do – I let my wife handle all the yard work." He reached down and plucked a fluffy white-topped dandelion that had gone to seed. "Maybe you and Cookie should trade household responsibilities."

His idea had merit. Buck and his wife, Dolly, own an older motel out on the highway. Whatever the tiny rooms lack in amenities is more than compensated for by the beautiful gardens Dolly has created throughout the property.

Buck blew the dandelion seeds into the wind, and we watched as they floated gracefully down the street, leaving tiny deposits on each of my neighbors' lawns. As if alerted by some internal radar, people began racing out of their homes, trying in vain to catch the dreaded spores with butterfly nets before they could land. Billy Rose, hindered by his arthritis, just stood there weeping forlornly, banging his head against his garage door.

I sank lower in the lawn chair and pulled my hat down over my eyes. "I don't know, Buck," I said. "That means I'd have to do the cooking. I think my wife would rather have malnourished plants than food poisoning."

He shrugged and opened up a bottle of dandelion wine he'd brought along with him. "I made it from your last crop," he explained. Taking a long swig straight from the bottle, Buck smacked his lips contentedly. "Not bad, if I do say so myself." He offered it to me. "Wanna sip?" I shuddered and shook my head.

"Suit yourself." Buck nodded towards the top of my hedge, where we caught a glimpse of the fiercely knitted eyebrows of the Slumberland Gardening Club Committee ducking down out of sight. "Don't look now, but I think the vigilantes are ready to make a move." The sounds of shovels and rakes could be heard rattling behind the hedge like sabers before a battle.

I told Buck not to worry, that I was moving on to Plan B. "And that is…?" he wondered.

"The local carpet store has a clearance sale on artificial turf." I shrugged. "It'll be expensive to start with, but just think of the money I'll save on fertilizer and lawnmower gas alone."

Buck cocked an eyebrow. "You got a point there. Tell you what – get it scotch-guarded and you won't have to worry 'bout the dogs, neither."

The only downside of replacing my lawn with fake grass is that it will spell the end of my love affair with dandelions. But such are the sacrifices one must make to be a good neighbor.

Back on Hunchback Mountain, the wind had turned chilly. Judging by the stiffness of my fingers, I realized that I'd been clutching the handrail for quite some time. The surrounding quietness told me two important things: first, the annoying children had grown tired of throwing rocks down onto the roof of my shop, and second, all the families had long since departed. That meant I could safely begin my descent without endangering anyone.

About to turn away, I noticed something at my feet, waving gently in the breeze. My heart pounded as I reached down and plucked the biggest, whitest, fluffiest dandelion I'd seen in years. Could it be? Yes, there was no doubt! It was one of the rare exotic strains I had imported from Italy two years previously, the same ones my neighbor had annihilated in one night with a banned substance.

Well, almost annihilated. Clearly one seed had escaped and somehow found its way to the top of this very mountain. And here I was, holding the results of that courageous journey in my own two hands. Tears welled up in my eyes at the magnitude of this serendipitous moment.

Glancing furtively from side to side, I made up my mind: it was time to set this flower free. Taking a deep breath, I was about to disperse the fertile spores to the wind when a small, annoying voice piped up behind me.

"Hey, mommy, that strange man is still here, and I think I recognize him. Doesn't he live down the street from us? And look – he's about to spread that weed all over Slumberland! Why would he do that?"

With a shudder, I realized that not everyone had left the mountain. Glancing nervously behind me, I found myself locked in the glare of the president of the Slumberland Gardening Club – I recognized her eyebrows.

"Oh, he wouldn't do that, Dilbert," she declared in icy tones. "*Unless...*" She paused for emphasis. "*...unless* he's not from here."

CHAPTER 3

❧ NEWS TRAVELS FAST ❧

News and rumors are difficult things to tell apart.

Now, if there's a politician nearby, it gets easier. The large media scrum, complete with yelling and fisticuffs, is a dead giveaway that a major rumor announcement is about to be made. On the other hand, if the press gallery consists of one solitary reporter with a Polaroid camera, then it's only news.

But in Slumberland, where rumors and news items enjoy equal rights, it's harder to tell the difference. The only sure way I can discern between a rumor and a piece of news is to stand in the middle of my shop and drop them both on the floor at the same time: whichever one makes it out the door first is the rumor.

When I first opened up Slim Shambles Auto Repair, things happened so quickly that there was no time to order a proper sign and have it installed. So I called upon a local artist to quickly create something that would get me over the initial hump of business startup. I was impressed with the work, but Buck Pincher was not.

Buck and his wife Dolly run The Happy Peasant Motel, a fine establishment where weary travelers can stop for the night and find fresh incentive for moving on the next morning. The Pinchers have been friends of Cookie and I for quite some time now, and as a rule I consider friendship a wonderful thing. Friends are supportive; they're sensitive about the things that matter deeply to you; they know when to keep their opinions to themselves.

Of course, none of this applies to Buck: he redefines the word 'friend.' But I let him hang around anyway.

"You call that a sign, Shambles? Looks like something a five-year-old would do in kindergarten." Buck was standing outside my office having a coffee while he waited for Basil to finish changing the oil in his car.

I followed his gaze to the cardboard and crayon creation hanging above my front door. "Yes, and I think my daughter did a lovely job, don't you? I'm not sure why there's a pony and a flower on it, but she got most of the letters right."

Buck stared at me for a moment. "Oh. Uh, well…what I meant was, now that you're all moved in and such, maybe you should think about updating it with something a little more permanent. After all, winter is coming and the cardboard…well…"

He was right. Already the rain had washed away part of my phone number. *Maybe that's why we aren't getting as many calls lately*, I thought. Out loud, I said, "What kind of sign should I have?" I knew Buck fancied himself as something of an expert on advertising. I, for one, was terrible at it. I knew that because Buck had told me so just a few months ago.

"What do you think of my motel sign?" he asked me one day as we lounged around his pool. The question hit me completely out of the blue – we'd been discussing local politics at the time. Clearly this was a friendly test of my skills of observation, so I decided to play along.

Squinting up at the large piece of plywood mounted securely between two poles at the edge of the highway, I scrutinized the sign carefully, as if seeing it for the first time. Not wanting to appear flippant, I took in all of its features with a critical eye and prepared my case.

"A few changes would certainly be in order," I began. "That green paint on the background…" I shook my head sadly. "Well, that certainly has got to go. It blends in too easily with the surrounding grass and trees. And the pale yellow lettering looks like something hung over from the '60s. Give it some color, man! Make the people sit up and take notice!" I settled back into my deck chair and delivered the clincher.

"Why, I drive this highway almost every day, and I never even notice this sign. Yep, I'd definitely say it's time for a new one."

Buck looked at me queerly and rolled his toothpick over to the other side of his mouth. "That is a new one," he said dryly. "I just put it up yesterday."

Since then I have left the subject of signs and advertising up to Buck. I mean, if I can't even notice a new sign when it's right in front of me (and brought directly to my attention, as Buck pointed out), then what do I know?

I took notes as Buck described what kind of sign would bring dozens of customers rolling up to my shop, ready to spend their hard-earned dollars on vehicle maintenance and repair. I stopped writing – it was time for a reality check. "So…are you saying they'll come and spend money like you do?" I asked carefully.

"Heck no," replied Buck. "They'll actually do some of those annoying maintenance items you always pester me about. Now where's that coffee pot? I need a refill."

I heaved a sigh of relief and went in to phone the sign company. It was good to know my new sign would actually pay a return on investment.

After lunch, Al from Artsy Al's Sign Company arrived, parking right in front of the office door. His eyebrows shot skyward as he caught sight of my homemade creation.

"You've got to be kidding me," he growled as he climbed down from the cab, a short stub of cigar clenched tightly between his thick lips. "You said it was urgent, but I didn't know it was an emergency." He pulled his ladder out of the back of the truck. "First things first: this has got to go."

"Why? Can't it stay there until you get the new sign ready?" I glanced around nervously. "You know how quickly rumors start in this town."

Al shook his head grimly and climbed up the ladder. "That's exactly what I'm afraid of, Slim." He waved his stogie in the direction of his brightly colored sign truck. "It's only been 30 seconds, but I'll guarantee you the whole neighborhood already knows I'm working here. If I drive away and they see this…this…" He shuddered. "Well, let's just say they'll think I had something to do with it." He ripped the offending parchment off the wall and held it gingerly between his thumb and forefinger as he climbed down. "Can't have that. It's bad for business."

I gulped. "But when will my new sign be ready?"

Al looked his watch and then squinted up at the sun. "Hmm, how 'bout tomorrow afternoon – is that soon enough?"

I nodded in resignation, but I couldn't shake the sense of foreboding that began to creep over me. Already things seemed quieter around the shop.

"Hey," inquired Basil at coffee break, "what happened to all our afternoon appointments? Nobody's showing up."

"I know," I said. "It's downright scary. At least we've got that brake job to do, the one that was dropped off this morning."

Basil shook his head. "Actually, we don't. The owner rushed back to pick it up, saying he didn't want his vehicle sitting here when the repo guys showed up. I wonder what he meant by that?"

I shrugged. "Beats me."

Things were still quiet the next morning. The only work we had all day was a kid whose bicycle tire went flat while he was riding past the shop. "I'm sure glad you can fix my tire right away, mister," he said, as Basil examined the tube for holes. "I didn't think anybody was open up here until you threw that sharp rock in front of my bike to slow me down."

"Well, it's a good thing you stopped when you did, kid," I said. "That gash in your tire could have caused a severe accident."

"Yeah, no kidding!" He poked at the jagged tear in his jeans. "An' it's a good thing I was wearing my helmet, too."

Finally the telephone rang around 3:15 that afternoon. "Slim," crackled the voice of Artsy Al. "I didn't get that sign finished yet, and my plane is leaving for Hawaii in an hour. I'll call you in two weeks when I get back."

"But…but…"

"You'll be fine," Al assured me. "Now, give me your credit card number so I can run the payment through before I go, just in case you're out of business by the time I get back." Al had a funny way of putting his customers at ease.

After hanging up, I went to see if the garbage truck had been by recently. The way things were going, I might have to go dumpster diving for my old sign.

The next morning I arrived at work to find Basil standing outside the door, waiting to get in. "What are you doing out here?" I asked.

He shrugged. "Can't get in. The door's locked."

"Of course it's locked. Why don't you use your keys?"

He pointed up at the blank spot above my door. "I stopped by Rolf's diner this morning for a coffee. Rumor has it that the business is sold, so I assumed all the locks have been changed. I was just waiting for the new owner to show up."

"THERE IS NO NEW OWNER!" I hollered. "Now unlock that door and get to work!"

The phone was ringing by the time we got inside. "Hey, Slim, how ya doin'?" It was Brakeline Bob, a mechanic friend who ran a brake and muffler shop in nearby Panicton. "Heard ya closed down yesterday. Got any good equipment left I can buy cheap?"

"Yeah," I replied sarcastically. "I got this nice ball peen hammer, and if you drop by, I'll use it to remind you not to listen to rumors."

"Sheesh! Are we having a bad day?"

"You don't know the half of it!" I slammed down the phone.

The next call came from Cheery McLundy, advertising manager at the local radio station. "Slim, honey, is it true that you're turning your shop into a used car lot? Why didn't you tell me, sweetie? We need to change the ads."

To escape the rumor mill, I drove downtown to Herkle's Auto Parts for a few supplies. When I walked in, Herk stared at me like he'd seen a ghost. "Is it really you?" he gasped, grabbing onto the counter for support. "Thank goodness! They said you'd left town during the night." He pushed my monthly statement across the counter. "Here! If you pay your account in full, I'll knock off an additional three percent."

By the time I'd reinstated my post office box, got my telephone reconnected, and convinced my dog that I was still its master, it was almost noon. When I finally got back to the shop, I discovered the first piece of good news I'd had in two days: Artsy Al was there putting up my new sign.

"What happened to your flight to Hawaii?"

"I canceled it." Al took his stogie out of his mouth and waved away a cloud of smoke. "Tried to put your credit card through, but it was denied. Head office in Toronto heard you were going bankrupt, so your credit's been frozen until your signs are fixed." He started up the ladder. "This'll cost you extra, by the way. And I'll need cash."

At that moment, a familiar rusty blue Topaz pulled into the parking lot. Buck Pincher had arrived and was snooping around my pickup truck. "What are you doing here," I snarled, hinting that I was not in the mood for any more nonsense.

One of Buck's strong points is that he's totally immune to hints. "I heard on the radio that you're now operating a used car lot. I'm looking for an old beater to haul garbage to the dump." He poked at some rust over my rear tire. "Whatcha asking for this worn-out GMC?"

Just then Buck noticed Al up on his ladder, installing my new sign. "Well, what have we here? Looks like a grand re-opening!" He rubbed his hands together with glee. "Say, you got any hot deals on service work, Slim? Some free coffee and donuts? Or, maybe a rebate on that oil change you overcharged me for the other day?" I don't recall the rest of the conversation, but I know I felt better when he left.

By the middle of the afternoon, Basil was ready for a well-deserved break. "That new sign sure made a difference," he groaned, wiping the sweat off his forehead. He reached for his coffee mug. "Ever since Al left, we've had cars lined up for two blocks." His face brightened noticeably. "Say, who bought the jelly donuts?"

"I did," I said. "We're celebrating our survival from an entrepreneurial near-death experience."

Basil went over to the pastry box and chose a particularly plump specimen. "Speaking of near death, don't you think chasing Buck off the property with a tire iron was a little extreme? I mean, he is your friend, after all."

I sank into my chair. It had been non-stop oil changes all day and I was exhausted. "No, he deserved that, seeing as how my business almost tanked after he suggested I replace my sign."

Basil shrugged. "Even so, I think it was kind of mean to start that rumor about his motel."

"Rumor?" My tired brain struggled to take in what Basil had just said. "What rumor? All I did was chase him off the property and tell him to get back to his flea-bitten motel where he belongs." A sudden chill numbed my spine. I lowered my voice. "Do you think somebody heard me?"

Basil licked his fingers. "Well, I did notice Dutchy loitering around his office window." He gave me a significant look. "*And* the window was open. Rumor now has it that the health inspector is closing down The Happy Peasant Motel on account of a bedbug infestation."

I winced and stirred my coffee slowly. "Yikes, that is severe. I'd better get over there and see if I can clear things up. No doubt there's already a crowd gathering for the bankruptcy auction."

"You're probably right," agreed Basil, reaching for his second donut. "Do you mind if I come along? I'd like to put in a bid on one of his used TVs before they're all gone."

CHAPTER 4

❧ A CHILLING MYSTERY ❧

Now, I've seen dramatics before – just watch Basil lose it when the coffee wagon drives by without stopping – but the scene taking place in my front office bordered on the ridiculous.

"Ease up, Clem," I said. "If you drink any more water out of my cooler, I'll have to charge extra for shop supplies."

The weather-beaten rancher unsuctioned his lips from the spigot and gasped incoherently. "Gotta…fix…air conditioning…dying… heat…"

To be fair, the temperature outside had reached the mid '90s, and Clem's dude ranch didn't have any shade in the pasture where he'd been haying. Not only did his Ford pickup have a non-functioning air conditioner, his power windows didn't work either. From the looks of it, he'd barely survived the drive to town. I tossed Clem a wet rag for his forehead, then went looking for Basil to get an updated weather report on Clem's A/C problem.

A furnace-like wind blew in through the open bay door, which only made it hotter inside the shop. Dust devils whirled in the gravel parking lot, and as I looked across the street, I could see the heat rising in shimmering waves from the pavement that separated my shop from Dutchy's Towing. This was normal summer weather for our valley, which is why so many tourists flock here this time of year. The only smart place to be on a day like today was down at one of the sandy beaches lining Hollownoggin Lake. Unfortunately, we locals had to work in this withering inferno to keep our bills paid.

The back end of Clem's truck was sticking out of the shop in a futile attempt to keep exhaust fumes from filling the building – the hot wind blew them in anyway. A set of air conditioning pressure gauges were duct-taped to the outside of the truck's windshield so Basil could take the readings from inside the cab, while at the same time checking the air temperature coming out of the dash vents. The big V8 engine rumbled away at a fast idle, and looking under the hood, I could see that the A/C compressor was running full time. Normally it would cycle on and off as the system came up to pressure. That wasn't happening today.

I tried to get Basil's attention. "Hey, got any cool air?!" He couldn't hear me over the sound of the old truck, but one look at the sweat pouring off my technician's forehead told me what I wanted to know. Basil shut off the engine and clambered out of the hot cab, gasping for breath. I handed him a cold soft drink from the shop fridge. "Let me guess," I said. "Not exactly the results you were hoping for?"

"No!" Basil mopped his brow and took a long swig. "Clem should relabel his heater controls to *Hot* and *Hotter*." He waved the can in the direction of the pressure gauges. "And I'm not surprised it isn't giving out cool air, not with pressure readings like that. The low side is up to 80 psi, while the high side hovers around 250."

I frowned. We'd seen enough A/C pressure readings to know what normal was, and this wasn't it. Clem's low side was more than 50 pounds per square inch higher than it should be. "Could there be too much refrigerant in the system?"

Basil shook his head. "I've evacuated the system twice with the recharge machine and refilled it both times with the correct amount." He drained the pop can and tossed it into the garbage. "There's something else wrong here, and I'm starting to get suspicious."

"Suspicious? About what?"

Basil pointed to the engine compartment. "We're not the first ones to pass this way." He lowered his voice. "Note the shiny new parts."

Sure enough, somebody else had been under Clem's hood recently. A brand new compressor and receiver/drier stood out in stark contrast to Clem's otherwise filthy, grime-covered engine. The average Slumberland farmer wasn't known for cleanliness when it came to his farm machinery, and Clem was no exception.

The new parts also revealed a common problem in the auto repair business: you don't always get the full story behind a mechanical breakdown. I'm all for saving money, but sometimes the discount repair done by a friend or relative isn't really worth it.

It reminded me of a certain customer whose name I hesitate to mention…

"So Buck, tell me again how this happened?" I held the tattered remains of an almost new fan belt in my hands.

"Dunno." My friend shrugged and dropped three more sugar cubes into his coffee. "That fan belt you sold me just fell apart. Must be defective."

Buck was always blaming his troubles on a defective part or person, so I ignored him and leaned under the hood for a closer inspection. "Hey, how did this fan pulley get so battered and bent?"

Buck peered over my shoulder. "Ah…that would be Cousin Elmo. He likes hammers."

"Hammers?! What on earth was Elmo doing in here with a hammer?"

Buck took a sip of his coffee. "Changing the water pump?" he suggested. "Say, got any rum to go with this?"

"Don't change the subject," I growled. "So you got your cousin to change the water pump…is that why there's a bolt missing from the alternator bracket?"

"Only one?" Buck was surprised. "Not bad, eh? Elmo usually loses three or four per job." He bent over the fender for a closer look. "I thought Elmo said he was gonna weld that bracket back into place."

"He did," I said, gritting my teeth. "But the weld broke. Which made the alternator come loose. Which is why the belt came off the pulley." I glared at him. "The pulley that was bent by the hammer."

"Tsk, tsk." Buck drained his cup and frowned. "So…you ain't gonna give me warranty on the defective fan belt?"

"No!"

He tugged on an earlobe. "Then how about a discount on a new one?"

Dragging myself back to the present, I headed for the waiting room. Clem had recovered from his sunstroke, and instead of draining my water cooler, he was now emptying my coffee pot. I even caught him stuffing sugar cubes into the pockets of his farm overalls. "Clem, quit stealing my supplies and tell me straight: did you already have somebody else look at this A/C problem?"

"Yeah," Clem acknowledged sheepishly. "I got a buddy who used to do refrigeration for the supermarkets. No offense, Slim, but his rates are a whole lot cheaper."

"No doubt." I'd heard that tune before. "How much did it cost you exactly?"

Clem shuffled his feet uncomfortably and glanced out the window. "Just the parts...and two cases of beer."

"Right." It wasn't hard to guess which had come first – installing the new parts or emptying the beer cans. "Clem, has your friend *ever* worked on automotive air conditioning before?"

"Well, not exactly. But it was such a deal, I couldn't pass it up."

"A deal?! You call it a deal when you pay for something and it still doesn't work?" I was incredulous. "Clem, if I charged people for repairs that didn't fix their problems, I'd be run out of town on a rail!"

Clem knit his eyebrows together and looked at me strangely. "Well, of course you would – and rightly so. What's your point?"

I gave up and sent Clem back to his hayfields. "I'll call you when we figure out what's wrong with your truck."

He hesitated. "Is this gonna cost me money?"

"Do horses eat sugar cubes?"

At noon, Basil came into the office to have his lunch. Setting his lunch kit down on the small coffee table next to his easy chair, he picked up his mug and headed over to the coffee machine. "I see we're out of sugar," he commented, rummaging through the cupboard below. "Clem's horse must love it when that wreck of a truck breaks down and needs servicing."

One of the things about Basil that impressed me the most was the way he always seemed to know what was going on. In the short time we'd been working together, Basil had consistently revealed this uncanny ability to figure out a situation with almost no clues to go on. He'd done it again just last week.

"So, Cookie has gone to visit her mother again, has she?"

I stopped chewing my sandwich and stared. "How did you know that?"

Basil put down his magazine and pointed at the food in my hand. "That cheddar cheese and strawberry jam sandwich gave you away. Cookie can't stand the combination, but you love it. So obviously you made the sandwich yourself."

"Yes, I did," I protested, "but that doesn't mean…"

Basil held up his hand to stop me. "Plus, it's on white bread. That means she's been gone for at least a day, because you've had time to buy white bread to replace the whole wheat brand that she normally makes you eat."

"Anything else?" I asked testily.

He thought for a moment. "Well, she didn't go off mad, because you have a piece of chocolate cake for dessert. That means she prepared a few things before she left."

The blatant transparency of my personal life was beginning to unnerve me. "I suppose you know when she's coming home, then?"

Basil looked me over. "I'd say tomorrow night at the latest." He laughed at my surprised expression. "You've worn that shirt for three days straight now, which signifies there are no clean ones in your closet. That means she'll be home soon to do laundry, because Cookie doesn't trust you near her washing machine."

He had me there. "Okay, I can see how you figured all that out. But there's no way you could know she's gone to her mother's. Why, she could have taken the kids to Disneyland for all you know."

"Oh, I'd know," he chuckled. "If they went someplace fun, you'd be griping about it from the moment they left." He spread out his hands in triumph. "It's simple. No griping? It's the mother-in-law's house."

I felt like a chastened Dr. Watson in a Sir Arthur Conan Doyle novel.

Since Sherlock Basil hadn't fixed Clem's truck yet, I took a stab at being the hero for once. "Say, those new compressors come filled with more oil than they need, right?" I turned our small office fan up to *High* and leaned back in my chair to catch the breeze. "Maybe Clem's buddy didn't take out the extra oil before he installed the compressor on the truck, and now there's too much."

Basil pulled out his pocketknife and sliced up an apple. "I've already considered that. I completely flushed the system and reinstalled the correct amount of oil. The results are the same." He popped the slice into his mouth and chewed thoughtfully. "Not to worry. A good meal always relaxes my mind. I'm sure something will come to me after lunch."

An hour later, Basil had the truck running once more and the air conditioning set on *maximum*. When I went over to see how things were going, I found him staring into space, deep in thought. "Any ideas yet?" He raised an index finger in the air and shook his head silently. It was his polite way of telling me to shut up.

Basil closed his eyes and began to feel his way along the A/C hoses, chanting to himself as he went. At one point, he opened an eyelid to find me staring at him. "One should expect the unexpected," he explained cryptically. "To do that, I must first clear the mind." He went back to his meditations. Suddenly his hands stopped and hovered over the evaporator inlet pipe. "Ah, I detect a disturbance in the Force. It's time to check out the orifice tube."

I protested on principle. "That doesn't make sense, Bas. If the orifice tube is plugged, the low side pressures would drop out of sight. But you saw the readings – if anything they're too high."

Basil smiled at me condescendingly. "I didn't say it was plugged; I said let's check it out."

I shrugged and wheeled over the recharge machine to empty the refrigerant one more time. When Basil finally disconnected the hose containing the orifice tube, we discovered that he was right: the tube wasn't plugged – it wasn't even there.

"And I wonder how that happened," I said sarcastically, knowing full well who the culprit was. Basil read my thoughts.

"I agree. Clem's buddy most likely took out the orifice tube for cleaning, and then forgot to put it back in." After installing the correct part, we recharged the system. Now the low side dropped to 25 psi, the compressor cycled properly, and we could finally chill out.

"How's it now, Basil?" I hollered jealously, tapping on the driver's window as I sweated in the smothering heat. Inside the cab, Basil was shivering away in his coveralls, a woolen scarf wrapped around his neck as he cleared frost off the dashboard.

Opening the door, he grinned. "It looks like I've found a new setting on Clem's heater controls: it's called *Der Friezen Yer Heine!*"

Clem was ecstatic when he came to pick up his truck. "Slim, I can't tell you how good it's gonna feel to have cool air on the drive home!"

"I was going to ask you about that. Why don't you have us fix your power windows as well? That way, if the A/C ever quits again, you could at least open a window."

Clem waved a gnarled hand in the air. "Naw, I've got me a friend who's gonna look into it next week. He's an expert – used to work for a glass shop installing windows in apartment buildings."

After he'd left, Basil came into the office for his coffee break. He stopped abruptly and scanned the room. "Hey, who took my other apple? I left it right here on the table after lunch!"

I chuckled. "Old Clem is at it again. I swear that horse of his gets more than his fair share of treats."

That's when the dramatics really kicked into high gear – you just don't come between Basil and his food. Ignoring the ranting going on around me, I opened the appointment book to pencil in a spot for Clem around the middle of next week. *Basil's not the only one with the powers of deduction*, I thought. *Clem will be back, once his friend gets finished 'fixing' the power windows on his truck.*

I also made a note to hide the sugar cubes.

CHAPTER 5

✎ A FINE DAY FOR A DRIVE ✎

The minute Buck Pincher pulled into my parking lot, I got the feeling it was going to be one of those days. And when I saw that his wife was in the car with him, the feeling quickly turned into a certainty. Dolly was expanding Buck's knowledge of the English language by filling his right ear with as many choice words as she could think of. And if I knew Dolly, she could think of quite a few.

After detaching his wife from his ear and himself from the car, Buck sauntered into the office like it was business as usual. But I could tell from the beads of sweat on his forehead that all was not well in Pincherville. After filling his coat pocket with mints on his way past the candy dish, Buck poured a large coffee and helped himself to three sugar cubes and two stir-sticks. Sufficiently reinforced, he sank into one of my waiting room chairs.

"Buck, why do you always take two stir-sticks?" I complained. "You only need one to stir the coffee." Granted, they aren't expensive items, but Buck's freeloading habits get on my nerves.

He took a large slurp of coffee and smacked his lips. "Well, I'll tell you, Slim. The first one is for stirring this here muddy concoction you misrepresent as coffee, and the second one is for removing the grinds from my teeth when I'm done choking it down."

I shrugged. "If you don't like my coffee, then quit drinking it."

Buck rolled his eyes. "I ain't saying I don't like it; it's just labor intensive, that's all." He jerked his thumb over his shoulder and changed the subject. "Slim, I've got a problem. Old Betsy out there has got a few quirks that'll require your legendary talents to rectify."

My defenses went up immediately. Buck's compliments always

come with a price. "I hate to tell you this," I replied cautiously, "but Old Betsy's quirks are far beyond my ability to repair. And besides, I thought your wife's name was Dolly?"

A long-suffering smile graced his craggy features. "Ha, ha. Good one, Slim. As I was about to explain, Dolly and I decided that today would be a fine day for a drive through the valley. Unfortunately, my car has decided to think otherwise. It coughs and sputters and barely makes it up any kind of an incline that ain't inclined downwards."

I rubbed my chin. "Kind of reminds me of you."

But Buck was not to be deterred. "Now, my car should be running perfectly, since I bring it to you for all its normal maintenance." He held up a hand as I began to protest. "I ain't blaming you – after all, you're only human. But it's gotten so bad now that I can't even rev it up enough to drown out Dolly's nagging."

Buck's interpretation of 'normal maintenance' was to open the hood once a year and look around, whether it needed it or not. "When's the last time that old jalopy had a tune-up?" I asked, knowing full well that the spark plugs in Buck's car were so old and rusty it would take either a cutting torch or minor explosives to remove them.

"Now hold on there," he said quickly, nearly choking on one of his stir-sticks. "Don't you go spending all my hard-earned money on stuff my car don't really need. Just make it run decent so's Dolly and I can take a little cruise. I ain't made of money, you know."

With a sigh, I put aside the paying work I was doing and went out to take a look at Buck's car. Climbing into the driver's seat, I stole a sideways glance at the other half of the equation. "Nice day, Dolly," I ventured. "Taking a little break from the motel?"

"Harrumph," she replied, arms crossed and jaw line set. "Look, Slim, it's nothing personal. But if there's anything you can do for the old wreck, then let's cut the small talk and just get at it."

I looked back through the office window where I could see Buck snooping around in my coffee cupboard. He was trying to find the bag of mints. "Look, Dolly, Buck might be a little out of shape, but I wouldn't exactly call him a wreck..."

She glared at me. "Not him, you nut – the car! Ever since he brought this thing home last fall we've had nothing but problems!"

I had to admit that their car was a real winner. Rumor had it Buck discovered Old Betsy under a pile of used drywall during a visit to the secondhand building supply yard. Being the shrewd bargainer that he was, he bought the whole pile of used drywall for his motel renovations and got the rusty old car thrown in on the side.

The owner of the supply yard was happy with the arrangement. He told me later that Old Betsy had been home to a family of pack rats. But under Buck's new ownership, all the pack rats moved out in less than a week. If there's one thing a pack rat can't stand, it's a bigger pack rat.

I started the engine and revved it up a few times, but to my surprise it sounded fairly normal. *Drat! I'm going to have to take it out for a test drive.*

With great misgivings, I convinced Dolly to wait in the office with Buck. Knowing that she can be just as frugal as her husband, I did a quick inventory on the levels in the coffee pot and the mint bowl. By my calculations, I had about five minutes to test drive, diagnose, and fix their car before my supplies ran out.

Heading out to the highway where I could find a few good hills, I rolled down the window to let in some badly needed fresh air. The sun was warm and the air was clear, meaning Buck was right about one thing at least – it was a fine day for a drive.

Getting away from the shop always puts me in a better mood, even if it means driving a car like Buck's. I do enjoy my trade – after all, I became a mechanic because I like to fix things – but sometimes the hassles of running a small business can wear you down. In a town like Slumberland, you don't just get stuck in routines; you often get buried in them.

That's not to say that life here is boring. Slumberland has its own share of local color, and Buck and Dolly Pincher are prime examples. They're about as colorful a pair as you can find, though most of it can't be blamed on Dolly.

I could understand their need for a break. During the summer months, they spend most of their waking hours operating The Happy Peasant Motel. The modest establishment is situated near the crest of Slumberland Hill, a section of the highway whose steepness of grade astounds engineers and infuriates truck drivers to no end.

To make it even better, the highway authorities installed a traffic light directly below the motel, about two thirds of the way up the steep incline. On a clear night, guests are lulled to sleep by roaring engines and howling transmissions as the truck drivers struggle to get their rigs moving again. By morning, some of Buck's customers have learned several descriptive new phrases from the truckers, and pass them on quite freely as they check out. Lately Buck and Dolly have refrained from renting rooms near the highway to families with small children.

However I, for one, like The Happy Peasant Motel. Every year near the end of summer, Cookie and I pack up the kids and spend a blissful weekend at what I like to call 'Pincher Palace.' We specifically choose that time of year, partly because it gives the kids something to look forward to just before school begins. But the main reason is that by the end of the summer, Buck has finally figured out how much chlorine to put in his outdoor pool.

One time we made the mistake of trying out the pool at the beginning of the summer. The fact that nobody else was in the pool area at the time should have served as a warning. But I wasn't paying attention, and did a perfect cannonball into the deep end wearing navy blue swimming trunks. When I climbed out, they were bleached pure white. Cookie had to point this out to me because my eyes stung so badly I couldn't keep them open. I concluded that Buck must be having trouble with the chlorine content.

When I mentioned this to him later, he nodded. "Yeah, I might have overdone it. But you gotta admit there ain't a pool in the valley with water as clear and sanitized as mine. Why, you can make out every bottle cap and bit of broken glass on the bottom of the deep end from halfway across the sun deck."

One year Buck got busy with other things around the motel and forgot to treat his pool for a couple of weeks. He failed to notice that the water was taking on a greenish tinge. The algae, which had lain dormant in the pool drains for many years, was at first baffled by the fact it wasn't being attacked by a barrage of chlorine crystals. Sensing new freedom, it began to grow with a vengeance. Actually, it was more like a deep-seated grudge. After completely overtaking the pool one night, it headed for the house. The Pinchers awoke in the morning to find writhing green algae lapping around the foot of their bed. Fortunately, Buck keeps a private supply of chlorine in his night table, so he was able to fight his way clear before things got ugly.

Thinking about Buck's pool made me suddenly realize the real reason Dolly was in such need of a break. It wasn't just the normal stress of operating a motel; it was what had taken place only a couple of days earlier.

It just so happened that the family and I had been relaxing by Buck and Dolly's pool that day, catching a few carcinogenic rays from the sun as the temperature hovered around 92°F.

Without warning, Dolly burst out of the house wearing her brand new swimsuit and headed for the pool at full charge. After cleaning 18 rooms, doing 36 loads of laundry, answering 42 phone calls, and chasing Buck out of the fridge for the 10th time that morning, she was ready for a cool dip.

None of us had been in the pool yet, for upon arrival I had noticed three empty 20-pound chlorine bags lying just inside the pool house door. The *half-price* sale stickers were still attached. Better judgment on my part suggested that we let somebody else test the waters first.

Well, Dolly tested them, all right. She did a beautiful half gainer off the diving board and was just straightening out nicely when her fingertips touched the surface of the crystal clear water.

It amazes me what the human body can do when the need arises. It certainly arose at that moment. I have never seen a more magnificent display of hand-walking on water than I did that day, as Dolly scooted right across the surface of the pool to the other side. Her high-pitched yell for Buck caught him sneaking a piece of turkey out of the fridge. He came to the front door looking guilty, but took off running for his life with Dolly in hot pursuit. I suppose she was a little upset at how close she'd come to having her new bathing suit bleached beyond recognition. Or maybe she didn't appreciate the way the pool water had sucked all the red nail polish right off her fingernails in less than two seconds. Whatever the reason, it was as plain as day that Dolly was feeling stressed.

My thoughtful musings were cut short by a loud bang from under the hood, accompanied by a sudden loss of power. I pulled over to the side of the highway. Smoke and rude noises began to pour out of the vehicle, and when I finally calmed down, I could hear that the car was sounding awful as well. I shut it off, got out, and opened the hood for a closer look. It didn't take long to discover that, once again, Buck Pincher had left his mark.

You see, Buck has this aversion to fixing things properly, especially if it's going to cost money. On the other hand, Dolly just loves to fix everything, especially in the area of Opinions. Buck explained it to me once. "Yessir, my perfectly good Opinion might be working just fine, but then Dolly will decide it needs fixing. And it won't do me a lick of good to raise an Objection, because she'll just fix that, too."

As I'd suspected, Buck's old car needed a tune-up. The unfortunate part was that Buck had tried to do it himself. From what I could see, the cracked distributor cap had been glued back together and the frayed ignition wires were wrapped with duct tape. It was a mess. Sparks were jumping to any metal surface within reach.

By the time I limped the car back into my parking lot, real smoke and rude noises were coming from under the hood, putting a definite end to the idea of 'it's a fine day for a drive.' Dolly also noticed the smoke and must have realized the same thing. Even though I couldn't hear her yet, I could see her through the office window. She was already fully engaged in fixing Buck's Opinion of his own mechanical abilities.

I suppose I should have felt sorry for my old friend. But I knew my mint bowl would be empty by now, the coffee pot drained, and even the sugar cubes would be safely stowed away in Dolly's purse, ready to be reused at the motel.

Yes, Buck and Dolly Pincher are a colorful pair, but most of it can't be blamed on Dolly.

CHAPTER 6

⊰≫ STAIRWAY TO HEAVEN ≫⊱

Cookie," I declared, "it's time we bought a motorhome." My wife walked over, peered into my eyes and sniffed my breath. "Well, that's a relief," she said. "For a minute there I thought you'd taken on some new habits." She went back to cooking supper. "Why in the world would you want a motorhome?"

"Well, you're always complaining that we never go camping," I said. "And with my back the way it is, you know I can't survive in a tent."

Cookie raised an eyebrow. "And you think our marriage can survive an RV?"

"You just watch." I rubbed my hands together. "We'll have so many family outings, you'll wonder why we didn't do this years ago."

So I got my wish…sort of. Cookie had a few ground rules. "But we'll never find a decent RV for under $5,000!" I protested.

She was firm. "There's no sense spending a fortune on a motorhome until we know if we like it. Besides, you're a mechanic; you can fix it up."

"But that defeats the whole purpose of taking time off," I argued. "I don't want to spend my entire vacation fixing things."

Cookie flashed her winsome smile. "Right. So tell me again why you want an RV?"

Eventually I found something that fit within the budget – a Flintstonesque relic that had been upgraded by installing a motor and brakes. The body was a little rough, but at least most of the cylinders were still firing. "Pile in," I shouted to the family as I pulled up in front of the house. "We're going camping!"

Cookie was doubtful. "This is pretty short notice. Are you sure we have everything we need?"

"You bet," I replied confidently. "The old couple who sold it to me promised to leave all their camping gear in it for us to use. Let's go!" So after a quick stop at a convenience store for groceries and a coffee, we headed off to find a campground we could get to and still be home by Sunday night.

"Where exactly are we going?" Cookie asked an hour later, as she turned the road map sideways to get her bearings.

I handed over a brochure I'd picked up at the gas station. "It says here this campground is perfect for families. There's even a day hike to the top of a waterfall."

She frowned. "Hiking? What about your back?"

"No problem," I beamed. "The waterfall's got stairs."

Cookie was impressed. Looking in the rear view mirror, I could see the kids enjoying themselves at the dinette table, coloring pictures and reading comic books as we rumbled down the highway. Life was great. Then Tipper had to go to the bathroom.

I looked in the mirror again. "No problem, Tip. Just go to the back. The toilet is behind the door on the left." I smiled at my wife. "That's the beauty of travelling in a motorhome."

Tipper ran to the back. "On the left?"

"Yes, on the left."

A few minutes later, he poked his head out. "I'm done," he called. "But I can't find the flush handle."

I was busy fighting with traffic. "What do you mean you can't find it?"

"Well, it's dark in here."

"Turn on the light!" I hollered.

"There isn't one!" he hollered back.

I glanced in the mirror again. "There isn't one...? Well, open the door wider and tell me what you see."

Tipper climbed out and pulled the door completely open. "I see a broom and some hangers." He looked at me. "I think this is the closet."

Cookie glared in disgust. I'd forgotten that left and right are reversed when you look in a mirror.

It was getting dark as we pulled into the campground. We were tired but excited to be close to nature. Perhaps a little too close, judging from the snores coming from the campsite next door. And that was just their dog.

The kids jumped out and began opening all the compartments on the motorhome, looking for camping gear. There wasn't any.

My oldest daughter stood there frowning at me, a trait she'd recently picked up from her mother. "Dad, did you actually see any gear, or did you just take their word for it – again?" Cache is a great kid; just way too perceptive for her age.

"Let's see…" I climbed back inside and rummaged through a cupboard under the sink. "We've got three paper plates, a pot with no handle, and half an eggbeater."

"Great," said Cookie, rolling her eyes (a trait she'd recently picked up from the kids). "Put them together with these two bent forks and a butter knife, and we've got everything we need, just like you said." She found a battered flashlight and tried the switch. "Well, Mr. Eveready, I don't suppose you thought to buy batteries?"

I didn't reply. Instead, I tried out the propane stove. These amazing devices bring the wonders of home cooking to the great outdoors… provided you fill the propane tank first.

After digging out the cold cereal and warm milk ("So…," observed Cookie, "the fridge is propane powered as well, eh?"), we sat the kids down to a late supper.

"Camping is cool, Dad," said Carrie. "I've never eaten cereal with a bent fork before!"

"It's all about new experiences," I said, waving my eggbeater philosophically.

"I'll give you a new experience," said Cookie. "Somebody's got to clean out the broom closet, and it's *not* going to be me."

After settling the kids into their bunks, Cookie and I sat down at the dinette for a game of Hearts. Halfway through the first hand the lights went out. "Hmm, the camper battery must be low. I'll go plug us in." On the way out the door I grabbed the useless flashlight in case I had to beat off any bears.

I tried to unlock the hatch for the power cord, but of all the keys the old couple had given me, this was one they'd forgotten. That was when I finally discovered a use for the flashlight.

"Hey," called my neighbor, as I stood there panting. "No need to beat your motorhome to a pulp. All those compartment keys are the same; next time just ask and I'll lend you mine." I nodded and threw the flashlight into the bushes before I was tempted to redeploy it elsewhere.

Soon the snarly black power cable was pulled out and coiled around my legs like a black mamba. I looked over at my neighbor again, who sat by his campfire watching me with keen interest. "Hey, where do I plug this in?"

With a snort, he reached into the cooler beside him for another cold one. "Into that tree, for all I care. Government campgrounds don't have services. If you want power, you have to go private." His dog woke up briefly and snarled. Dragging himself over to our motorhome, he shared his opinion of greenhorn campers on one of my back tires before flopping back down beside the fire for another sleep.

Climbing back into the darkened interior, I suggested to Cookie that we retire early. "Might as well," she said. "There's nothing else to do."

I looked around in the quiet darkness. "Well, we could..."

Cookie snorted. "In your dreams, lover boy. We're packed like sardines into a crowded campground, in a vehicle with three kids and squeaky springs. Do I have to spell it out for you?"

Having gained some clarification on that subject, I turned my attention to wrestling the retractable bed out from the wall. After finally climbing under the covers, I reflected on the day. It had been a shaky start to the weekend, but I'd learned much. Like, don't drive with the roof vents up. "Just look at those stars," I whispered to my drowsy wife.

"Where else can you view the night sky while lying in bed?"

"Yeah," she replied as she contemplated the gaping hole in the roof. "What'll we do if it rains?"

"Relax," I assured her. "I checked the forecast before leaving home – it called for clear skies all weekend."

The only good part about listening to the pounding rain on the aluminum roof was that it drowned out the snoring dog next door. Climbing onto a roof in the midst of a torrential downpour was no easy task. "Why don't you use the ladder on the back?" called Cookie from inside, as I slipped off the hood for the second time.

I soon had the skylight duct-taped back into place. Climbing down, I comforted myself with thoughts of drying out in front of the furnace… until I remembered that it was a *propane* furnace. It was the one time in my life where I contemplated selling my soul for bottled gas.

By morning the sun was out again, so I rallied the troops for a brisk hike after breakfast. "Let's head to the waterfall," I declared. "The one with stairs!"

Cache looked at her sister. "This is gonna be good."

"Why?" asked Carrie. "Because of the stairs?"

Cache shook her head. "No. Because it's Dad's idea."

The waterfall was easy to find – all we had to do was follow the creek from the lakeshore back towards the side of the mountain. There we discovered a small sign that read "Shorty's Creek Waterfall Stairs." They looked wet and slippery, so like a gentleman I stood back and let the others go first. "That way I'll be here to catch you in case you slip," I explained. Cookie said nothing. She can be extremely gracious at times.

And so the climb began. "…98, 99, 100!" announced Tipper, jumping up and down on the wooden stairs above me. To my left, the roaring water threw billowing clouds of mist into the air as Shorty's Creek thundered past. Only four years old, Tip was proud of his counting abilities. I was just glad to have made it that far.

"Take a picture, Dad!" squealed Cache and Carrie. With aching sides

I puffed my way up the last few steps to the small landing perched on the rocky hillside. My lower vertebrae were screaming under the weight of the heavy pack, which was half-filled with snacks, juice boxes, and other hiking essentials. The other half was filled with Tipper's rock collection.

A quick search through my bulging coat pockets revealed that the camera was gone. "It must have fallen out," I groaned, collapsing onto the damp wooden platform.

Cookie was sympathetic. "Not to worry, dear. We'll wait here while you go back and find it." She joined the kids at the railing to admire the falls.

The lost camera was finally located on Step 32, where I'd stopped in a previous life to tie my boot lace. Crawling back up to the landing, I was just in time to hear the family say, "Let's go higher; it'll make a better picture."

"Go…ahead…without me," I wheezed, gasping for air like a carp out of water. "I'm right behind you…" Grabbing the railing for support, I wracked my brain trying to remember who the idiot was who'd suggested this hike in the first place. My brain didn't appreciate being wracked, especially in its tired condition. It responded by slapping me upside the head, reminding me that this hike of death was my own stupid fault.

"Thanks a lot," I snarled. "If you're so smart, then next time talk me out of it."

An ethereal voice drifted down from above, cutting through the mists like a revelation from heaven. "Hurry up, Dad," called Tip. "We're waiting. And who are you talking to, anyway?"

Gritting my teeth, I resumed the climb. It was obvious a different carpenter had built the next set of stairs, someone whose tape measure had more inches per foot than the last guy. It's the only reason I could come up with to explain why the steps grew higher the further I went.

My upward progress was also hindered by an annoying squirrel who leapt from branch to branch, badgering me for handouts. A lively discussion ensued between us about the benefits of earning an honest living as opposed to begging, but my brilliant arguments fell on deaf ears. When I expressed my opinion of panhandlers, he responded by tossing a pine cone under my feet. Once my vision cleared and the pain subsided, I could make out the number painted on the step three inches in front of my nose. It was 200. *Thank heavens; surely we're almost there!*

Pulling myself over the edge of the next landing I found my family leaning nonchalantly against the railing, gazing at wild flowers blooming in the mist. They were bored. "You just missed the hummingbird, Dad," complained Carrie. "Now we'll have to go higher for our picture."

"Higher?" I croaked. "You mean there are more stairs?"

"Yep," smiled Cookie, holding out my camping brochure. "392 all together."

"Race you, Dad!" called Tip, scampering upwards out of my clouded vision.

Ascending the last 192 steps was a trial by fire. By this time, it was obvious the carpenter had tossed his tape measure into the falls and used star measurements to lay out the last section. The kids did their part to lighten my load by eating most of the snacks in my backpack, although it aggravated me how effortlessly they ran up and down the stairs to retrieve them. I hate showoffs.

By the time I made it to the top, the sun was starting to set. "We've been waiting so long, I'm cold," complained Cache. "Can we go back now?"

I lay on my back, counting the spots floating before my eyes. "Can't we just spend the night here?" I hollered over the noise of the falls. "It's so peaceful."

But nobody was listening. Tipper scooted past me and ran down a few steps before turning around. His eyes grew wide. "Hey Mom," he said in awe. "There must be bears around here, and they're hungry!"

"Bears?" Cookie gathered the kids in close. "Why do you say that, dear?"

Tip pointed excitedly. "Look at these stairs! They're all clawed up and some even have teeth marks in 'em."

Cookie sighed with relief. "Oh, that's just your father, Tipper. Now put your new rocks in his backpack; it's time to get back for supper."

I would have protested, but I was too busy pulling splinters out of my gums. Besides, I needed all my wind for the return trip – which went much quicker than I expected. Halfway down, the grumpy squirrel snuck up behind me and tossed another pine cone in my direction. Gravity did the rest.

Limping into the campsite later, I found the family lined up and looking serious. All the other holidayers in the campground were busy cooking their dinners, but around our motorhome things were strangely quiet. "Glad you could finally make it, dear," greeted my sympathetic wife, her hands on her hips.

"Yeah, Pops," echoed Carrie. "Where've you been the past hour? We're hungry."

Struggling out of the backpack, I collapsed into a lawn chair and looked around. "I was giving you a head start," I said. "You could have had supper ready by now."

"Oh, is that so?" Cookie proceeded to give me a rundown of our situation. "We've got no power and no propane; without refrigeration the meat went bad, so I threw it out; we have no eating utensils to speak of; and to top it all off, there are no matches to start a campfire." She dangled the keys in front of my face. "We've taken a vote. It's time to hit the road, Jack."

Half an hour later, we checked into Zeke's RV Village. I left Cookie and the girls at the small store while Tipper and I went to dump the holding tanks. For the past few miles, Cookie had been complaining about a disturbing odor coming from the bathroom area, something more than just my wet hiking boots and dirty socks.

We pulled onto the concrete apron, and Tip and I got out to take stock of our situation. Squatting down on our haunches, we spent some time contemplating the two big black-handled valves dangling from underneath the rear of the motorhome. We couldn't decide which one to pull first. "I think it's this one," I said, glancing at my young son to see if he agreed.

He looked dubious. "I think I'll stand way back here, Dad. I wouldn't want to get in your way."

I grabbed the handle and began to tug on it. "Don't…be…so…silly… you're not…in my…" Suddenly it popped open. *Amazing*, I thought. *I didn't know these tanks could hold so much.*

Zeke didn't share my sense of wonder. "Most idiots connect the drain hose *before* they empty their sewage!" The campground host muttered vague obscenities as he tossed another shovelful back onto the apron. "Have you got no mechanical sense at all? What do you do for a living, anyway?"

Tipper was about to open his mouth and explain, so I squirted him with the garden hose. "Oh, look at that! My mistake, son. Why don't you head off to the hot showers and wash off some of this smell before your mother gets here. I'll join you shortly."

Things went much better after that. With a hot meal and some outdoor pool time, the family actually began to enjoy the trip. In fact, it became a weekend of discovery for my children. "Hey, Mom, look what we discovered!" The kids were gathered around the rear of the motorhome. "Dad says all this brown powdery stuff falling on the ground is called dry rot. It's probably why the old geezers sold this motorhome so cheap in the first place."

"Old geezers?" echoed Cookie. "Children, where are your manners!"

"Those are Dad's words," explained Cache.

I learned some other valuable RV tips as well. "And it's very important to put the awning up *before* driving away," I instructed the kids.

"Yeah," interjected my wife. "Otherwise you get people chasing after you with sticks because you damaged their trailer on the way by." She looked in the side mirror. "Could you speed it up a little, dear? They're getting closer."

Carrie put down her comic book. "Hey Pops, what's with the loud bang

I heard as we pulled out, the one just before the awning hit the trailer?"

I glanced at the black mamba bouncing down the road behind us. "It's just the power chord, sweetie. We'll stop and coil it up once the mob thins out."

By this time, my credit card was suffering from severe overexposure. My expenditures for the weekend included a battery, two new tires, a full set of dishes, and a case of duct tape to keep the siding in place while driving. The awning repairs were still to come.

We were just about back to Slumberland when Cookie suddenly hollered for me to pull over. Expecting to find another piece of the body going south, I grabbed the duct tape off the dash and jumped out. But to my surprise, everything was in its proper place – except for my wife. She was nowhere to be found.

The kids had their noses pressed against the side window. "Mom went that way," they said in unison. I nearly had heart failure as I followed their gaze. Next to the highway was a huge sales lot full of brand-new motorhomes.

Climbing into a forty-foot diesel-pusher motor coach, I found Cookie relaxing in a leather recliner next to a marble gas fireplace. "Now this," she smiled dreamily, "is RVing."

I looked at the price tag on the window and gasped. "What about the $5,000 budget?" I squeaked.

She put on her pouty face. "Are you saying our marriage isn't worth a few extra dollars?" She closed her eyes and snuggled in deeper. "Besides, it's your fault for bringing up the subject in the first place. You were right; we should have done this years ago."

Being right can be costly. Oh, somehow we'll find the money to buy a better rig, but it certainly won't be like the monster we were standing in. In fact, my list of 'must-haves' had been pared down to a few basic essentials: it goes out, it comes home, and it has propane.

But the next time we do any hiking, I'm going to insist that we visit a pond. As far as I know, they don't build them on vertical slopes.

CHAPTER 7

❧ DEVELOPMENT DAZE ❧

In a small town like Slumberland, there are certain phrases that, if spoken in just the right circles, can really get the citizens out of their rocking chairs and off their porches in a big hurry. *Yard Sale* is one such phrase.

One summer Cookie decided we should have a yard sale to get rid of a few unused items. "Honestly, Slim, this stuff is just collecting dust in the garage. It's time it went to somebody who will actually use it."

"No way!" I declared, looking down at the pile of weightlifting equipment. "This *stuff*, as you call it, has sentimental value." I picked up a small dumbbell and flexed my arm. The only response was a loud pop from my elbow.

Cookie observed my pitiful efforts. "I think you mean *sedimentary* value."

"Very funny." I tried to lift one end of the weight bench and drag it back towards the house. It wouldn't budge. "Say, how did you get these heavy things out to the curb anyway?"

She blew a strand of hair out of her eyes. "Tipper helped. He's a lot stronger than you look."

With the assistance of a furniture dolly, I moved the Buff Bubba Championship Weight Training Kit back into the garage, hiding it under the table saw where it belonged. What Cookie didn't understand was that actually using the weights wasn't the issue. The simple fact that I owned them made me feel more manly.

After rescuing a few other important items from the curb-side pile, I drove down to Main Street to drum up some business. Climbing onto the hood of my truck, I rubbed my sore elbow and hollered, "Yard sale today at 3212 Crabapple Drive!" Returning home, I got caught in a traffic jam of automobiles, bicycles, wheelchairs, and baby carriages. I barely arrived in time to break up a bidding war over my youngest child.

"Thanks, Dad," said Tipper. "I owe you one."

"You'd better believe it," I replied. "But the next time you try to help mom sell my Buff Bubba gear, you're history."

So the kids were now safe, but the annoying budgie we kept in the kitchen wasn't so lucky. To this day, Cookie maintains that I was the one who wrote *Free* on the bird with a magic marker. "Why would I do that?" I protested, hiding the marker behind my back.

Cookie glared at me. "You've never liked Sparky, especially once he learned to talk."

"Oh yeah? And how would you like to be greeted three times a day with 'Hey, Fatso, how's the paunch today?'"

"Eight times a day," corrected my wife. "He only said it when you were snooping in the fridge for snacks."

Well, not anymore.

Budgerigars and yard sales aside, there is also a word that can really stir up the hornet's nest around town – the word *Development*. Whisper the D-word quietly in Baldy's Barbershop and riots break out in front of town hall. Say it aloud on a street corner and you'll cause a minor traffic accident. In fact, there is such a local aversion to the D-word that folks here have adapted their speech patterns.

Instead of saying *development*, our schoolteachers will refer to a child's academic *process of advancement*. The public health nurses show pregnant mothers flip charts, illustrating a baby's progressive stages of *growth enhancement*.

Local businesses have to be especially careful. Recently, the drugstore advertised the following special: *Film Developing, extra prints only 10 cents each*. Before the police could get the situation under control, three windows were broken and all the chocolates went missing on aisle six.

Therefore, it was with great interest (and wearing protective headgear) that I recently attended a town council meeting. A variance application to add a storage shed to the back of my repair shop was on the agenda, and I was hoping Mayor and Council would lend me their support.

On most council nights, you could fire a cannon through the visitors' gallery and not hit anyone, provided our town reporter Rover Dangerphrase ducked first. But tonight was different. The room was packed to capacity. Outside, boisterous picketers spilled down the steps and into the street waving their placards and shouting slogans. Three extra patrol cars brought in from Panicton were slowly circling the block, while inside two stern-faced RCMP officers stood at the back of the room, decked out in full riot gear. The night held much promise, so I found a seat next to Buck and settled in to observe.

"Nice goalie mask you've got there," I said in admiration. "Did those thick shin pads come with it or were they extra?"

"It's a package deal," he replied. "You can buy them local, but they're cheaper at Big Box Mart in Panicton. Say, you wouldn't have an extra can of mace, would you? I hear things could get ugly tonight." He offered me a chocolate from the brown paper bag he was holding.

I chose one filled with caramel. "Why? What's on the agenda?"

Buck was incredulous. "What! Ain't you heard?" Leaning closer, he lowered his voice. "They're discussing the D-word tonight. Some out-of-towner wants to put up an 18-storey hotel out on the highway, right where the tourists can see it. Can you imagine the audacity?"

I chewed thoughtfully and reached for another chocolate. "Uh huh. And would that, by any chance, be somewhere close to your motel?"

"You're dang right it is." Buck's beady eyes darted suspiciously from side to side. "Right across the road, from what I hear."

I sighed. "Why does everyone get so riled up whenever somebody wants to build something in this town? Don't they realize that everything we take for granted in life – the grocery stores, the office buildings, even our houses – have all been built by devel..." Buck shot me a warning glance. "Er, I mean, by structural assemblers and providers? People should learn to appreciate the benefits of a free-market economy."

Buck looked at me with disgust. "Oh yeah? And I also hear they're putting in a 12-bay repair shop on the ground floor."

"What!" I leapt to my feet. "Let's hang 'em right now from the flagpole; let's boil up a bucket of tar, let's..."

Buck pulled me back down. "Shut up," he growled. "We ain't even seen the guy yet. If you make a fuss before the meeting starts, he'll sneak out. Then we won't know who we're supposed to run outta town." He passed the bag of chocolates my way again. "No sense ruining the night's entertainment before we even get started."

As usual, Buck's cooler head prevailed. I picked out a hazelnut cream and took a bite. "Say, these aren't bad. Did you get them at Big Box Mart as well?"

He coughed and looked the other way. "No, I...uh...picked them up locally the other day while I was getting some film processed. Now shush up and keep your eyes peeled for that D fellow."

Just then a side door opened and Hank Brink entered the room. Wearing an umpire's vest and carrying a thick sheaf of documents, our town planner went around the council table distributing an agenda package to each councilor's place. You could feel the tension rising in the room as the riot police took a tighter grip on their nightsticks.

"Hey Hank!" called someone from the back of the room. "Is that a copy of the proposed DEVELOPMENT you're passing out? I hear they're asking for 500 acres of top grade farm land to build it on!"

Hank began to perspire. "Ah, no, actually," he answered nervously. "You're mistaken there. They only want to..."

Somewhere to the left, a chair crashed to the floor as a concerned citizen jumped to his feet. "Yeah, and I heard they want t' pump all the sewage right into the city reservoir!"

An ominous rumble of voices filled the room. "Don't be absurd," protested Hank, mopping his forehead with his handkerchief. "The fact is..."

But the floodgates had cracked open and the comments came

fast and furious: "...overpass right through the schoolyard...won't be using any local staff – bringing in his relatives from Toronto to run the joint...our taxes are gonna increase by 200%...I hear they wanna build 80 condos right next door..." Like distant thunder, a low chant began at the back of the room, growing with intensity as more people joined in. Throwing aside all earlier reserve, Buck jumped onto his chair and pumped his fist into the air. "Down with the D-men!" he hollered. "Down with the D-men! Down with the D-men!"

Much to the relief of the anxious police officers, Mayor Dewgood and his council members chose that moment to enter the room. Dewgood swept the room with a fierce gaze as he sat down, and the place went quiet. Our mayor may not be a big man, but what he lacks in stature he more than makes up for in personal presence. A single word from his lips has been known to silence baying hounds; a stern glance from his eyes can make a car salesman lower his asking price; and his diatribes on the finer points of municipal law have caused many a seasoned lawyer to soil themselves. On the other hand, his toothy smile and firm handshake have charmed more than one citizen out of their vote at election time. Let's just say Mayor Dewgood knows how to keep Slumberland in line.

After calling the meeting to order, Dewgood pointed his gavel at a meek little man trying to hide behind a briefcase in the front row.

"Mr. Peatmoss," he boomed, "we will now consider your development proposal. Would you like to make your presentation to Council at this time?"

At the mere mention of the D-word, the whole room collectively sucked in its breath. I shuddered at the thought of what would happen next, and even considered leaving while I had the chance. But Peatmoss had already risen on trembling legs, and was clearing his throat to speak. Before he could get a word out, a familiar voice from the chair next to me cut through the stillness. "There he is, boys – get 'im!" The occupants of the room exhaled as one and the chase was on.

What happened next is still a blur, but I do recall the headlines from the next day's edition of the *Slumberland Rebuttal*:

> **Big city developer run out of town on a railroad tie; extra police brought in to quell riot!**

In the article, Rover Dangerphrase went on to write how the proposed development was actually nothing more than a hot dog and cider stand, to be built on a vacant lot next to Deth Pallor's Funeral Home. They'd even planned to use local apples to make the cider.

What I do remember is that after the majority of the crowd left in hot pursuit of poor Mr. Peatmoss, Mayor Dewgood had no choice but to move on to new business.

"Slim Shambles," he boomed again loudly. "I do believe you have a proposal before Council concerning your repair shop." He leaned forward and slid his bifocals down his nose. "Now what, exactly, might that be?"

I gulped and looked around the council chambers. At the sound of the mayor's voice, a bunch of stragglers, mostly old men with canes, stopped and sniffed the air like hound dogs picking up a scent. Several shuffled in my direction, jockeying to get within cane range. A sudden disturbance startled me, and I looked down to see Buck crawling out from underneath his chair. "Buck? I thought you were out leading the riot."

"Naw, that's too much like work. I just do the inciting." He brushed himself off and eyed me suspiciously. "Now what's all this talk about development at your repair shop?"

I realized that if I wanted my variance permit, I would first have to clear all the opposition from the room. Climbing up on my chair, I summoned my courage and in a loud voice uttered the bravest words I have ever spoken: "There's an all-night yard sale at The Happy Peasant Motel, starting right now! All furniture and fixtures half-price!"

"That was a dirty trick," grumbled Buck sourly. It was three weeks later, and he was still sore at me. "Do you realize I was up all night chasing them yard salers off my property? They even tried to sneak off with my outdoor pool."

"I apologize," I said, banging in the last nail of my new addition. I stood back. "Well, how does she look?"

Buck squinted at my new storage shed while he sipped some coffee. "Fine, I guess. But what are you gonna keep in there? I thought you already had a parts room."

I went over to my truck and pulled aside the tarp that was covering the box. "It's not for parts; it's to store this stuff." There in the back of the truck, in all its glory, was my Buff Bubba Championship Weight Training Kit. "I had to get it out of the garage before Cookie went on another spring cleaning binge. I can't believe I almost lost it."

Buck raised a shaggy eyebrow. "That would have been a shame. I'm feeling more manly just sitting here looking at it." He drained the dregs of his coffee and looked around for a refill. "Are you really gonna pump some iron?"

I laughed at Buck's attempt at jocularity. Lifting out a couple of other items I had rescued from the last yard sale, I put them in the shed for safekeeping. Buck went over to inspect the brand new mountain bike and the sturdy pair of cross-country skis. Neither item had ever been used. "They're beautiful, Slim," he breathed in awe and amazement. "Would it be okay if I came by to gaze at them every now and then?"

And there's another reason why I'll never pump iron; I wouldn't want to be accused of *developing* some muscle tone. It might cause a riot.

CHAPTER 8

⊰ COOKIE'S VALENTINE ⊱

I t was a Wednesday morning in mid-February, and the winter sunshine sparkled brightly off the banks of newly plowed snow. I love snow banks: they're a lot more forgiving than concrete barriers when I take the corners a little too fast.

Not many people hang around an industrial park that early in the morning, so the road was my own and I was having a blast driving to work. But as I completed a perfect 360 into the parking lot, the nagging suspicion that I was forgetting something returned like a dark cloud. The suspicion first appeared that morning as I was leaving for work.

"Here's your lunch, sweetie." Cookie smiled at me as she thrust the brown paper bag into my hands. "I know you'll be busy over the lunch hour, so I packed light."

I frowned. Cookie never pays much attention to my appointment schedule, so her comments were puzzling. Just then the phone rang, and as Cookie went to answer, she called back over her shoulder, "Don't be late for dinner; I'm planning something special!"

Now I was really worried. Her birthday wasn't until August and our wedding anniversary was still over a month away, so I checked my day-timer. Nope, it wasn't even time for my own birthday. The fact that my wife was planning a special dinner meant something important was up, but hanged if I knew what it was. I also knew better than to ask.

"Morning, Basil," I said, as I hung up my coat in the office. He nodded absently, deeply engrossed in a magazine article about disc brakes. He makes a point of looking wise and mature when people are watching, but I know better. From what I'd just seen in the snow, he'd done a nice little figure 8 in the parking lot with his Fiat before I arrived.

Pouring myself a cup of coffee, I decided to check out the appointment book, looking specifically for any jobs booked in around noon. But there were none.

"Basil," I asked casually, "do we have something coming in over the lunch hour today, something we forgot to write down?"

He glanced up, a knowing smile on his face. "Let me guess – Cookie dropped a hint this morning."

I shrugged my way into a pair of clean coveralls. "Don't know what you're talking about. Want a refill on your coffee?"

Basil chuckled and held out his mug. "Have it your way. Most stores are sold out by now, but I hear Fuzzyberries might have something left. That's where I always go when I forget."

There was no way I was admitting to Basil that I'd forgotten something, especially where it concerned my wife. So I changed the subject. "Well, we might as well get started. These cars aren't going to fix themselves."

We spent the rest of the morning fighting seized spark plugs and rusted bolts, all under a shower of melting snow and ice. Winter has got to be the worst time of year to be a mechanic. By the time noon rolled around, I was soaked and ready for a break. But when I opened up my lunch bag, I discovered what Cookie meant by packing light.

Basil inspected the scrawny piece of meat I held out and shook his head in disbelief. "I didn't know it was possible to deep fry the hind legs of a mosquito." He inhaled deeply. "However, I do believe I smell apple pie."

I looked hopefully into the bag again, but there was no pie. Apparently, the aroma was all I was going to get. "Well, there's a carrot here," I said in resignation. "At least I won't starve. Just the same, I think I'll head downtown and pick up something for dessert."

Basil just smirked. "That Cookie is one smart gal. Remember what I said: start with Fuzzyberries. They're your best bet."

A few minutes later I slid to a stop in front of Fuzzyberries Ice Cream & Eatery. Pulling my winter hat down low over my eyes, I jumped over the slush by the curb and then sauntered inconspicuously into the popular ice cream and candy store. I knew I was on a mission, but for the life of me I couldn't figure out what it was. So until I knew how things were hanging, I had to play it cool.

"Hey, Slim," greeted Mike, the owner. "Those big chocolate hearts are popular this year. Got one left!"

"No thanks," I said. "Not a big chocolate fan. But I'll have a coffee and muffin to go." I glanced around the store, curious what Basil had meant when he said that this place would be my best bet.

"Hmm. Okay." Mike shot me a sideways glance as he poured the coffee. "Say, you *do* know it's Valentine's Day, don't you?" He set the pot back on the burner.

"Do I know…?" I rolled my eyes. "Sheesh, what kind of an idiot do you take me for?"

Mike threw up his hands. "Hey, I'm just making conversation, that's all." He nodded towards the display case. "But I think Bavarian Fudge is one of your wife's favorites."

His insinuations were beginning to annoy me. "Are you implying that I'm not ready for Valentine's Day?" I pointed to the coffee. "I'll have some extra cream, please. And don't forget that muffin: blueberry, if you have it."

He shrugged, added the cream, and put a lid on the coffee cup. "Some guys wait 'til the last minute, you know." He put my muffin in a bag and set it beside the coffee.

Digging in my pocket for some change, I agreed. "Yeah, the sops. They never learn, do they?"

"Nope, they never do." Mike counted the money. "Hey, you gave me too much."

"Oh, did I?" I reached into the display case. "Well, keep it. I'll just take this chocolate heart here to make up the difference."

"Why not?" grinned Mike. "It's the last one."

Mission accomplished, I pulled a slushy u-turn in the middle of the street and drove back to the shop. As I did, I reflected on my first date with my own special Valentine, my wife Cookie. It seemed like only yesterday...

"Hello...is this Slime Shambles?"

My heart skipped a beat as I clutched the telephone receiver with both hands. It was her! Cookie McDream, the girl I adored, but never had the courage to talk to. And she was calling me!

"Y-yes, this is Slime...er, Slim...ah, I mean me." I gritted my teeth. *What a ditz!* "And thank you for calling!"

"Huh?" There was a long silence. "Well, whatever. Listen, Sam, this is Cookie McDream, and I need a favor."

"The name's Slim," I squeaked. "A favor? Sure, anything you want!"

There was a heavy sigh on the other end of the line. "What I want is no longer the issue. It's a question of desperation now."

Playing it safe, I said nothing.

She continued. "Look, Kim, it's my company's annual Christmas party, and I vowed I would never go alone again." She paused for an agonizing moment, and then blurted out, "Want to take me?"

There it was, our first date. I felt honored, and I told her so.

"Well, don't be," she replied. "All my friends are busy, and Rent-a-Date is completely booked. You're last on the list."

Being a man of pride and principle, I accepted the invitation in a heartbeat. I might have been last, but at least I was on the list.

At this point in my life, I had just graduated from automotive trade school, and was therefore completely broke. So much so, that I had moved back home to live with my parents on their apple orchard in Narymatter, a sleepy little farming community just across the lake from Slumberland. Although I was now a fully-licensed automotive technician, the economy had taken a downturn and there were no jobs to be had. So I was down to fixing the neighborhood tractors in Pa's workshop. To be honest, life was looking a tad bleak.

But then Cookie came along. I first noticed her sitting with her friends in the little church I attended on the weekends in Panicton. She was hard to miss, a petite blonde with heart-stopping blue eyes. My valiant efforts to strike up a conversation with her in the foyer afterwards always seemed to end with my tongue tied in knots around my left shoe. I once overheard her comparing notes with her friends. "Yeah, that tall guy with the dorky glasses and a beard is okay; I just can't understand a word he says. Do you think he actually knows English?"

Cookie's phone call gave me renewed hope, and I was determined to make this first date a roaring success. Someone once told me that first impressions are very important, so as soon as I hung up the phone I ran outside to wash The Truckinator.

Now, The Truckinator, or TT for short, was a work in progress. Originally a 1956 Chevrolet pickup, TT was slowly being transformed into a street-dominating, tire-smoking hot rod, piece by chrome-plated piece. Slowly is the operative word here. Finances being what they were, I often had to settle for primed metal instead of chrome.

No, in those day the Truckinator was what we called a *sleeper*. The non-descript exterior concealed a thundering mass of raw power beneath, just waiting to unleash itself upon any unsuspecting motorist foolish enough to challenge me at a stoplight. That's provided I don't stall the engine when the light turns green.

Under TT's hood sat a bored-out Chevy 283 with 10:1 pistons, a racing cam, and a Holley 4-barrel carburetor. The rebuilt Turbo 400 transmission had a nice little shift kit installed, which gave it a solid grab between gears. The loud cherry bomb mufflers made The Truckinator fun to drive, albeit most of the neighbors held an alternate view on the subject.

Now Pa Shambles had a unique relationship with The Truckinator – mostly he tried to ignore it. Some days I wished he would learn to avoid it instead. "Hey," I cried one day, "there's a new dent in my truck! Did you hit it with the tractor again?"

Pa shrugged as he polished the candy apple red paintjob on his fully restored Buick. "A new dent? How can you tell? They all look the same to me."

But today as he came out of his workshop, Pa just stopped and stared. "What are you doing out here in the snow?" he asked in disbelief.

I dropped the sponge into the wash bucket and wiped my frozen fingers on my jeans. "I'm shining up my truck. Got a hot date tomorrow night."

"Shining it up?" He shook his head. "What's to shine? Don't you need paint first?"

I looked at my pride and joy, and realized he had a point. The Truckinator was a patchwork of brown, black, and gray primer. A real paint job was still light-years away. The only shiny parts showing were the chrome wheels, which I'd already washed six times. I had to face it: this was as shiny as TT was going to get. "Well, I just wanted to make a good impression, I guess."

Pa grunted and shook his head. "If you want to make a good impression, take her in something else."

I couldn't believe what I was hearing. "Great idea, Pa! Does that mean I can borrow the Bui…?"

"Nope," he said, cutting me off. And on that note, he stumped up the stairs and disappeared into the house for dinner. Typical Pa Shambles: always long on advice but short on solutions.

I could hardly concentrate on my work the next day. The two farm tractors I was rebuilding were caked in old grease and other farm residue, and by the end of the day I had to shower twice to get rid of the stains and smells. After decking myself out in a festive holiday sweater and my best pair of jeans, I fired up The Truckinator and rumbled around the lake to Slumberland, where Cookie lived.

Pulling into her driveway a few minutes early, I found Cookie waiting anxiously by the front door. I started to get out of the cab, but she was already climbing in the passenger side.

"Wow," I said. "Are we late or something? You seem to be in a hurry."

Cookie slammed the door, and then slammed it again when it wouldn't close the first time. "Let's just get moving before my parents see this wreck," she said. "It'll give them one more thing to worry about."

One more thing? I wondered. *What does that mean?*

She glanced around. "Where's the seat belt?"

"Uh, they didn't have them in 1956."

She stared at me. "How lovely." Then she sighed. "Well then, drive slowly. I, for one, plan to survive the evening." I gulped and shifted into reverse. As far as first impressions went, this was *not* one of my better ones.

We headed for the restaurant, me clutching the steering wheel nervously and Cookie clutching the dashboard in terror. "You should relax!" I shouted above the loud exhaust. "It won't blow up – it's supposed to sound this way!"

But a hard knot was forming in the pit of my stomach as I tried to figure out why Cookie's parents would already be in a state of worry. As far as I knew, we'd never met.

Once at the restaurant, however, things began to look up. Her boss had gone all out, reserving the entire party section. "Wow," I whispered to Cookie as we ate. "Your boss is a great guy. Talk about sparing no expense – I got to super-size everything!" I squirted more ketchup on my fries. "Uh, sorry about the Coke I spilled on your dress when I choked on the Big Snac."

"Don't worry about it," she replied graciously. "It'll make it easier to remove the grease stain I got from your truck seat." She nibbled at her hamburger. "So how come your truck always jerks when it shifts gears? Is there something wrong with the transmission?"

Dinner was only the beginning of the evening's events. From there we moved on to the main party at the boss's house. Before leaving the restaurant, Mr. Big himself gave me the privilege of leading the rest of the group to his home. He even gave me a hand-drawn map on a napkin. "Shouldn't be too hard," he said. "It's only six blocks away."

An hour later, I pulled off the road, trying in vain to read the map in my hand. "I'm sure we're getting close," I muttered. A long line of cars driven by the other employees waited behind us, angrily honking their horns. "It's just so hard to read this map he drew."

"I'm not surprised," declared Cookie icily, "considering you used the map to clean the inside of your windshield."

"Sorry," I said lamely. "The defroster is broken right now." Her cold stare verified that I wasn't warming her up, either. But eventually we found the right house...or at least I thought we had.

"Why are all the lights out?" I asked. "Did we really take that long?"

But after waking up the boss and his wife, everybody piled through the front door and headed for the bar in the recreation room. From all accounts, a great time was had by all. Although Cookie and I didn't partake, the rest of the staff consumed enough alcohol to forget that I was even remotely associated with their fellow employee in any way, shape, or form. That cheered her up considerably.

Driving home afterwards, Cookie was in a jovial mood. "Well, that didn't go too badly," she commented. "They really loved your standup comedy routine."

I gripped the steering wheel and swallowed hard. "Actually, I was reciting a sonnet," I said. "It was about a jilted lover who killed himself rather than live with rejection."

Cookie yawned and waved a hand. "Yeah, whatever." We pulled into her driveway once more, and as she opened the door to get out, she said, "Thanks for the ride home, Dim."

"The name is Slim," I mumbled in resignation, banging my head against the steering wheel. I had never felt so low in my entire life. There was no doubt that if things were left as they were, I'd never hear from Cookie McDream again. In desperation I blurted out, "Say, would you like to go out with me again sometime?"

The minutes ticked by slowly as I waited for Cookie to regain her composure. Wiping the tears from her eyes, she finally managed to gasp, "My goodness, Bim, you sure know how to make a girl laugh. I almost passed out with that one!" Then she paused and looked at me thoughtfully. "Sure, let's do that. I could use a good laugh once in a while. See you next Saturday?"

Just like that, Cookie McDream got out of my truck and walked into my life. And after more than two decades of marriage, she still likes it when I make her laugh.

And me? I just like it when she remembers my name. No one else says it better.

CHAPTER 9

❧ ALL MAKES AND MODELS ❧

The brightly-painted vehicles created a rainbow of vibrant color as they lined the streets around Mumbleton Park. It was the May long weekend, time for the annual Orchard Run in Slumberland. By Saturday morning hundreds of hot rods and classic cars had inundated the town, most of them sporting more chrome than a '57 Buick.

"Mish ish awshum, Shlim!" exclaimed Buck through a mouthful of cotton candy. His motel was jammed with the out-of-town hot rod owners, drawn in by the low rates posted on his sign. But so many had complained about paying extra for running water that Buck called me up, looking for an excuse to get off the property.

I didn't mind having him along while I took photos of the cars. The only problem was that he managed to get the back of his head into every picture I took. Some people are photogenic, but with Buck, it's more like a photo-genetic disorder. And once you've seen it, you'd rather not see it again.

"We need more of these events around this town," I declared, adjusting the polarizing filter on my camera. "Car shows are clean, safe, and great fun for the whole family. And I'll bet it's good for your motel business."

Buck shrugged. "That's debatable. To be honest, I'm getting tired of all the complaining."

I raised my eyebrows. "Yeah, I heard there was a bunch of partying going on there last night. You'd better crack down on that."

Buck was indignant. "What for? It's my own property – I can have a party if I want to!"

I chuckled to myself and moved on to the next car in the lineup. "Hey, nice '32 Ford Deuce Coupe. I definitely want a picture of this baby. Now move."

Buck ignored me. Pressing his sticky fingers against the side window of the flaming yellow hot rod, he peered inside at the fancy leather seats and custom dashboard. "Maybe I should do something like this with my Merc."

"Don't touch the cars, Buck," I cautioned. "You're getting fingerprints all over the place." Lying down on the pavement, I angled the camera upwards for a better shot.

"Oh." Buck looked at the mess he'd made. "Well, no problem – I'll just wipe 'em off." He pulled up his shirttail, exposing a large western belt buckle studded with gaudy sequins.

With a yell, the Coupe's owner scrambled out of his lawn chair, spilling his drink in the process. His eyes bulged as the belt buckle drew closer to his expensive paint job.

I jumped up and grabbed Buck's arm, dragging him away. "Say, how about a candy apple – there's a booth over by that tree."

We beat a hasty retreat and got lost in the crowd. "I still don't know why my car was banned from the Show & Shine." Buck glowered as he tossed the empty cotton candy tube into a nearby trash container. "I betcha I could've won first prize."

I glanced over to see if he was serious. "Buck, they don't hand out prizes for rust." We stopped to examine the engine compartment of a blue 1968 Corvette. "Now here is something that deserves a prize – an L88 427 cubic inch big block. Did you know that only 115 of these engines were ever sold that year?" I adjusted my camera lens for a close-up shot. "This thing is rare."

Buck sniffed. "Yeah, well, my Topaz is rare, too. There just ain't many cars left like Old Betsy."

I tossed a cynical smirk in his direction. "Thank heaven for small mercies."

We were standing in front of Memory Lane Retirement Centre, a venerable old building located right across the street from the park. The aging residents were out in full force, enjoying the fine collection of automobiles. Some folks were in wheelchairs, but others were sunning themselves on park benches, their canes and walkers within easy reach. Many of these cars hailed from the days of their youth, and seeing them again brought back happy memories.

I recognized one long-time resident right away. "Morning, Hooch. How's the arthritis today?"

Hooch Rambler didn't answer right away – his mind was on other things. His rheumy eyes glistened as he gazed upon the collection of vehicles filling the street. It was nostalgia at its best...or perhaps at its worst.

You see, Hooch used to be a race car driver back in the Forties, although rumor has it his driving skills were honed running moonshine with his pa during the prohibition years. After hanging up his racing goggles, Hooch moved to Slumberland and ran a mechanic's shop until his aching joints forced him to retire. Now the closest he ever got to a vehicle was when the Sunshine Bus came around on Bingo Night. I think his lack of mobility weighed heavily on him.

But Hooch was in a good mood today. "I used to drive a truck just like this, Slim!" he declared. His cane thumped up and down in excitement as he ogled a customized 1928 Model A pickup that bore little resemblance to anything ever produced by Henry Ford. I took a closer look at the old man. Hooch was wearing his ancient leather driving helmet, with a pair of old goggles perched on top. Seeing him dressed this way made me apprehensive. *Something doesn't seem right here*, I thought.

"You drove one of *these*? I doubt that, Hooch." I pointed to the powerful engine with chrome exhaust pipes bulging out the sides. "This is nothing like the cars you used to race. There's about 600 more horsepower here than you've ever dreamed of."

Hooch just waved me off. "Ah, shoot, I won lots o' races in one o' these rigs," he bragged, his eyes glazing over with ancient memories.

"Bet I still could."

"Yeah, too bad those days are long gone," said Buck, yawning. "It's gotta be twenty years since they took your license away, ain't it?" He pulled a toothpick out of his shirt pocket and bent over the small chrome side mirror to get a better look at his teeth.

"Harrumph! Who needs a license? It's like ridin' a bicycle – ya never forget how." Hooch pushed himself upright and hobbled towards the vehicle. "An' I'll prove it to ya."

"HOOCH!"

For an old guy, Hooch could move pretty fast. Within seconds, he'd slid his arthritic frame under the dashboard of the Model A and disappeared. Obviously, this had been planned well in advance. All it took was a couple of dummies to come and stand in the right place to screen his getaway – dummies like me and Buck.

Whipping out a pair of small jumper wires, it took Hooch only seconds to bring the engine roaring to life. Grinning from ear to ear, he straightened up behind the wheel and snapped his goggles into place. Mashing the gas pedal to the floor, he dropped the truck into gear and lit up the rear tires, filling the street with choking blue smoke. Buck jumped back from the mirror, but not before Hooch laid a strip of rubber right across his sneakers.

When the smoke cleared, all that remained were twin tire tracks that clearly marked the escape route. Hooch had crossed the street, vaulted over the sidewalk and gone right through the middle of Mumbleton Park. The wide path of destruction was marked by overturned vending booths and scattered folding chairs. Not only did the Pony Ride turn into a chariot race, but the hot air balloon sheared its moorings and soared skywards, taking Mayor Dewgood with it. Our illustrious politician had been giving a speech from inside the gondola, but he was now bellowing orders to his lackeys on the ground as they ran back and forth, trying to grab the dangling ropes.

Buck stared up at the balloon as it drifted east towards Hollownoggin Lake. "Sheesh, with all the hot air coming outta Mayor Dewgood, he'll be up there for a week!"

Behind us, the geriatric crowd of spectators in front of Memory Lane broke into a rousing cheer. Clearly, their sympathies lay with the escapee, and Buck and I were now unwitting heroes for helping him do it.

After a long and circuitous chase through the side streets of Slumberland, the RCMP finally cornered Hooch in the parking lot of the grocery store and returned him to the care of the Memory Lane staff. A victory celebration awaited him in the activity room, and I'm sure the Ovaltine ran high that night.

"So much for the Orchard Run being a clean and safe event," said Buck later, as we surveyed the damage outside the Bean Dust Café. Hooch had managed to miss only one of the planters on his third run past the popular hangout. "But I agree it's great fun for the whole family. I know I got a kick out of it!"

We sat down at one of the outside tables and ordered cappuccinos. "So how's your foot?" I asked.

Buck examined his shredded sneaker. "Not bad. Good thing I wore my steel-toed models."

I stared at him. "You wear steel-toed footwear? Buck, you run a motel, not a welding shop."

"So? You think motel work doesn't have its dangers?" He sniffed indignantly. "Sometimes it gets so bad I gotta wear ear protection *and* a hardhat."

"I can understand the ear protection," I replied, "considering what some of your guests say about your motel. But why the hard hat?"

Buck lowered his voice and leaned close. "Tell you what – just go and nick Dolly's flower beds with *your* lawn mower and see what happens." He shook his head. "It's a good thing I can run fast."

Down Main Street, the hot rods were pulling out one by one for a sunset cruise. The excitement was over for the day and Slumberland was once more settling down for the night. I chuckled at the mental image of Buck running to escape his wife's wrath. Then I thought about

Hooch's glorious bid to escape the confines of retirement. On top of that, there was the mayor floating high above Hollownoggin Lake, no doubt devising painful and diverse punishments for all those responsible for his current predicament.

The Orchard Run might bring together different makes and models of classic cars, but Slumberland…well, Slumberland has just as many makes and models of classic characters – people like Buck, Dolly, Hooch, and Mayor Dewgood.

Reaching for my cappuccino, I took a moment to reflect on my good fortune. Slumberland is an ongoing drama, with a new act offered every day.

And I get a front row seat to it all.

CHAPTER 10

❧ THE BRITISH ARE COMING ❧

*W*ow! *This V12 is really smooth.* I pulled onto a straight section of highway and put Sir Rodney's '87 Jaguar through its paces. *Got to get me one of these!* Jaguars were not a common vehicle around our shop, but I hated to turn away work, no matter how strange it was. I recalled the elderly gentleman's complaint when he showed up that morning.

"The strangest noise appears when I throttle out of a right hand curve." Sir Rodney was perched on the edge of one of our office chairs, primly holding his teacup in one hand as he adjusted his monocle with the other. "And it's not coming from under the bonnet, either. In fact, I should think it will be difficult to locate, as I've had several blokes attempt it already."

Sir Rodney was a fine example of old British gentry. It showed in everything from his impeccable manners right down to his tweed hunting jacket and handlebar mustache. I don't really know if his title indicated actual knighthood or not, but he certainly conducted himself as such, and who were we to argue?

"We'll do our best," I assured him. "Would you like a warm-up on that tea?"

He frowned. "Warm up my tea? I should think not!" He set down his half-empty cup and picked up his umbrella. "Actually, it's been a poor excuse for elevenses around here. Not a bickie in sight." He stood to his feet. "Now give me a lift home, old chap, and I'll let you get on with your work."

After dropping him off at his orchard – which he referred to as his country estate – I made my way back to the shop…with a little detour for a test drive, of course. Throwing the car into a right hand corner, I accelerated hard. A loud tapping noise appeared instantly and I groaned – it sounded like it was coming from inside the wood-grained shifter console right beside me. *Great – I hope we don't have to take that whole console apart.*

I glided noiselessly into the shop and shut off the engine. Basil came over from the workbench where he'd been overhauling a carburetor. "Well, Squire Shambles, what do you think? Is our Duke of Earl Grey Tea just hearing things, or does he have a legitimate complaint?"

"He most definitely has a problem, but I sure don't know what it could be." I climbed out of the low-slung vehicle. "Never heard anything like it. Let's put it on the hoist and do the transmission service first. We'll check out the noise later."

Once the car was in the air, I took a trouble light and inspected the automatic transmission. "Are you serious?" I muttered. "Do we really have to remove the crossmember before we can get at the oil pan?"

Basil smiled. "Welcome to the world of British automobiles." He dug around in the bottom of his toolbox for his near-new set of Whitworth standard wrenches. Since they only fit British cars, they rarely saw the light of day. "I actually enjoy working on these vehicles from time to time. Come to think of it, aren't you a bit of an expert on them yourself? As I recall, you became rather intimate with Land Rovers when you were in Africa."

"Thanks a lot!" I shuddered. That was a memory I was hoping to forget…

Cookie and I had been married only two years when we volunteered to work on a relief project in Kenya, East Africa. We were assigned to a remote mission station in the northwest corner of the country called the Turkana District, named after the dominant tribe of the area. It was a hot, dusty place that grew an abundance of scorpions and thorn bushes. It also had an abysmal lack of paved roads, which made the durable four-wheel drive Land Rover the vehicle of choice. My job was to keep the project vehicles running, and over the next two years the majority of automobiles that crawled through my workshop door were Landys. I even got to own one.

"Well, here it is!" said Wendell, the veteran missionary and project manager. He had come all the way down to Nairobi to meet us when we first arrived in the country. He'd also brought our transportation, a Series II Land Rover station wagon. "I had my helpers go over it from front to back. Anything that needed fixing, we did it."

We looked at the battered grey vehicle sitting before us in the guest house parking lot, and wondered what we were getting ourselves into. "It's a good thing you're a mechanic," Cookie whispered in my ear, "or I wouldn't go ten yards in that thing."

I gulped and walked around the Land Rover. The suspension sagged a little to the left, and one of the ten-ply tires was worn down to ply #8. Opening the hood for a peek, I caught sight of duct tape and mechanic's wire holding a number of crucial items in place. I quickly slammed the hood before Cookie had a chance to see: there are some things you just don't want your wife to know. "Well, it's a beauty, that's for sure. How does it run?"

Wendell rubbed the back of his deeply tanned neck. "Well, we had to make a few repairs on the way down," he admitted. "But I'm sure it'll be fine for the return trip." He smacked the front fender with his hand, promptly causing the tailpipe bracket to break loose. "Now, if you'll excuse me I've got to finish up a little paperwork. We've got a three day drive ahead of us, so we don't want to dawdle."

Once he was gone, I gave the vehicle a quick going over. From what I could see, if this was the type of workmanship Wendell was getting from his local help, then it's no wonder he'd put in a request for a mechanic. I knew that back in Canada there was no way we'd be taking a 500-mile trip in this bucket of bolts. "But this is Africa," I explained to Cookie. "Around here, they'll drive just about anything."

Soon it was time to leave. Backing out of the parking stall, I noticed a puddle of oil on the ground. I called over to Wendell, who was driving his own vehicle. "Uh, is that us?"

"Oh that." Wendell waved a hand dismissively. "There's a slight leak from the transmission, but we can fix it when we get back to our station."

The slight leak turned out to be more severe than Wendell thought. About every 100 miles we had to stop and refill the transmission with 90w gear oil. That was fine when we could find a service station and borrow their service pit. But when we hit the final off-road section of the trip, it meant crawling in the dirt under the Landy in 110° heat, and pumping in the thick oil with a large plastic medical syringe. It didn't help matters that the oil filler plug was right next the hot exhaust pipe. By the time we were in the final throes of our journey I was covered in oil and sand and burn ointment. I'd had enough.

"Slim, aren't you going to stop and put in some more oil?" shouted Cookie over the noise of the screaming transmission.

"No!" I hollered back, throwing the shifter into high gear and mashing the gas pedal to the floor. "I'm sick of this piece of junk! It either gets us home or it blows up – and I don't care which!"

We made it, but just barely. After unpacking our supplies, I parked the Land Rover in the workshop compound and ignored it for two weeks. We both needed some space.

By then, I had determined that the oil was leaking from the front transmission seal, and the only way to replace that seal was to remove the transmission from the vehicle. I threw down some grass mats and crawled underneath the station wagon to size up the situation. "Hmm, looks like I'll have to remove this crossmember and then…hey wait! The crossmember doesn't come out – it's welded to the frame rails."

"Yes, *bwana* Slim," replied Francis, who had crawled under there with me. "You have to take the transmission out from the top."

Francis was a local villager whom Wendell hired from time to time to do simple maintenance on the project vehicles. His limited automotive training had come from the days when he'd worked for a road construction company. I stared at him. "From the top? You mean from *inside* the vehicle?"

He nodded. "*Ndiyo* (yes). You must remove the seats, then the floor, and then the doors. Next you remove the transfer case and the drive shafts. Only then can you unbolt the transmission and lift it out through the passenger doorway."

We climbed out from underneath the Landy and looked inside. Removing the seats and the floor to work on the transmission? I had never heard of anything so ridiculous in my life. "That looks like about a week's worth of work," I observed. "Have you ever done this before?"

Francis smiled modestly. "*Ndiyo*, once or twice. It can be a difficult job, so instead of paying me by the hour, you should do this as a contract. It might save you lots of money."

I looked at him narrowly. "Okay, how much?"

He spread his hands and shrugged. "Not very much. Perhaps 500 shillings?"

Although that translated into a little less than $50 at the time, it was still more than most of his fellow tribesmen made in a whole month. But then, being goat and camel herders, not many Turkanas had ever driven a car, much less fixed one, so my options were limited.

How long this job was going to take was anyone's guess – I just knew I wasn't eager to do it myself. "Okay, it's a deal. You remove the transmission and put it back in. But call me when you've got it out, so I can replace the damaged seal."

I showed Francis where my tools were and left him to the job. Before long, it was midmorning, and braving the blistering African sun I headed across the compound for the main mission house. It was time for tea and biscuits.

Figuring my vehicle would be out of commission for most of the week, I asked Wendell if I could borrow his Datsun pickup in case I needed to go somewhere.

"Sure," he said, "but what's wrong with your Landy?" When I explained the situation, he raised his eyebrows, a hint of a smile tugging at the corners of his mouth. "500 shillings, eh?" He blew on his tea to cool it down. "I should have warned you about Francis."

I looked at him in surprise. "How come? Are you telling me he doesn't know what he's doing?"

Wendell laughed. "Oh, he knows what he's doing, alright – in more ways than one."

When tea break was over, I followed Wendell out to the workshop. I'd only been gone about an hour, but Francis had put the word out and a whole gang of his relatives had appeared out of nowhere, ready to follow his instructions. From what I could see, they'd been working feverishly, and making good progress, too. They were just lifting the transmission out onto the ground as we strolled up.

I was shocked. "Out already? I thought you said this would take all week!"

Francis smiled a big toothy grin. "No, you said that, *bwana*. I just said it was a big job and I wanted 500 shillings." He shrugged. "You agreed to it."

"Yes, I did," I spluttered, "but you said I would save money this way."

He shrugged again. "I said you *might* save money; I didn't say you would for sure."

By now, Wendell was beside himself. "Slim," he wheezed between fits of laughter, "you've just had a lesson in the art of bartering. You never, ever agree to the initial price. In Africa, negotiation is the name of the game."

It also pays to know a little about the local economy. As I soon discovered, the average laborer around those parts made about five shillings a day. It didn't take long before I had a lineup of villagers sitting outside my workshop gate every morning. Everyone wanted to work for the crazy rich *mzungu* (westerner) who paid too much.

I left Basil to finish the job on Sir Rodney's Jaguar. My two years in Africa had given me my fill of British vehicles. They might be nice to drive – some of them, that is – but I'd rather let someone else do the actual repairs. After all, isn't that why you hire staff?

Later that morning, when the Jag was back together, Basil came by my hoist. "Did you want to look into that tapping noise, or shall I?"

"Be my guest," I grunted as I fought with a stiff set of brake shoe return springs. "You'll hear the noise on right hand turns." As he turned to go, I added, "Oh yes – it only happens when you're accelerating."

That put a big smile on his face.

But when Basil returned, he looked concerned. "I thought you said the tapping noise only occurs on right hand corners?"

"That's right."

"Well, something has changed, then. That noise is there every time you accelerate, whether the car is taking a corner or just going straight."

"Oh no," I groaned. "That's terrible!"

"No, that's progress," countered Basil, the eternal optimist. "Now we know where to start looking for the cause of the noise." Basil was right, of course. Because the noise had changed after we'd disturbed the transmission and its crossmember, it had to be related to that area of the vehicle. "I think we need to inspect the entire driveline," he added.

Up went the Jaguar on the hoist again. "Wow, look at all that metal shielding!" I exclaimed. "There's so much tin under here you can't even see the driveshaft." I looked at Basil. "I guess that's all got to come off if we're ever going to inspect anything."

Basil sighed. "I'm afraid you're right. I must admit that even I am beginning to develop a slight dislike for British engineering."

After exposing the driveshaft, Basil found the source of the noise. A plastic fuel line running through the driveshaft tunnel had come loose and was hanging just a fraction of an inch away from the driveshaft. Stepping on the throttle made the tail end of the transmission torque to the left, which caused the fuel line to rub on the spinning front universal joint. If things had gone on much longer, the fuel line would have rubbed through, resulting in a major gasoline leak.

"By Jove, that's amazing!" exclaimed Sir Rodney, when he came by later to pick up the car. "Awfully glad you found it, old man. Could have caused a nasty fire if that plastic fuel line had ruptured." He hung his umbrella over his arm. "Oh, and book me in next Friday, would you? My other vehicle has developed a small problem."

"Your other vehicle?" I asked. "I didn't know you had another one."

"Oh yes, my dear boy. It's just an old thing that I use around the farm. Those Landy's are just ducky for getting through the dodgy spots in the orchard come springtime, don't you know."

I gripped my pencil so tightly it snapped in two. "And what seems to be the problem with your Land Rover?"

Sir Rodney removed his monocle and polished it with a silk handkerchief. "Oh, not much, really. My foreman tells me there's just a small oil leak coming from the transmission."

As Rodney and his Jaguar purred out of our yard, Basil came out to stand beside me, coffee cup in hand. "Not drinking tea today?" I asked.

Basil wrinkled his nose. "No. I've had enough British influence in my life to last me a month." He took a swallow and grimaced. "But I think this coffee needs more sugar. Say, what was Sir Rodney saying about coming back next week? I didn't quite catch that."

I looked back at the Jaguar disappearing down the street and sighed. Flashbacks of rough roads, dusty workshops, and Land Rover transmissions being lifted out through passenger doors filtered through my brain.

"Basil," I said, slapping him on the back. "You really don't want to know."

CHAPTER 11

⊰ MEET THE PARENTS ⊱

There is nothing quite like an early morning drive along Hollownoggin Lake. The springtime sun rising over the eastern hills can take your breath away, but today I had no time for sightseeing. The winding highway hugging the shoreline demanded my full attention as I sped past the slower cars in the right hand lane. Lucky for me, none of them had red or blue lights on the roof.

The reason for my haste was a special order part that was waiting for pick-up at the bus depot in Panicton. Our customer was the provincial ambulance service, and they didn't like to be kept waiting for their vehicles. My plan was to be back in time for Basil to install the part first thing when he arrived for work that morning.

But the quick flash of a road sign prompted me to ease off the gas. I glanced sideways just in time to catch a fleeting glimpse of a rest stop, a small park on the lake complete with picnic tables and a few trees. It caught my attention because it brought back memories of Cookie and me during our courting days.

Although our first date was a borderline disaster, Cookie agreed to go with me to a movie the following weekend. From what I've been told, it was a great picture – but it was totally wasted on me. Sitting that close to Cookie completely blew my concentration. "Here, would you like to share my popcorn?" I nervously shoved the bag under her nose, spilling buttery kernels onto her lap.

"No thanks." She looked closely at the bag. "Hey, where did this come from? I thought you decided not to buy popcorn when we came in."

I, too, looked at the bag. The truth was I hadn't a clue where it came from. I looked around nervously. "Well, ah…"

"Oh, but I will have a sip of your root beer." She took the cup from my hands and wiped off the straw. I licked my lips and grimaced at the funny taste in my mouth. *I don't even like root beer!* I slunk lower in my seat and avoided looking behind me, where an animated discussion was going on between a guy in the aisle seat and the usher. The guy seemed pretty upset about losing something…

"What's all that commotion?" asked Cookie, looking behind us.

I shrugged. "Nothing that concerns us…oh, look, the movie's starting!" *Just in time, too.* I slid the bag of popcorn down to the floor and nudged it forward under the seat in front of me with my foot. I didn't want any evidence around when the lights came back on.

During the movie I wanted to reach over and hold Cookie's hand, but I was too nervous. With my luck, I'd grab somebody else's hand or kneecap (or worse) and get smacked for my trouble. So I sat in forced isolation until the final credits petered off the screen. As we jostled through the crowds and out the door of the theatre, I berated myself for my timidity. If this relationship was ever going to go anywhere, it needed a lot more help than I was giving it.

Fortunately, help arrived as we waited to cross the street. When the light turned green, Cookie reached over and took *my* hand. It was a good thing she had a strong grip because I almost floated away.

Over the next few months, Cookie and I snuck various outings into our weekend schedules: slow drives up and down the valley in The Truckinator; picnics by the lake; breathtaking hikes among the hills. It was a glorious time.

I say *snuck*, because for reasons we both understood but couldn't explain, we weren't quite ready to tell the world that Slim and Cookie were an item. It might have been a touch of shyness on my part and a whole lot of apprehension on Cookie's, but whatever the reason, we were very nonchalant about the whole thing. At least outwardly. Inwardly, I was a wreck. Any fool could tell that she was the girl for me; it was the wiser folk (like Cookie) who still needed convincing.

Things were also moving slowly because we lived in two different worlds. Cookie resided in Slumberland, while I boarded with my parents across the lake in Narymatter. However, I had full-time work as a mechanic at a busy service station in Slumberland. The half-hour drive every morning took me from Narymatter to Panicton at the south end of the lake, and then back north to Slumberland.

Cookie, on the other hand, worked in Panicton. So every weekday morning she would drive her white Volkswagen to work, and every weekday morning our paths would cross near the little highway rest stop. I would wave at Cookie and she would wave back. It was delightful, but it wasn't enough.

One night on the phone I made a suggestion. "Tomorrow morning, let's leave extra early and meet at that rest stop. It'll just be the two of us, enjoying the early morning sun before going to work."

Cookie giggled at the thought. "This sounds adventurous! I'll see *you* in the morning."

Up until this point, I'd had very little contact with Cookie's parents. Dr. and Mrs. McDream were well-respected long-time residents of Slumberland, as well as staunch members of the Slumberland Community Church. Cookie had been born and raised in the same town, had lived in the same house, and had graduated from high school with the same kids she'd gone to kindergarten with.

I, on the other hand, had lived in no less than six houses in two countries during my growing up years, and had attended five different schools. On top of that, during my four-year apprenticeship I had moved eight times and gone through at least a half dozen used cars (as a side note, only three of the accidents were my fault).

There was no getting around the fact that the differences in our backgrounds were significant: Dr. McDream had a PhD in plant pathology, whereas Pa Shambles was a self-taught carpenter with a bad back; Cookie's two brothers both had high-paying government jobs with nice retirement packages, while I was a schmuk pulling wrenches in a gas station where I didn't even get a discount on fuel.

As far as family heritage went, it was like comparing apples to left-handed lug nuts. From all accounts, stability and respectability were important facets of the McDream family lineage. I, on the other hand, was about as stable as a weather vane in a cyclone.

Oh, I had met Cookie's parents, but the meetings had been mercifully brief. One evening, as I stood awkwardly in the family room waiting for Cookie, I attempted to engage her father in a rare exchange of wit.

"Say, Doc, I heard this funny joke the other day: If a man is alone in his orchard and speaks, and there is no woman to hear him, is he still wrong? Ha ha, do you get it? Is he still...well, you know what I mean... right?" Cookie's mom frowned at me over her knitting. "Or maybe... ah...perhaps maybe you don't..." A bead of sweat trickled down from my left eyebrow as I contemplated making a mad dash for my truck, Cookie or no Cookie.

Dr. McDream lowered his newspaper to see what all the babbling was about. "How interesting," he remarked, as if noticing me for the first time. "Who are you again, and why are you in my house?"

Come to think of it, Cookie hadn't made much progress with *my* parents, either – at least not with Pa Shambles. Although my mother was one of God's special angels sent down to earth, Pa came from one of the lesser clouds.

One Sunday after church, I brought Cookie home to show her the sights of Narymatter. Leaving her to chat with my mother, I went to change into some hiking clothes. A few minutes later, Pa came into the house, stomped around a bit and then left. When I came out, Cookie was standing there looking confused.

"Let me guess," I said. "You've met my dad."

Cookie looked up at me, her lower lip quivering. "I think so."

"You think so? Did he speak to you?" She nodded.

"Does he know your name?"

She shook her head. "No, we didn't get that far..."

Later that evening, we all sat down for supper. Once again, Ma had done wonders with potatoes and gravy, roast beef, and fresh peas with carrots. She kept the conversation going throughout the meal, helping Cookie to feel at ease. Pa just kept his head down and consumed his supper one forkful at a time. The fact that he hadn't said much yet was a blessing.

When it came time for dessert, Ma brought out one of her prize-winning lemon meringue pies. Setting it on the table, she asked, "Now Cookie, when you bake a lemon pie, how do you make your meringue?"

For reasons still unknown to modern science, something in Ma's question sparked interest at the other end of the table. Cookie opened her mouth to reply, but Pa Shambles beat her to it.

Picking at his teeth with a toothpick, he snorted. "How d'ya know she can even cook?"

I was horrified, but I soon discovered Cookie was made of sterner stuff. The next evening I received a phone call. "Slim," she declared, "next weekend is Valentine's Day and you're coming over for dinner." It was a statement, not a request.

My heart skipped a beat. "That's wonderful! It will give me a chance to get to know your parents better and…"

"Forget that nonsense," interrupted Cookie. "I'm not inviting you to meet my parents; I'm making you dinner to prove to your father that I know how to cook!"

And prove it she did. The meal was fantastic, and it was a great opportunity for the two of us to spend some time together – her parents had been sent out for the evening under strict orders from Cookie about when they could return home.

But as a result, I still hardly knew her family, and they knew even less about me. Deep within was the urgent need to prove that I was a fine, upstanding young man worthy of their daughter's affections. The problem was, I didn't know if that would ever happen.

The next morning I could hardly contain myself as I left home and headed for Panicton. Fifteen minutes later, the highway turned north towards Slumberland, and at that very moment I pictured Cookie McDream getting into her car and heading for our little rendezvous.

My calculations must have been off, however, because when I arrived at the rest stop, Cookie's car was not there. *No matter. I'll just sit down by the lake and enjoy the sun until she arrives.*

I got out of my truck and walked through a small stand of trees to the water's edge. The sun was shining, the birds were singing, and the lake was…well, whatever lakes do, it was doing it. Overall, it was a glorious moment. *This is definitely one of my better ideas*, I thought.

Within minutes, I heard a car pull up in the parking lot. *Ah, Cookie's here.* I waited for the engine to shut off and for the car door to open, but neither happened. The car just sat there idling.

I'd assumed that Cookie would see my truck and come join me, but that wasn't happening either. Maybe it wasn't her. Maybe I was at the wrong rest stop. Maybe it was time to go find out.

On the other side of the trees, a little white car was indeed stopped in the parking lot. *Yes, that's Cookie's car, but why isn't she getting out?* I ambled over for a closer look. *And who is that beside her in the car?*

When she saw me coming, Cookie opened her door and jumped out. As she hurried across the grass towards me, I could see the agitation on her face. "Oh Slim, I'm so sorry I'm late," she cried as she got closer. "I didn't know what to do!"

"That's okay," I said, looking over her shoulder. "But who's in the car?"

Cookie blushed and looked away. "That's my dad," she admitted. "He came with me."

My mouth fell open. "Your dad? You brought your father with you for our rendezvous?" I was stunned. "You mean, like a chaperone?"

"Don't be silly," she said. "I didn't bring him: he invited himself. I was rushing around this morning, getting ready to leave, when my dad came down the stairs and announced he needed a ride into Panicton."

Cookie looked at me, her blue eyes pleading. "I didn't know how to say no."

I was flabbergasted. "But what happened when you told him we were planning to meet?"

Cookie sighed. "I didn't tell him. We just got in the car and came."

"What!" This was not going well. My chest tightened like a vise and I found it difficult to breathe. "So what did he say when you pulled in here?" I squeaked.

She glanced back at the car. "Well, he hasn't said anything yet. When we got to the turnoff, I just said, 'Dad, I have to stop here!' and pulled in." She looked back at me. "I think you should go and say hello."

I gulped. My chances of impressing the good doctor were plummeting rapidly. Sucking up my courage, I pasted a sickly smile on my face and walked over to the car. Dr. McDream was sitting there stiffly, staring straight ahead out the windshield. He seemed to find this whole affair as embarrassing as I did. In a twisted sort of way, that was encouraging.

I leaned over and tapped on the side window. "Good morning, sir!" I said loudly. "How are you today?" He turned his head slowly and looked up at me. A single nod was the only reply I got.

But it was enough – I could see it in his eyes. From that moment on, Dr. McDream and I understood each other. As a father, he loved his intelligent, vivacious, but sometimes unpredictable daughter. And here was I, falling in love with the very same girl. It was our common ground.

Though many years have passed since then, that incident at the rest stop dominated my thoughts as I went about my business in Panicton. In fact, I didn't realize how much it was on my mind until I pulled into the parking lot back at the shop. Basil met me as I got out of the truck.

"Here you go, Bas," I said, handing him the package. "I hope you like them."

"You hope I like...?" Basil stared at the package he was holding. Then he looked at me. "Well, I do appreciate the roses, Slim, but I really could use that part instead." He looked over my shoulder. "Did you leave it in the cab?"

Rats, I fumed as I climbed back into my truck. *It's hard enough for a guy to keep his mind on his work these days.* As I headed back to Panicton, I thought, *Whoever put that flower shop next door to the bus depot should be shot.*

CHAPTER 12

✆ IT'S NEWS TO ME ✇

A nd for another twenty bucks we can outline the whole ad with pictures of tiny oil cans – the readers will find the imagery irresistible!" Rover Dangerphrase mopped his forehead with a handkerchief as he ended his feverish sales pitch. "I guarantee you won't be able to keep up with all the customers."

Basil coughed politely from his easy chair in the corner of the office. "I hate to mention the obvious, Slim, but do we really need another oil change ad? No offense to Rover here, but we can't keep up with the flow of customers as it is."

He was right. My problem wasn't a lack of business – it was finding enough help to keep up with our existing work. I'd been holding off hiring another mechanic, but maybe it was time to give it more serious thought.

Rover began to sweat more profusely as he watched his sales opportunity slip away. As the sole reporter and ad salesman for the *Slumberland Rebuttal*, the success and viability of our local newspaper rested upon his shoulders. This was his paycheck we were talking about.

"Okay, let's drop the oil cans. How about a nice black border to make the ad stand out? No extra charge!"

Always a sucker for a deal, I signed the proof and sent him on his way. "Just make sure you get the spelling right this time!" I called after him. The *Rebuttal* was known for its unique interpretations of the English language in written form – not to mention a tendency to massage the pertinent facts from time to time.

Personally, I have my own method of reading the local publication.

First come the comics, followed by the classified ads. Then if I still need a touch of humor, I'll turn to the front page and catch the headlines. Such was the case at Baldy's Barber Shop a week earlier, where I was patiently waiting my turn to go under the scissors.

"Did you hear the news?!" Buck Pincher burst through the door, wheezing worse than an accordion on Polka Night. Whatever was on his puny mind, it had to be big: Buck would never expend this much energy on a trivial matter.

"What news?" I asked, looking up from my newspaper.

Buck held up a shaky hand while he bent over and dragged lungfuls of air into his chest. "Just…wait…(gasp)…need air…!" Baldy cleaned his razor and returned to the mountain of shaving cream adorning the customer in his chair. I returned to my comic strip.

Finally the color returned to Buck's face. "Okay…get this. Rumour has it that Mayor Dewgood is gonna be impeached for corruption." All seven eyes of the room's four occupants jerked quickly in Buck's direction as he continued (you couldn't count Ropey Lewis's glass eye – it never moved). Buck lowered his voice conspiratorially. "It seems Dewgood took kick-backs when Council was handing out contracts during the sewer project last year."

I tried desperately to get Buck's attention, but he was so excited with his news that he ignored me completely. Rubbing his hands gleefully, he continued. "Now Mick McYodel, a local contractor, is bringing a lawsuit against the whole town council. He claims that because of the mayor's actions, his trucking company has missed out on all the work!" Buck hitched his thumbs in his suspenders and beamed with importance. Ropey's eye popped out in surprise and rolled across the room.

Wow, I thought, *this is news! An honest-to-goodness corruption scandal, right here in Slumberland – life doesn't get any better than this.*

Suddenly a great spray of shaving cream erupted from the barber chair. Baldy jumped back in surprise, checking the razor in his hand for signs of blood. A muffled voice bellowed with rage from beneath the mound of white lather. I had tried to warn Buck: the mayor was in the building.

"What in blue blazes are you blathering about, Pincher?" Mayor Dewgood grabbed the towel Baldy offered him. "Did one of the tacky tourists from your motel make this up, or has your imagination finally kicked in after all these years? I've never heard such hogwash!"

Buck turned beet red. "I…I…I read it in the paper," he stammered. "It's all there in black and white." He fastened his eyes on my newspaper like a drowning man clings to a piece of wreckage. "There!" he cried, pointing. "It's the front-page story! Slim, you've read it, right?"

"Not yet," I admitted sheepishly, turning to the front page. But there it was, a headline-grabbing article backing up Buck's wild accusations. Pasted beneath it was a picture of the mayor's smiling face.

"Yep," I confirmed. "It's all here. Say, Mayor, if you're done, can I get my haircut now?"

Mayor Dewgood leapt from the chair and grabbed the paper out of my hands. After scanning the story furiously, he turned so red in the face that Baldy had to give his razor a second look. "It's ridiculous, it's poppy-cock, it's…it's…" Just then the door chime tinkled as some unfortunate soul picked an inopportune moment to enter the premises – a soul by the name of Rover Dangerphrase. The mayor glared at him. "It's you, Dangerphrase!" he shouted accusingly. "This is *your* fault! Where did you get this drivel?"

Rover tried to backpedal his way out of the shop, but tripped over Buck who was doing the same thing. He tugged at his shirt collar and tried to explain. "I'm just reporting what my sources told me. They claim they overheard you bragging to Mick about the kickbacks!"

All of us winced. We'd seen what happened at council meetings when anyone brought up something the mayor didn't agree with. This had the potential to get messy.

Rover ploughed doggedly onwards, digging his grave even deeper. "And…and then Mick replied that he was going to bring a lawsuit against Council." Rover wrung his hands. "I'm just doing my job. You know – reporting the facts!"

The mayor slowly and purposefully crossed the room, waving the rolled-up newspaper threateningly as he came. We all ducked. Baldy's dog, Closeshave, slunk out the back door – he knew what a rolled-up newspaper meant.

"The facts," began the mayor, hissing through his tightly clenched teeth, "are about as far from your article as news is from your newspaper." He thumped the paper against Rover's chest. "What I said was..." He pointed the paper directly at Rover's nose for emphasis. "Let me repeat that. *What I said was*, now that the sewer project is almost over, we can all *kick back* and take it easy." Rover backed up against the door, now possible because Buck had long since disappeared.

Dewgood continued, his voice rising. "And then Mick replied that he was going to put on his *best suit* and come to the next council meeting to express his *gratitude*. He wants to thank the town for using local contractors, because his employees *haven't missed a day of work all year!*" A solid whack with the paper to Rover's left ear added final emphasis to the mayor's words.

By this time Rover had found the door knob. After a quick "I'll print a retraction!" he was gone.

The mayor stomped back to the barber chair to finish his shave while I retrieved the newspaper from the garbage can. After all, I hadn't read the classifieds yet. Closeshave snuck back in and assumed his normal position – asleep next to the baseboard heater. Ropey located his glass eye under the magazine rack and life returned to normal. Let me rephrase that: life continued as usual. Scenes like this happen a lot around here.

No doubt Rover's retraction will be even more colorful than the original headline:

> *Politician goes on rampage in local business. Mayor seen foaming at the mouth, man loses eye. Witnesses claim local residents and pets were seen running for their lives...*

Yes, it'll all be there in black and white. And come to think of it, my oil change ad will be right behind it on page two. I can see it now:

Slim Shambles Auto Repair Oil Change Special – Pay for the first one and get the second pair of pants free.

I shook myself back to the present. "Basil," I said, "where's that old sandwich board we used to advertise last month's special? I'm thinking it might be safer than one of Rover's ads."

He smiled. "I've already got it out and ready, sitting beside my tool box. I knew you'd come to your senses."

Typical Basil – always a step ahead of me. "And would it be safe to assume that you've got a line on someone to help with our existing work load?"

"You're close," he replied. "I've taken the liberty of drafting a *help wanted* ad for a new technician. Would you like me to phone Rover and have him put it in the next edition in place of our oil change ad?"

I shuddered. "No, I'll call up the *Panicton Herald* instead." At least the *Herald* would spell 80% of the words correctly. Not only that, there's a good chance they'd put the ad under the proper heading as well. The last thing I needed was a bunch of résumés from out-of-work plumbers and eager-faced shoe salesmen.

The bigger problem is what to do about the oil change ad in the *Rebuttal*. Knowing Rover, if we just canceled the ad outright, he'd turn it into some front-page story about Slim Shambles Auto Repair going out of business.

With a sigh, I decided to leave the ad as it was. But I made a note to stop by the local thrift shop and pick up a dozen pairs of second-hand pants, just in case.

CHAPTER 13

❧ NAME THAT TOON ❧

H ey, when am I gonna get some service around here?" Buck thrust his empty coffee cup under my nose, making it very tempting to angle the grease gun slightly to the right and pull the trigger. With any luck I'd fill his shirt pocket before he could jump out of the way.

"Make your own coffee. Can't you see I'm busy?" I wiped the sweat off my forehead with the sleeve of my dirty coveralls, promptly smearing grease all over my face. With a groan, I moved to the other side of the truck to finish lubing the ball joints. It was my fifth oil change that morning and it wasn't even coffee time yet – for me, at least. Buck, on the other hand, had already polished off two full pots and he'd only been here an hour.

My cheapskate friend looked glumly into his empty cup. "I would make my own, but you're all out of fixin's." He tossed the styrofoam cup into the trash. "You'd think a decent shop would take better care of their preferred customers."

I tightened the drain plug, and then pushed the oil bucket off to its place beside the workbench. "Yeah? Well, any shop decent enough to have a preferred customer list wouldn't have you on it, now would they?"

Buck's eyebrows shot up. "Whoa, aren't we testy this morning. What's eating you?"

Waving my wrench in front of his face, I cried, "Are you blind? Take a look at that parking lot – the cars are stacked up three high!" I tossed the wrench onto the workbench. Unfortunately, it slid right off the other end and disappeared into the bucket of used oil. I felt like punching something, and Buck was standing dangerously close. "Look, I've got so many customers waiting that Basil and I could be here all night and still not get finished. And you want me to stop and make you coffee?"

"No need to get snarky," Buck sniffed. "Some businesspeople *I* know think having lots of customers is a good thing." And with that, he slouched back out to my office in search of my secret stash of day-old donuts. He'd sniffed their presence when he arrived earlier that morning.

Basil came by a few minutes later with an armload of ignition parts for the tune-up he was doing. "I overheard your little tête-à-tête with Buck," he said. "I know he can be a bother, but he's right: having lots of work is a good problem to have. We just need to hire another mechanic."

I flipped the release lock and lowered the hoist. "Yeah, I know. I just haven't had time to go over those résumés we got in last month."

Basil shrugged. "Why don't you take a break after this job and do that. We're behind schedule anyway – another hour won't make much difference."

Soon I was sitting behind my desk, reading the résumés through one by one. Buck was his usual annoying self, rereading and commenting aloud on the ones I discarded. "Hey, what's wrong with this guy? Says here that he'll work below the going rate if you pay him cash under the table." He nodded approvingly. "Sounds like my kind of guy."

I grunted. "Yeah, and if you'll notice, he's also not a licensed technician. That's fine for old jalopies like yours that still have wooden-spoked wheels. But with these new fuel injected vehicles, I need someone who's up on the current stuff." Not only were cars getting more and more complicated, but so was the process of finding qualified staff. Concentrating on these résumés would require some peace and quiet, so I got up and walked over to the filing cabinet. Opening the top drawer, I located the donuts in the "B" section, filed under *Babysitting Supplies.*

Buck's eyes lit up. "Oh, so that's where you keep 'em."

I tossed him a stale sour cream glazed. "Here – stuff this in your mouth and keep quiet. You've been more distracting than usual today, and I have work to do."

Reclaiming my chair behind the desk, I picked up the next résumé and began to read. Suddenly I sat bolt upright. "Hey, this looks interesting. Says here this guy has worked at car dealerships as well as independent shops like mine...I'll bet he knows a thing or two about electronic fuel injection."

"What's his name?" mumbled Buck, dropping crumbs down the front of his shirt.

"Name? Why do you want to know his name?"

Buck rolled his eyes. "Any idiot knows you can tell a lot about a person by their name."

"Well, I guess if you're using yourself as an example, then you've got a point." I looked at the top of the page. "His name is Tooner Bocksend."

"*Tooner*? What kind of name is that?" Buck snorted and slapped his knee. "Why don't he just call himself *Sparkplug* or *Tailpipe*. Ha! Let me guess – I'll bet his specialty is 'tune-ups'!" He collapsed into a fit of laughter at his own joke.

"Well, if it is, then I'd like to see what he can do." I reached for the phone and dialed the number at the bottom of the page. Tooner wasn't home, but his wife said she'd give him the message. I hung up and looked at Buck. "Well, that's that. I wonder what this guy will be like?"

Buck just shook his head and chuckled. "*Tooner*! Slim, you're killing me." He wiped the tears from his eyes. "I'll bet you the only thing he can 'toon' is the radio."

Tooner Bocksend arrived the next morning in a Chevy pickup that was even older and rustier than my own. "I'm Tooner," he growled as he came in the office door. "Where d'ya want me to unload?" The toolbox strapped into the back of his truck had seen better days, and to be honest, its owner looked about the same. Wearing a pair of patched-up coveralls and a greasy ball cap, Tooner looked like your typical middle-aged, old school mechanic; a guy who'd seen it all, had probably worked on it all, and was no doubt tired of it all. But fixing cars was what he did and what he planned to do until he retired.

I coughed politely. "Ah, good morning. I'm Slim Shambles." I poured a cup of coffee and offered it to him. "I thought we might start with an interview first. You know, get to know each other a little."

Tooner ignored the coffee. "Well, here's what I need t' know. D'ya need a mechanic or don't ya?"

"We do!" said Basil, choosing that moment to enter the room and take over the conversation. He reached out and shook Tooner's hand. "I'm Basil, and you can back your truck right into the bay. We'll use the hoist to unload your tools."

And just like that, Tooner was on staff. How long he'd last, I didn't know, but like I told Buck later, "If Basil thought it was a good idea, then who was I to argue?"

Buck stared at me. "You're the boss."

To start him off, I gave Tooner the task of rotating and rebalancing four tires on a small sedan. He grabbed the floor jack and started lifting one side of the car. He looked around the shop. "Where's yer stumps?"

"My what?"

"Yer stumps. The big blocks of wood that hold up the car so's I can jack up the other side." The toothpick in Tooner's mouth waggled up and down as he waited. Apparently, he wasn't joking.

I pointed to the far wall. "Around here we use metal jack stands, not stumps."

He let out a low whistle. "Wow. Goin' for the fancy stuff, eh? I like that!" That's when he caught sight of the tire balancer. "An' you'll have to show me how t' use this here dynamic model. All we had up north was a bubble balancer."

"Up north?" I asked cautiously. I hadn't seen anything about that on the résumé.

"Yep. Northern Alberta. Spent the last five years in a loggin' camp, fixin' skidders."

When the lunch hour arrived, we discovered another interesting facet of our new employee's personality. "Phew, Basil, open the windows!" I exclaimed as I came in from the shop. "What's that horrible smell?"

"Oh, sorry 'bout that," said Tooner. "I was just airin' out my socks. Mabel didn't have time t' wash 'em last week." He put his work boots back on and laced them up. Out of the corner of my eye I could see Basil in his easy chair, shaking with silent laughter. What he found so funny about Tooner's lack of personal hygiene was beyond me. All I knew was I'd lost my appetite for solid food.

Pouring myself a coffee, I asked Tooner about his work experience.

"Well, let's see now." He took a bite of his egg salad sandwich and thought for a moment. "I guess you could say I done a bit of everythin'. Worked the rigs; worked in some loggin' camps; did a stint in one o' them big box stores..." Although the list was extensive – Tooner had certainly been around – I found it difficult to pin down what he'd actually done at all those places.

"So, do you specialize in anything?" asked Basil, voicing the question that was foremost in my mind.

Tooner took another bite. "Specialize? What d'ya mean?"

"Like tune-ups," I interjected. "We sort of had the impression that you were an expert at tune-ups. I mean, with your name..."

Tooner's eyes narrowed. "Somethin' wrong with my name?"

"Not at all," I backpedaled. Basil just shrugged and smiled. It was a good time to change the subject.

"Basil, after lunch, why don't you show Tooner how to hook up our coolant flushing machine."

"Coolant flush?" Tooner reached for his coffee mug. "Why d'ya need a machine for that? Back on the prairies we just stuck a garden hose in the radiator and let 'er rip."

If I was having any doubts about Tooner's suitability for our shop, they were reinforced later that day when I caught him spreading used oil on the parking lot. "Keeps the dust down," he grinned. "Heck, we coat whole roads with it back where I come from."

"But you can't do that here!" I protested. "This is British Columbia, the Green Province, where every second person is either a tree hugger or married to one. If the environmental people ever catch us dumping oil on the ground, we'll either be shut down or fined into bankruptcy!"

After showing Tooner where the used oil tank was, I stumbled back into the office in search of some strong black coffee. "Basil, what have we gotten ourselves into?" I drank the scalding liquid straight down without stopping.

"He's just not used to the way we do things, that's all." Basil poured me a second cup. "I kind of like the guy," he added. "Let's give him a week."

It wasn't that Tooner's work was poorly done, or that we had any comebacks on the vehicles he serviced; it was just that his ways were what you'd call unconventional. Buck, on the other hand, called them entertaining.

"Slim, did you see that?" he exclaimed later that week. "I didn't know you could seat the bead of a truck tire with lighter fluid and a match! I'm sure glad you hired that Tooner guy: he's very educational." He rubbed away the ash from his singed eyebrows.

"Yeah, well, school's over. I told Tooner to use the air blast on the tire machine from now on – it's a lot safer."

"Too bad," replied Buck. "That was the most fun I've had all week."

Two days later the opportunity arrived to really see what Tooner was made of. "I've got a Chevy Astro van that's idling too fast." I handed Tooner a set of keys. "So much so, that it jerks badly every time the owner puts it in gear. We can't seem to slow it down, so check it out and let me know what you think."

Tooner opened the hood of the van and looked at the V6 engine almost hidden from view in the tiny engine compartment. "Hmm, ain't never worked on one o' these fuel injected models before," he growled. "Should be interestin.'"

My mouth dropped open. "You've never...? But...but didn't your résumé say that you worked in a dealership once?"

Tooner grabbed some tools from his box and climbed inside the van to remove the engine cover. "Yep," he called over his shoulder. "About

10 years ago I spent six months in a Lada dealership back east – right before they got sued and went bankrupt."

I stared at Basil. "Lada? Those tin cans made in Russia?" Any form of computerized engine control would have been unheard of in a Lada dealership, especially a decade ago. Again, Basil just shrugged and smiled. I was amazed at his calmness. He patted my shoulder. "Patience, Slim. Tooner might surprise us yet."

I had my doubts. Basil and I had already spent time on this van two weeks before and had gotten nowhere. This computerized fuel injection was just too new and was coming at us too quickly. In those early days, almost every drivability problem that came through our shop made us feel like we were back in trade school – only this time there were no textbooks and no instructors to help us.

"Fine," I said. "Since you've got such confidence in him, then you work with him on this problem." Burying myself in a brake job, I tried to forget about Tooner and his lack of credentials.

Basil showed Tooner how to connect our scan tool to the van so that he could read the data stream – a bunch of numbers and readings related to the onboard computer. Not that seeing those numbers ever seemed to help us much: in those days we were still scratching our heads over phrases like *long term fuel trims* and *O2 sensor cross counts*. But even if most of the numbers on the screen didn't make sense yet, Tooner took a keen interest in it all. "What's that mean?" he asked, pointing to one of the readings.

Basil adjusted his bifocals. "That's the reading for the IAC, or idle air control motor." He explained how the IAC motor opens and closes to control the idle speed. "A low number means the computer is closing it to lower the idle, and a high number means the computer is telling it to open and raise the idle."

Tooner stared at the screen for a few moments and then looked at Basil. "Well then, there's yer problem."

Basil was taken aback. "Excuse me?"

"Look at the numbers," said Tooner. "It's readin' zero. Don't that mean yer computer is tryin' t' lower the idle by closin' off the air passage?"

"Well, yes, but…"

"Well nothin'," said Tooner. "Obviously that ain't workin'. This engine's runnin' faster than a preschooler on sugar cubes."

Basil pursed his lips. "And so…"

Tooner rolled his eyes. "It's as plain as skid marks on a piece o' road kill! Either ya got an IAC motor that ain't doin' its job, or ya got a vacuum leak." He shut off the van. "To be idlin' this fast, this engine is gettin' extra air from someplace."

Basil smiled grimly. "I agree with you, Tooner, but we've checked everything we can think of. If you've got any great ideas, I'm all ears!"

Tooner ruminated on that for a moment. Then his eyes lit up. "I'll be right back." He disappeared into the parts room.

I came over to where Basil was standing. "Well, has he got any miracles hiding up his sleeve?"

Basil shook his head. "I highly doubt it. As I was explaining to him, we've already…"

Suddenly Tooner reappeared carrying a small box in his hand. It contained a new PCV valve, a little plastic device whose sole purpose in life was to suck oil fumes out of the engine. Tooner climbed back inside the van, replaced the valve, and then started up the engine. To our amazement, it purred like a kitten on granny's lap, and at the right speed, too.

Basil and I just stood there with our mouths hanging open. "How… what…but…" spluttered Basil. "But I checked that valve already – it looked fine!"

Tooner grunted. "How things are lookin' and how they is, well, that's two different things." He took the old PCV valve out of his coveralls pocket and held it up. "I've only been t' one trainin' course in the past twenty years, and for the most part it was nothin' but a waste o' my time. But the feller did show us one thing that night – he showed us how t' test PCV valves."

He certainly had our attention. "How?" we parroted in unison.

Tooner put the valve on the floor and stomped on it with his heavy work boot, smashing the plastic device into tiny pieces. "That's how," he said with a grin. "Truth is, there ain't no way t' tell how much vacuum they're suckin' just by looking at 'em, so the best thing is t' replace 'em on a regular basis."

Well, that settled it. With a two-dollar part, Tooner had solved a major shop headache *and* proved his worth. Even if he wasn't up on all the latest automotive trends, he was willing and able to learn.

The other thing that one little demonstration did was to prod me into action as far as training courses were concerned. Instead of ignoring them under the excuse of being too busy to attend, I started signing us up for the odd night course. The new trend in vehicles wasn't going away, and only a fool would choose to ignore the writing on the wall.

Going over a list of courses one afternoon, I came across one dealing with customer relations. *Hmm, Tooner can be a little on the gruff side*, I mused. *Maybe I should sign him up.*

Suddenly a heated discussion out in the parking lot interrupted my thoughts.

"But all I want is one new spark plug…"

"An' I'm telling ya it's time for a full tune-up!" Tooner waved a dirty air filter under Buck Pincher's nose. "How d'ya expect this car t' get any decent mileage if you keep ignorin' the basic maintenance?"

"But I changed that air filter three years ago! And besides…"

"Quit yer whinin.'" Tooner slammed the hood down. "Come back this afternoon and I'll have this bucket o' bolts runnin' like new." He stalked back into the shop, leaving Buck standing there with his mouth flapping uselessly like a fish out of water. My tight-fisted friend had finally met his match.

I grinned. Tooner didn't need a course on customer relations – he was doing just fine.

CHAPTER 14

⊗ A BAD DAY GOLFING ⊗

Forget it, Slim. I ain't going golfing and that's final." Sweat dripped off Buck's scowling face as he swung his pickaxe. The tool bounced off the rocky soil and vibrated painfully in his hands. "If I don't get this broken irrigation line fixed, Dolly's flowers will dry out." He hefted the pick over his shoulder for another swing. "And if they go, you can bet who's gonna be next."

I surveyed the manicured grounds of The Happy Peasant Motel. Dolly had spent untold hours creating a floral masterpiece on the property. Rock walls lined the terraced hillside, and explosions of color filled the flowerbeds. It was easy to see why the water supply was such a big concern, especially in this summer heat.

"Relax," I said. "I've already cleared it with your wife. She's going shopping tonight and says she doesn't mind if you work under the floodlights, so long as you finish the job."

Buck just glared at me. Sometimes he fails to appreciate my ingenious solutions to his domestic dilemmas.

"Tell you what," I continued. "We'll go golfing, and if you win the round, I'll dig up your waterline myself."

That caught his attention. Buck can't turn down an opportunity to avoid manual labor. "Sounds tempting," he acknowledged, thoughtfully rubbing his chin. "But I've never even played golf before."

Buck is so gullible. Out loud I said, "No problem; I can teach you. A multi-talented person like yourself will pick up the basics in no time. And you know the old saying – 'A bad day golfing is better than a good day working.'"

The appeal to his ego hit home, and Buck climbed out of his hole.

"Well, maybe you're right – it's time I learned a new hobby. It can't be all that hard to hit a little ball with a stick." He surveyed the pile of earth and stones in the middle of his lawn. "Besides, it'd be a hoot to win that wager and see you working for a change."

I whistled cheerfully as we headed out to the Slumberland Golf and Country Club. Buck studied the front nine as we drove by on the way to the clubhouse. "This don't look so bad. Nice and flat, not too many trees…" Then he caught sight of the large water hazards and sand traps strategically placed around the fairways. "Hey, I don't like the look of them things." He glanced at me with suspicion. "Are you setting me up or what?"

I brushed off his concerns. "Relax, buddy; you'll do fine. I rarely lose a ball on this course. The secret is in having the proper gear." What I didn't tell Buck was that my Arnie Palmer monogrammed golf clubs were tucked away in the trunk. Since Buck didn't own a set, he'd have to use rentals. *Hah! Winning this wager is going to be child's play.*

We had a small moment of confusion when it came time to rent Buck's clubs. "What would you like in your bag, Mr. Pincher?" asked Todd, the young assistant at the pro shop.

Buck's eyes lit up. "You mean I get a choice? Let me see…how about a couple of beers, some of them little sausage rolls, a burrito, and…"

"Buck," I interrupted. "I believe he means, what selection of clubs would you like?" Turning to Todd, I winked and said, "Just give him the usual assortment – it's his first game." Todd winked back. This wasn't the first time I'd brought a newcomer to the course. He drew me off to one side as Buck picked through the pail of used golf balls.

"Have you got any money riding on this one, Slim?" he asked.

I smiled. "No money, Todd. Just a little competition between old friends."

He nodded knowingly. "Then I'll give him 'the usuals' just like you suggested."

We warmed up on the practice green before heading to the first hole. Buck took out one of his clubs and sighted down the shaft. "Say, is there supposed to be a bend in this here iron?"

I pulled out a kid leather golfing glove and fit it to my left hand. "My goodness, Buck, you're a lucky man. You managed to get one of those special clubs that Todd keeps around for important guests! From what I hear, those babies give you a huge advantage when you have to hit around a tree or some other obstacle."

Buck relaxed visibly. "Huh. Glad to see something going my way for a change." He swung the club around like a baseball bat. "Okay, pitter patter, let's get at 'er!" He paused as a thought hit him. "Or should I say, 'pitter putter?' Ha, ha, ha, ha!"

I smiled at Buck's little joke. "Now for the rules," I said. "First, golf is a gentleman's game, so no loud, offensive language on the course."

He shrugged. "Sounds fair. If I forget, you can remind me."

Oh, I will, I thought smugly. "Secondly, if you're too slow, let the other golfers play through." I took out my favorite wood and buffed it with a soft chamois. "And thirdly, be careful with the greens. Repair your divots, and watch your cleats when – oh, I'm sorry; you don't *have* any cleats. Tsk tsk!"

Buck looked down at his black high-topped running shoes. "Is that gonna hurt my game?"

"Not at all," I replied casually. "Not at all."

I won the toss and took the first drive. Then it was Buck's turn. He didn't do too badly for a beginner. "Can I hit it again, or do I have to wait for you to catch up?" he asked.

"Just wait by the cart," I growled, heading over to a line of Ponderosa Pines. Taking a few deep breaths, I reminded myself that it was only the first swing of the day. My next shot placed me right up beside the green, and I began to relax.

Buck's putting was terrible, so I still won the hole. But at the next tee-off, my drive was worse than the first. "I guess we'd better park the cart further back next time," Buck commented, examining the crack in the windshield. "Will this be covered by the damage deposit?"

For a novice, my friend's luck was uncanny. On the third hole, he skipped his ball right across the water hazard and rolled it up six inches from the flag. My own ball plunked into the middle of the pond, quickly followed by my woods. "Don't you need those clubs?" Buck wondered.

"Not anymore," I declared. "I'm going back to my irons."

By the ninth hole, Buck was offering me his rental clubs. "There must be something wrong with yours – I've never seen a ball curve so much in my life." Neither had I. The severe hook that I'd spent hundreds of dollars on golf lessons to eliminate had suddenly returned to haunt me. It was a good thing the windows on the pro-shop had wire mesh.

By the time we drove out to the back nine, Buck was really getting into the game. "Am I ever glad you dragged me out here, Slim. This is way more fun than digging ditches." He hopped out of the cart before it even stopped. "Mind if I go first?"

"Be my guest," I hissed. "You've got the honors." It was a phrase I would never have imagined applying to someone like Buck Pincher.

On the next two holes, I followed Buck's beautiful lofts with blistering grounders that burned skid marks in the fairways. By the time we putted out on the 11th green, he was crowing so much that I had to say a few words. "Gosh, Slim," he responded in surprise. "I ain't never heard you talk like that before. If the lineage of that ball is so bad, maybe you should use another one." He picked it up for a look. "Oops, I forgot; this *is* your sixth ball!" I drove off in a huff, leaving him rolling on the grass laughing. At least my favorite hole was coming up next.

The 12th fairway was 356 yards and a par 4. The best part was the scenery, one of the main reasons I loved golfing at this course. The canyon dropped 400 feet off the right-hand side of the fairway and the view was spectacular. Today we could see a herd of wild horses grazing on the lower plateau over on the other side. Buck watched them with interest as I set up for my second shot.

After hooking to the left all morning, I decided to compensate. I lined up my shot directly at the canyon itself and let go with a powerful swing. That's when my hook suddenly disappeared. The ball rocketed straight out into space far above Buck's head. He whistled in appreciation. "Nice shot, Slim. That herd will be running for days."

Hole 13 was hardly worth mentioning, although Buck did anyway. "Slim, I don't think you can blame that marmot for stealing your ball. After all, when you hit him in the backside with it, he probably figured you didn't want it anymore." On the 14th, Buck offered to drive me over to where my ball lay. "Don't bother," I sighed. "These electric carts don't come with four-wheel drive and off-road tires."

The 15th fairway also followed the canyon closely before doglegging back to the left. Buck peered down at the creek far below with a pair of binoculars. "Yep, you're right; there *is* a ton of golf balls down there," he said in awe. "Seems kind of pointless to keep adding to the pile." He lowered the field glasses. "Do you wanna try that shot again or should we just move on?"

"Shut up and get in the cart," I muttered darkly. "This ain't over yet."

Fairway 17 can be tricky, and in spite of myself, I felt obligated to give Buck some advice. "Keep to the left," I cautioned, "and for heaven's sake, what are you doing with that 9 iron? The green is still 275 yards away!"

Buck glanced at the club and shrugged. "It's the only one I've used all day – I thought they were all the same." He promptly laid up a perfect shot three feet from the pin. I stomped off to drop a ball at the spot where my last drive had left the universe.

Right then a couple of elderly women pulled up alongside Buck with their cart. "Young man, do you mind if we play through? It's very hot today, and we're getting tired of waiting for your friend. Is this his first time?"

Miraculously, the score remained tied by the eighteenth hole, thanks to Buck's poor putting game and my creative scorekeeping. Buck's drive put him in a sand trap, the first bad shot he'd had all day. Mine landed on the green, which was also a first. It looked like my game had finally returned. "Go ahead, Tiger," I sneered. "Let's see what you can do."

Buck shuffled apprehensively over to the sand, dragging his trusty 9 iron behind him. He knew that the entire fate of his household chores was on the line. Closing his eyes, Buck took a wild swing. When the shower of sand finally settled, his ball lay only one foot from the pin. Suddenly I was having trouble breathing.

But I managed to calm myself. My own ball sat just five inches from the cup. Yes, it had been a tough battle up to this point, but victory was in sight. Muttering to myself, I reached for my putter. I couldn't believe how much this game had unnerved me today. It was time to put it to bed…

The worst part was listening to Buck's advice. "Watch your grip, Slim. And don't choke up on the handle." He sipped his lemonade and leaned back in his lawn chair. "Nice night, ain't it?" Getting up to adjust the floodlights, he continued. "Too bad they kicked us off the golf course; I was really having fun." He sighed. "But I guess they didn't appreciate the damage you were doing to that last green. Ten putts – is that a course record?"

I muttered dark, useless threats as I swung the pickaxe again, striking yet another buried boulder under Buck's lawn. Sparks flew as the impact sent shockwaves up my arms so severe that my glasses rattled halfway down my nose.

"Hey, be careful with my pick!" he exclaimed. "That's the special one I reserve for guests." Buck peered into the hole. "Should only be another foot or so. Do you need more light?"

What I needed was to have my head examined. Never again would I make a wager against Buck Pincher. His raw luck is so uncanny that it borders on voodoo.

And forget the clichés – as far as I'm concerned, a bad day golfing is just a bad day.

CHAPTER 15

〰 A ROMANTIC EVENING FOR FIVE 〰

Basil shook his head as he folded up the newspaper and tossed it aside. "I don't know about you, Slim, but I'm getting weary of all these newspaper ads." He took a tomato slice out of his lunch kit and salted it lightly. "It appears that all the special days of the calendar year have become nothing more than opportunities for retailers to inundate the public with a glut of overt advertising and bald-faced commercialism."

I stopped sucking on my juice box. "And this is a bad thing?" I asked.

My usually upbeat technician rolled his eyes in disgust. "Of course it's a bad thing! Just look at today's paper." He waved a hand over the *Slumberland Rebuttal*. "It's jam-packed with nothing but ads for Mother's Day, and the blessed event is still three weeks away!" He picked up a piece of celery and waggled it in my direction. "Did you know that even the founder of Mother's Day, Anna Jarvis, became so upset over the mushrooming sales of greeting cards, that in 1948 she protested the commercialization of Mother's Day and was arrested for disturbing the peace?"

I was astounded. "But I thought it was a good thing to buy your mother a card."

Basil snorted. "Mrs. Jarvis saw it differently. To her, it was a sign of being too lazy to write a personal letter." He looked at me grimly. "Slim, according to the media, if you don't overwhelm the women in your life with armloads of flowers and caseloads of chocolate, then you're the most ungrateful piece of humanity on the face of the earth." Basil slammed his lunch kit closed. "Now I ask you, who needs all that rubbish?"

I do, I thought, jotting down a note in my day-timer: *Order flowers and chocolates for Cookie*. Basil's ranting aside, if it weren't for all this outside assistance from the media, I'd forget every special event there was, from birthdays and wedding anniversaries to case lot sales at Big Box Mart.

This minor character flaw was something my wife discovered not long after we were married, but she didn't let it discourage her. In fact, Cookie has some very effective ways to make up for my negligence in these matters of the heart – she turns them into matters of the stomach.

"What's this?" I asked last August, as a pile of greasy potatoes and barely-singed beef slid onto my dinner plate.

"It's my birthday dinner," Cookie announced dryly, tossing the frying pan into the sink. "Cold hash. How do you like it?"

Note to self: Cookie's birthday was yesterday. "Ah, it looks interesting," I ventured.

"Yes," she agreed. "But far too interesting for me. I'm going out to Chez Roberto's with my girlfriends. Enjoy."

Where's the half-page birthday notice in the newspaper when you need one?

Due to further negligence on the part of the advertising industry, the same problem arose with our wedding anniversary.

"You'd think that after this many years, you'd finally remember!" exclaimed Cookie, breaking her vow of silence two days after the devious event disguised itself and snuck by me without leaving so much as a muddy footprint.

"But I had no warning," I protested feebly. "I had the car radio on all month and not one DJ said a word about it."

"Well, here's a warning for you," she replied coolly. "Use two blankets: the couch is cold this time of year. I'm going to snuggle in with a good book, and later on I'll have a headache."

But that was last year. This year I'm a new man. This year our anniversary will be the mother of all anniversaries, the one that will make up for all my past sins. Never again will Cookie feel neglected and unappreciated. Never again will I have to suffer through cold hash, cold couches, and even colder shoulders.

I cashed in a savings bond and booked the honeymoon suite at the fanciest hotel I could find in Panicton. A few more phone calls got me the largest fruit basket and darkest chocolates available. I even arranged for an entire wall of flowers to be pre-delivered to the room.

"Oo, where are we going?" Cookie squealed with delight when I broke the news.

"It's a secret," I answered mysteriously. "But pack lightly."

Every base was covered: the babysitter was coming to spend the night; Chez Roberto's had our favorite table reserved; and I even exhumed my dinner jacket from the back of the closet and had it dry-cleaned.

We were just getting dressed for dinner when the phone rang. I picked up the bedroom extension, only to be assaulted by a raspy voice breathing heavily on the other end of the line. "Buck, is that you?" I asked. "Look, I can't talk right now – Cookie and I are just about to…"

"Hello, Mr. Shambles?" croaked the voice, followed by a round of coughing so violent I almost hung up and called 911. When the caller could finally speak again, I discovered that it was Darla the babysitter, calling to say she was deathly sick and that she wouldn't be able to babysit that night.

Cookie looked up as I slammed down the phone. "That's the babysitter!" I hollered in a panic. "She's got the bubonic plague or something. I've got to find a replacement!" A mad scramble ensued as I went through my phone list of friends and relatives. "Everyone's busy," I muttered, crumpling the list and opening up the telephone book. "But don't worry – I'm starting with the A's. I'll have someone here in no time!"

Cookie came over and took the receiver out of my hand. "Calm down," she said. "We'll just take the children with us."

Dinner at Chez Roberto's was passable, although the kids shot spit wads at the waiter's back all night and kept asking for more ketchup for the baked salmon. I scowled towards a darkened table in the far corner of the room. "I'm sure that's our babysitter over there," I hissed loudly to Cookie. "I think that whole bubonic plaque thing was a ruse." My wife just shushed me and continued eating. She seemed to be enjoying herself.

Pulling up in front of the hotel later, I shifted the minivan into park. "Are you sure about this?" I asked Cookie. "Maybe I could get the kids their own room at the motel down the street."

She laughed. "Slim, you're talking about three children under the age of twelve. You can't send them off to their own motel."

The kids and I wanted to take a vote, but Cookie was adamant. So I got out and went looking for the luggage trolley. "Do you require help with your bags, sir?" asked the bellhop.

I waved him off. "It's not for the bags," I said. "I got three kids who like to ride." Our entrance into the hotel was anything but quiet.

Once we got to the suite, the real fun began – starting with the jacuzzi. "Not so many bubbles!" I hollered at Tipper as he dumped the whole bottle into the tub.

"Relax, dear," my wife soothed. "They're having fun." She hummed to herself as she turned back the covers on the bed.

"Hey Dad, I've never seen a heart-shaped bed before!" exclaimed Carrie, escaping from the tub in her dripping wet bathing suit and taking a running dive onto the bed. "Can we all sleep on it?" She began bouncing up and down, foamy bubbles and all. Suddenly she flopped on her back and stared upward. "Wow, this is way cool. Look, Cache, there's even a mirror on the ceiling."

Her older sister just nodded and continued surfing every channel on the television for the ninth time in a row, and at full volume no less. It wasn't a case of nothing to watch, but rather too much to see.

Suddenly a commercial for vacation getaways popped onto the screen. "Hey Dad," said Cache. "Isn't it your anniversary soon?" She looked up at me. "Are you gonna do anything special for Mom this year?"

I sank down into an overstuffed easy chair and looked around the room. A ravaged box of chocolates lay in tatters on the coffee table, next to the picked-over fruit basket. What wasn't fully eaten had at least been tasted. The wall of flowers had turned into a carpet of weeds, thanks to the flower fight that erupted when the kids first entered the room. I reached down and picked up a red rose with a broken stem. "So much for a romantic evening with my wife," I sighed, holding out the flower.

Cookie took the rose and sniffed it contentedly. "Let's call room service and order some nachos. Then we'll watch a movie with the kids."

"But everything is ruined," I protested. "This was supposed to be special."

Her eyes twinkled as she planted a kiss on my cheek. "It is special," she replied. "At least you remembered."

Looking ahead to next August, I've taken the precaution of booking a table in advance at Chez Roberto's for Cookie's birthday. My wife loves the ambiance; I like the menu – they don't serve cold hash.

The restaurant even offered to give me a wakeup call two days ahead, provided I promised to leave the kids at home.

To be on the safe side, I called up the babysitter's boyfriend to make sure Darla's own birthday wouldn't interfere with our plans. "No problem," he said. "Her birthday comes later in the year."

I frowned at his arrogance. "Listen, just between us guys here – do you mean to tell me that you actually know when Darla's birthday is, and can remember it?"

"You bet," he laughed. "There's no way I could ever forget. Her birthday is on Christmas Day."

I hung up the phone in disgust. Some guys have all the luck.

CHAPTER 16

❧ IN PURSUIT OF CULTURE ❧

Accorting to my wife, I lack culture.

"You should learn to appreciate the finer things in life, like art and music." Cookie killed the sports channel with a casual flick of the remote.

"Hey, the playoffs aren't over yet!"

"No," she smiled. "But your days of boorishness are. In one month, I want to see a new man."

I gulped. "You mean you're trading me in on a new model?"

She sighed. "Alas, no. As mother always said, 'Better the junker that's paid for than a Jaguar with lease payments.'" She tossed the remote onto the couch. "But at least try to learn the difference between a Picasso and pizza. Remember, you've got 30 days."

Cookie's words rattled in my brain as I unlocked the office door the next morning. A complete makeover in 30 days? Who was she kidding? I'm a mechanic – I can overhaul a Borg-Warner transmission in about 10 hours. But undoing decades of misguided behavioral patterns in only a month is a bit of a stretch.

Besides, what was wrong with me the way I was? Clearly a second opinion was needed here, and it arrived a few minutes later as a familiar red Fiat pulled into the parking lot. "Basil," I said as he walked through the front door. "Do I lack culture?"

Basil paused mid-step. "Is this a trick question?"

I shook my head.

After taking off his coat and hanging it on a hook, Basil rubbed his chin thoughtfully. "Before I answer that," he began cautiously, "may I ask what initiated this train wreck of thought?"

I turned on the coffeemaker. "It's Cookie. She seems to think I could use a few improvements." I looked him square in the eye. "Basil, give it to me straight – do you think I'm uncouth?"

Basil held up both hands in self-defense. "Slim, I'm going to do us both a favor and leave that one alone." He shook his head and chuckled. "Cookie may be your wife, but I have to work with you. Let someone far wiser than I guide you through this minefield of introspection." He escaped into the shop on the pretext of finding a clean pair of coveralls, but I could hear him snickering as he went. "Slim Shambles…a man of culture? Ha ha…as if that could ever happen…oh my goodness, that's precious…!"

So much for the second opinion, I muttered to myself.

So like Don Quixote in pursuit of a windmill, I began my quest – although deep down I knew Cookie was dreaming the impossible dream. As far as I was concerned, Art was my neighbor down the street and culture was something that grew in a petri dish. Clearly I was out of my league and I knew it.

Time being of the essence, I took the afternoon off to go look for an alternate source of sagely wisdom. In Slumberland, few such options exist. So I headed over to the home of the one guy who could take any complex subject imaginable and break it down into its basic elements. This man could demonstrate quantum physics with a weed-whacker.

"You wanna learn about art?" Buck Pincher's face lit up. "Your search is over! I dabble in that a little bit myself. Why, next weekend I'm heading south for an artists' convention in Mud Flats, Idaho. You can be my guest."

I looked around Buck's cluttered studio. Half-finished watercolors and oils lay stacked on chairs and filing cabinets, layers of dust giving silent testimony to ambitious projects begun and then gleefully abandoned. I peered closely at the current project underway on the easel – it was a still life of three nine-volt batteries in an antique ashtray. Buck was in his 'acid and ash' period.

Scattered about the room were half-used tubes of acrylics, some of them uncapped with paint spilling out onto whatever surface lay beneath. From what I could determine, in the area of art Buck did more dribbling than dabbling. But then again, it was more than I did.

"Idaho? And I'm your guest for the whole weekend?" I was incredulous. "You mean you'll cover the hotel bills and everything?"

"Ha! Good one," Buck snorted. "Naw, we'll take your RV and park in my friend's barnyard. It'll only cost you the gas and the food."

I expected Cookie to be excited at my progress when I told her about my upcoming trip. She wasn't. "Buck Pincher? Is that the best you can come up with?" She turned the steak over on the barbeque and sighed. "Why do I get the feeling I'm going to regret all this?"

"Hey, that's not fair," I protested. "The worst that could happen is that I won't learn anything."

"No," she replied. "The worst that could happen is that you'll learn things you should never have known. Remember, you'll be in close quarters with Buck for an entire weekend."

I convinced myself that Cookie's misgivings were unfounded and started packing supplies into my brand new fifth wheel trailer. Our old motorhome had been put out to pasture – meaning I'd sold it to a local farmer to use as a chicken coop. If nothing else, the upcoming trip would provide an excellent opportunity to expand my horizons, to open new visual vistas, to experience life's invigorating sights and smells…in other words, it was a chance to get away and goof off.

The sights and smells that assaulted us a few days later when Buck and I pulled into Mud Flats weren't exactly the ones I had expected, especially when it came to pursuing culture. *Hmm…kind of a strange looking art gallery*, I thought to myself, as the hot wind blew tumbleweeds across the gravel parking lot of the Mud Flats Fair Grounds. A couple of horses tied to the fence rail nearby strained at their reins as they searched for something to nibble on, and for a moment I had the feeling I'd just stepped into the middle of the OK corral at high noon. Everyone who walked past us wore either western boots or a cowboy hat or both.

Fortunately, no six-guns at the hip were in sight.

The massive barn-like structure in front of us sported a large banner that read *Welcome to the Mud Flats Annual Mule and Draft Horse Show.* A small sandwich board off to one side added the following information in crude crayon letters: *DDDI Annual Convention Inside.*

"What's DDDI stand for?" I asked. "Is that the artists' convention?"

"You bet," confirmed Buck enthusiastically. "It stands for *Doodling Dudes in Dungarees International*, a great bunch of cowboy cartoonists. I'm telling you, Slim, these guys create some really cool stuff. Just wait till you see." He started for the entrance, but I grabbed his arm and pulled him back.

"Cartoonists? I don't know, Buck – something doesn't smell right. Maybe we should…"

"Relax," he sighed, rolling his eyes in exasperation. "You gotta trust me on this one. Just buddy up with these guys and before you know it, you'll be standing in the very grass roots of culture."

I lifted my foot and located the source of the disturbing smell. "Yeah?" I said, scraping my boot with a stick. "And exactly what kind of medium do they work in?"

Once inside, it didn't take long to locate Buck's friends. Decked out in red long underwear, cowboy hats and boots, the cartoonists were hollering and whooping it up over in one corner as they showed off their illustrations to any unfortunate rancher who wandered too close.

The ringleader was a scrawny runt with a handle bar mustache and a ten gallon hat. His red underwear had a few extra hand-painted stains strategically located to provide authenticity. At least, I assumed they were hand-painted. He was hard at work with a black marker, drawing graffiti on a canvas-covered outhouse that was set up on display. Buck dragged me over for an introduction.

"Slim Shambles, this here's Bender Cranium, one of the best western artists you'll ever meet. If it's culture you want, ol' Bender here's got slop buckets full of it."

"Howdy, boys!" Bender stuck the marker behind his ear and shook our hands vigorously, grinning like a maniac. He pointed at the outhouse. "How d'ya like it? Some lucky feller's gonna get this for a door prize at the end of the weekend."

I examined his sketch of a caricatured bull in the midst of a bowel movement. The other cartoonists had covered the rest of the structure with drawings along a similar vein. "Buck," I whispered. "I don't think hanging out with *Doodling Dudes in Dungarees* is exactly the cultural enlightenment my wife had in mind."

But Buck ignored me. He was in his element and the turkey buzzards of reason had long since flown the coop. Grabbing Bender by the arm, Buck dragged him over to some paintings on display. "Kinda been dabbling in watercolors myself, Bend, and I'm curious how you get the texture on those buffalo chips to look so real…"

Left to my own devices, I wandered over to the building next door to check out the draft mules, but not before a scrawny woman in long johns and heavy mascara tried to sell me one of her works of art. "Take this home for the little lady," she crooned, thrusting a gaudy painting in front of my nose. "She'll be speechless with delight."

The colorful piece illustrated the lively interaction between an old prospector, an outhouse, and a hornets nest. I knew what Cookie's reaction would be if I bought it, and 'speechless with delight' was not the term I would use.

My plunge into the world of artistic license continued that night out at a local ranch, where Bender had invited Buck and me to a barbeque. All the cartoonists were there, dressed to the nines in their best jeans, leather vests, and shiny belt buckles. When the cooks brought out a roasted pig on a huge platter, Bender and his buddies let out a raucous cheer of delight. My mouth watered as the delicious smells of roast pork filled the dining hall. I was just about to get in the food line when Bender decided the pig was looking a tad under dressed. A mad dash ensued as everyone rushed outside to grab twigs, wild flowers, tree bark, and pine cones – anything they could get their hands on. Then they piled back inside and went to work.

Buck was impressed. "I've never seen a roast pig with dandelions sticking outta his ears before. Just look at that color and texture!"

I stared at the pig, taking note of the bits of color and texture poking out of a lot of other places as well. "I think I'll just have the salad," I mumbled weakly.

Buck shook his head. "You're missing the whole point here, Slim. You gotta enter into the spirit of the thing. Take this pig for example. It was just dinner a few minutes ago, but now it's become what we artsy types call *Found Object Art*. Why, even guys like Pablo Picasso were into this kind of stuff!"

Picasso? That name sounded familiar – Cookie had mentioned it in connection with a pizza. I looked at the pig once more. Ham, pizza, Picasso…in a strange sort of way it was all coming together. *Maybe this isn't such a wild boar chase after all,* I thought.

After supper, we gathered outside around the campfire. Bender pulled a battered old guitar out of its case and tuned up. "Ah," I said. "Time for a little classical music?"

"Sure, I knows a classic," grinned Bender. "An' I even learnt all three chords." It wasn't long before we were hollering at the top of our lungs, "My name is Sue! How do you do!" The Man in Black would have been proud.

Sixteen songs later things were simmering down. That's when a muleskinner named Terry pulled out his whiskey bottle and passed it around.

"Buck!" I hissed as it came our way, "you don't know where that's been!"

"I don't care where it's been," he chortled, grabbing the bottle. "Question is, how far will it go?"

Buck's raucous singing put the finishing touches on the evening's performance as we drove back to our trailer that night. It also caused a small stampede in the dairy pasture next door.

Steering Buck towards the bedroom at the back of the trailer, I headed for the bunks up front in a vain attempt to escape his snoring.

Somewhere just before dawn I managed to drop off to sleep, only to be rudely awakened by loud braying right outside my window, courtesy of Terry's head mule. I fumbled for the clock. "4:30 a.m.?" *Forget this quest for culture; it's time to get back to civilization.*

I stumbled out into the cold morning mist and hooked up my truck to the trailer. 100 miles later it was time to stop for breakfast. Buck stumbled out of the trailer, holding his aching head. He opened his bleary eyes and looked around in confusion. "Hey, this don't look like Terry's ranch." He stared at the sign by the highway that read *Humpty's Dumpy Diner – Breakfast served all day until 3 p.m.* "And where's my buddy Bender?"

"Gone!" I growled, heading towards the diner. "I managed to lose him at the last freeway exit."

A few days later, I walked into Buck's kitchen, only to find him fishing behind his refrigerator with a bent coat hanger. "Now what are you doing?"

Buck sneezed as a dust bunny floated by his nose. "I'm looking for some culture."

"Please," I protested. "I'm done with that nonsense."

He stood up. "Got it. I knew it was here somewhere." He blew the dust off an old cassette tape. "It's a singer named Maserati, or something like that. I figured with you being a mechanic and all, you might like it. I know my wife does."

This sounded promising. I squinted at the faded label. "Actually, the name is Pavarotti. What's his musical style?"

"I'm not sure," admitted Buck. "Never bothered to listen to it. I'm guessing Country Gospel?" He opened up his old cassette recorder and stuck in the tape.

"That sure doesn't sound like Country," I said a few minutes later. "How come his voice wavers like that?"

Buck shrugged. "Maybe the tape's stretched. It was pretty warm behind the fridge."

In the end, my search for new cultural horizons brought me right back to my own living room, where our oldest daughter was practicing her piano pieces for an upcoming music festival. "What's that song Cache is playing?" I asked Cookie.

"That's Fantasia in D minor by Mozart," she replied. "Don't you just love the trills, the arpeggios, and the cadenzas of classical music?"

"Uh, sure." As far as I knew, a cadenza was a piece of furniture, but I didn't want to embarrass Cookie by mentioning it. "Well, I'm going down to the family room to view the arts on TV. Call me when supper is ready."

"Viewing the arts…?" Cookie's eyes lit up. "Oh Slim – you did it!" She threw her arms around me in a big hug. "Tell me, what kind of arts?! Theatre, ballet, symphony…?"

"No," I replied guiltily. "Martial arts – I rented a Jackie Chan movie."

Cookie has now resigned herself to the fact that the tuxedo I wore on our wedding day was a once-in-a-lifetime memory, never to be repeated. It's become obvious that I'll never be a Jaguar, or even a Maserati.

But that's okay. At least I'm reliable transportation.

CHAPTER 17

⮞ TOWED TRUCK ⮜

Dutchy chewed on one of his toxic cigarillos as he worked the controls of his deck truck. The hydraulics moaned under the load of the full-sized Suburban he was unloading.

"Ja," he grunted through clenched teeth, as his truck's suspension groaned in protest. "I mean, in Holland we drove sensible cars, little cars that were easy to park and good on fuel." He let go of the controls and began to unhook the safety chains. "And when they broke down, they didn't break the tow truck too."

Basil climbed up into the Suburban to steer it back down the ramp while Dutchy operated the winch. "Welcome to our Canadian lifestyle, Dutchy. Take these Suburban owners, for example. They have three active boys all in hockey – they need a big vehicle just to haul the gear to the rink."

Dutchy took out his cigarillo and spat on the ground. "Ja? Well, if their big cars break my truck, I'm gonna charge them extra!" He climbed into the cab, put the tow truck into gear and drove across the street to his other shop – the one with the yard full of wrecked vehicles. A simple sign that read *Dutchy's Towing* hung crookedly on the chain link fence.

I say his *other* shop, because Dutchy owned a few different properties in town, including the building I was renting. From all appearances, the towing business was just a sideline to keep himself busy.

Dutchy's wrecking yard happened to be located on higher ground than the rest of the industrial park, the reason being that his property ran right up against the base of Hunchback Mountain. Like a fortress wall, the rock cliff shot 900 feet straight up behind him to the summit. It was an imposing sight, and with a good pair of eyeballs you could see the tiny railings of the viewpoint perched at the south end of the plateau, directly above our two shops. I have stood at that viewpoint in the past, and the memory of it still rattles me. But I don't mind being at the bottom looking up – there's not as far to fall when I pass out.

Being situated higher than all the surrounding buildings suited Dutchy just fine. Like a liege lord surveying his fiefdom, he liked to sit at his office window with a mug of coffee in one hand and one of his thin little 7-minute cigars in the other as he kept a vigilant eye on his peasants below. When the time came to knock on his door at the end of every month, I felt like I was bringing tribute, not just the rent check.

Tooner brought a leaky radiator over to the tire machine where I was working. "What d'ya want me t' do with this thing?" he asked. "Should I take it over t' Charlie?"

Charlie ran a lawnmower repair shop in the building across the parking lot – a building also owned by Lord Dutchy. The mower business being slow lately, Charlie had decided to get into repairing radiators as well. At the strong suggestion of our landlord, we had sent a few rad repairs Charlie's way because, as Dutchy put it, "Ja, I mean, he's got to pay his rent too, you know."

But there was one problem with Charlie's radiators: they refused to hold water. In fact, almost every one of the units he'd repaired for us had to be removed again and redone. It was costing us time and money.

"Gee, I don't know, Tooner – I think we should send that rad downtown to Herkle's Auto Parts, like we used to." Herk had a deal going with a radiator shop in Panicton, where he would handle the pickup and delivery, and they would do the repairs. "The work from that other rad shop was a lot more reliable."

"Ya got a point there," he agreed. "We ain't had much luck with Leaky Charlie." He peeked across the street. "But how ya gonna get it past Dutchy? He's sittin' up there right now at his window, drinkin' his coffee and watchin' every move we make."

"Let me handle it." I called up Herkle's Auto Parts and asked if they could come by to pick up the radiator. "And make sure Rodney uses the back door," I added.

We worked out our strategy, and when Rodney skidded to a stop out behind our shop a few minutes later, we were ready. "Okay, Slim," called Basil in a hoarse whisper. "Make the call."

I hit the speed dial for Dutchy's Towing, and the moment Dutchy moved away from his window seat to answer the ringing of his phone, I hollered, "Okay – go for it!"

Basil held the back door open while Tooner grabbed the radiator and made a mad dash out to Rodney's truck. I had my hand over the mouthpiece of the telephone receiver, but I could hear Dutchy's voice on the other end. "Ja? I mean, who is this? Hello? Hello?"

Basil gave me the thumbs up as Rodney laid rubber down the back alley. I hung up the phone and mopped my face with a rag. *Whew! We got away with it this time.*

The morning passed quickly and before we knew it, Rodney had returned and dropped off the newly-repaired radiator without being seen. But there was one anxious moment when Dutchy swooped in after lunch on a reconnaissance mission.

"Ja, I mean, didn't I see a cooling system job come in here this morning?" He craned his neck in every direction, searching out the dark corners of my shop. He even sniffed the air to see if he could detect the sweet smell of hot antifreeze. "And if I did, how come I didn't see any radiators going over to Charlie?"

"Cooling system?" I echoed, leaning nonchalantly against a stack of new tires. "That's funny. It's been so busy all morning that I could hardly keep track of…"

"Bah!" Fortunately, Dutchy was in a hurry. He turned and headed for the door. "Must have been my imagination, ja?" He stomped out the bay door, mumbling something about prank phone calls throwing off his concentration that morning.

After he'd left, Tooner came over to help me move the tires. Behind them was the car my nosey landlord had been searching for. "Hurry up and get that radiator reinstalled," I muttered darkly. "His Highness might come back any minute!"

Tooner did his own muttering, throwing in a few choice words I hadn't heard before. He lifted the radiator into place. "Bein' the landlord don't give ya the right t' be snoopin' around another guy's shop." He reached down to reattach the lower hose. "If I were you, I'd tell him t' mind his own business!"

I agreed with Tooner, but sometimes things are just what they are. "He's only looking after his interests," I said. "He figures if he can keep everybody working, then his rents will get paid on time. Besides, he does send us some extra work now and then."

"Sendin' a guy work is one thing, but tellin' him how t' do it is another."

I glanced outside again to check on Dutchy, and it was a good thing I did. He was just about to enter his shop when he suddenly spun on his heel and began striding back across the road in our direction. Evidently he'd just remembered some other misdemeanor on my part that required his immediate attention. "Quick!" I cried. "Put the tires back in place!"

By the time our afternoon break came around, I'd had enough interaction with my landlord to last me for the rest of the year. Tooner was feeling it too, and stepped outside to soak up a little sun at the picnic table beside the shop. That's when he noticed the suspicious activity going on up at the top of Hunchback Mountain. "Hey Slim – Basil!" he hollered excitedly. "Come on out here. Ya gotta see this!"

Joining him around the side of the building, we followed his gaze to the very top of the mountain, where we could just barely make out a tiny rectangular white shape rocking back and forth on the edge of the cliff. "What is that?" I asked, squinting as hard as I could. "Some kind of big box?"

Tooner took another mouthful of sandwich. "Nope," he mumbled as he chewed. "It's a vehicle. In fact, I'd say it's a pickup truck."

"I agree," said Basil. "And from the looks of it, it's stuck on some rocks at the edge of the cliff."

"Do you think anybody is in it?" The thought of staring out of a windshield into empty space unnerved me completely. I almost passed out right there in sympathy.

Tooner munched on while he watched the truck rock for a few minutes and then stop. Then it would start up rocking again. Finally he said, "If yer askin' me, I'd say somebody's tryin' t' push that truck over the edge."

We forgot all about work and stood there mesmerized for the next ten minutes while the tiny shape wobbled back and forth. Though it was too far away for us to see them, it was obvious somebody was up there, and it certainly looked like they were up to no good.

"I'm calling the police," I declared, starting for the office.

All of a sudden Basil gasped. "Look out!" he yelled. "It's coming down!"

We watched in horror as the white truck broke free from the rocks and began its free fall into space. Halfway down the cliff it smashed into an outcropping of solid rock, flipped over backwards, and continued its rush towards terminal velocity. The hood came free and sailed off on its own like a hang glider. It was like watching a stunt show from a movie, only in slow motion and without the scary sound track.

After what felt like an eternity, the truck plowed into the shale at the bottom of the cliff and rolled down the incline, losing itself in the low brush and trees below. A lone front tire broke loose on impact and rolled down the shale slope, gathering speed as it went. I had visions of it blasting through the wall and destroying our shop, but fortunately it didn't come in our direction. Instead, it bounced and wobbled its way into an abandoned sawmill yard down the street, finally burying itself in a pile of old lumber.

We all stood there with our mouths gaping open, too shocked to move. Tooner was the first to speak. "Now, that's what I call off-roadin'."

"I'll say!" Basil removed his glasses and rubbed his eyes with a shaky hand. "I would never have believed it if I hadn't seen it for myself."

I dashed inside and dialed the phone number for the local RCMP office. "Uh, I'd like to report…well, I mean, we just saw…" Suddenly I wasn't sure what to say. This was Slumberland – things like this just don't happen here. I took a deep breath and started over. "Somebody just pushed a truck off Hunchback Mountain." I shut my eyes, waiting for the laughter to begin.

But it didn't. "Yes, we know." A tired sigh came from the receptionist on the other end of the line. "That was us."

"What! You mean to tell me your officers pushed a truck off the mountain?"

"Don't be silly," she replied dryly. "I mean that our members are there on the scene. The truck was stolen last night from a dealership in Panicton, and the thieves tried to push it off the cliff. We were trying to winch it back up when the cable snapped."

"Oh." I couldn't think of anything intelligent to say. "Oh," I said again, and hung up. Then it dawned on me: if the local police were involved, then they were probably using a local towing company for the winch work. I looked across the street at Dutchy's parking lot – his winch truck was nowhere in sight. I suddenly remembered seeing him drive it out of his yard about an hour before. *Oh boy – I'll bet Dutchy's not a happy camper right about now.*

Thirty minutes later we spied Dutchy sneaking down the lane behind the sawmill, a tangled mess of broken cable piled high on the back of his truck. He was making his way towards the base of the mountain, and it was obvious he didn't want to be seen. Just as obviously, we wanted to be there to rub it in. "C'mon, gang," called Tooner over his shoulder as he ran out of the shop. "Hop in the truck – it's time t' check out the carnage!"

But I was having second thoughts. "Easy, boys. Dutchy is likely to raise my rent if we get him too upset."

"Aw, come on, Slim – we never get to have any fun."

In the end, we didn't make Dutchy endure the embarrassment of having three hecklers watch him recover the mangled truck from the bottom of the cliff. But we did stand by the side of the road and give him a three-tech salute when he finally drove by, dragging the broken bits home to his wrecking yard. It was the least we could do.

"Hey, Dutchy," called out Basil. "I don't know how it is in Holland, but in Canada, if you break the little car with your big tow truck, you have to pay for the damages!"

Dutchy puffed furiously on his cigarillo as he got out to unlock his gate. "Ja?" he hollered back. "Well, in Holland this would never have happened!"

"How so?" goaded Tooner.

"Because there we have sensible mountains, little ones that don't tear your car to pieces!"

We collapsed on the ground laughing, but as we finally dragged ourselves back inside the shop, a sudden thought struck me. "Hey Basil," I said excitedly, "call up Dickie Dixon at the used car lot and tell him to get that Chevy up here right away, the one with the leaky radiator that he called about last week."

It would be a while before King Dutchy would forsake the safety of his castle walls to make a tour of the troops – his ego needed time to heal. That meant we had a brief window of opportunity to conduct business on our own terms, and it was an opportunity I didn't want to miss.

CHAPTER 18

DANGER: CURVES AHEAD

About a month ago, somebody snuck into an empty storefront in Slumberland and opened up a ladies-only fitness centre. They called it *Contours for Chicks*. As a businessman, I can appreciate good marketing techniques, but I think that's going too far.

To the average housewife, Contours for Chicks conjures up images of a safe place for women to get in shape. But to the average husband, it translates roughly into Trophy Wives 'R' Us. With a name like that, no red-blooded male is going to say no when the little lady comes and asks him to cough up the membership fees.

However, I took it all in stride, figuring it was just another passing fad, like the newest celebrity diet or the latest self-help book. And since it was for women and not men, I didn't feel threatened in the least.

But Buck Pincher was worried. "Our reputations are at stake here, Slim," he grumbled one day as we sat at the counter of Fuzzyberries Ice Cream & Eatery. "Once our wives get all trim and healthy-like, they'll be after us to change our ways."

"But Buck, Dolly's been after you for years to change your ways."

He glowered. "See what I mean? It's started already."

"Well, I'm all for promoting healthier lifestyles," I told him, taking a bite of my banana split. "Look at it this way. If our wives stay slim and trim, we won't have to spend all that money each year on new outfits in bigger sizes."

Buck looked at me as if I was brain dead – and considering what I'd just said, he had good reason. Dress size has precious little to do with a woman's need to shop.

"A healthy lifestyle is one thing!" he retorted. "But what's with all the secrecy?" He took a swig of coffee before digging into his cherry-covered cheesecake. Buck had a point – there was a lot of stuff going on behind closed doors lately. Even during the renovation stage, all the windows were covered with brown paper so that no one could see in. We were forced to wait for the grand opening.

Like every other Slumberland male over the age of 12, I was planning to join the crowd on the sidewalk and gaze in admiration at the trim and fit females pumping iron to the pounding beat of disco music. They would become role models to us, inspiring one and all to new heights of gazing and admiring. But as soon as the brown paper came down, the vertical blinds went up. Thus ended the fantasy.

"So you really think we should be worried about this place?"

"What do you think?" Buck scraped the last bit of cherry sauce from his plate. "You've seen the large sign on the door, saying no men are allowed inside." Buck lowered his voice. "Kind of makes you wonder what goes on inside those four walls, don't it?"

Indeed, it did. And I knew that if I was ever going to find out, I'd need someone on the inside. So when my wife mentioned that she wanted to sign up, I graciously agreed.

"What!" I hollered. "They want forty bucks a month, automatically debited right out of our bank account? Not as long as I'm king of this castle!"

Cookie smiled sweetly. "I knew you'd understand, Your Highness. Now finish up those dishes, and when I get back, I'll tell you all about it."

So she joined up, along with 80% of the other women in town. "It's a thirty minute workout where you rotate between eight or nine different machines," reported Cookie after the first session. "You only spend 30 seconds on each machine and then move to a 'recovery pad' to get ready for the next station."

"But how come it's for women only?" I stuck my hands in my pockets and tried to look pitiful. "I was sort of thinking it might be good for me to join a health club with you. You know – so we could be together."

She laughed. "Nice try, buddy boy, but that's not how it works. Women like this setup because it's a non-threatening environment where they don't have to impress anybody. Like it or not, that means keeping the guys out."

I was flabbergasted. "You mean other women feel the need to impress me?"

Cookie paused and gave me the once over. "Hmm… maybe not. It's all the other guys we're worried about."

Like I said, my wife was not the only one who signed up. Within weeks of the grand opening, you could hardly loiter on a Slumberland street corner without getting trampled by a gaggle of women in all shapes and sizes, jogging their way to the fitness club. Wearing headbands and spandex, the fierce glint in their eyes was enough to frighten small children and terrify grown men.

I think Buck was right. Now that our women were becoming fit and trim, the pressure was on us men to conform. Little add-ons like beer guts, love handles, and triple chins just didn't cut it anymore.

"It's been worse since they opened up that tanning salon right across the street," complained Buck. "It was bad enough being labeled a couch potato; now Dolly calls me her pet bleached whale."

I was having my own troubles back home – Cookie's muscle tone was improving at an alarming rate. The other day she was showing off her biceps to our son. Tipper was impressed. "You'd better watch out, Dad," he said solemnly.

"Whadda ya mean?" I blustered, flexing my right arm until beads of sweat popped out on my forehead. "I'm still in charge around here!"

He looked at me doubtfully. "Maybe you've got the voice, Dad, but Mom's got the muscle."

Clearly, things were getting out of hand, so I called an emergency meeting over at Rolph's Diner. About a dozen guys showed up, all showing signs of stress. "Slim, can you lend me two bucks for coffee?" whined Ropey Lewis. "Linda's used all my spending money to buy organic health food – I'm dying for some caffeine and white sugar."

Rolph set a large mug of steaming hot coffee under Ropey's nose. "On the house, Rope. And here – take a napkin. I can't bear to see a grown man cry."

I banged the salt shaker on the table. "Gentlemen, let's bring this meeting to order. There's only one matter of business on the agenda: we need to do something about Contours for Chicks."

"You got that right," whined Buck. "Dolly can beat me at arm wrestling now."

Baldy drained his coffee cup and held it out for seconds. "And exactly how is that different than before?"

Buck glared at him. "Because now she does it while she's knitting booties for the grandkids."

Rep Tyler rubbed the stubble on his chin. "Whoa – that is serious."

Even Hank Brink, our town planner, was there. He was also our bylaw enforcement officer. "Hank," I said, "isn't there something you could do over at city hall? Like maybe revoke their business license?"

He shook his head. "Sorry, Slim; I wish I could. My wife's been spending a fortune on new aerobics outfits, a different one for each day of the week." He sighed. "Much as I hate to admit it, Contours has complied with every bylaw I've thrown at them – even some I made up."

"Made up?" Baldy eyed Hank shrewdly. "Huh. I always suspected you of doing that." A few other businessmen around the table began to raise their voices in agreement. The meeting was in danger of falling apart.

I banged the salt shaker again. "Now calm down, fellas. Let's stay focused."

"There's only one thing to do," declared Buck. "If you can't beat 'em, join 'em."

"But that's the problem, Buck. Men aren't allowed to join."

A sly grin crept onto Buck's craggy face. "I'm not talking about *joining* Contours; I'm talking about *competing* with them. We'll open up our own place right next door and…" Lowering his voice, Buck filled us in on the rest of his idea. It sounded good, so everyone pledged to help out in any way they could.

A week later we were busy at work inside the commercial building next door to Contours. Buck had signed an open-ended lease with the owner, so we were painting walls and putting up sports posters in anticipation of our own grand opening. Rep Tyler was up front filling a large fish tank with water, getting it ready for some of his infamous wildlife. I took a closer look at the small, hand-painted sign taped to the front of the glass: *Danger – Piranhas. Keep yer stupid fingers out, buddy!* "Are you sure about this, Rep?"

"Them's a man's fish!" replied our local naturalist. "Don't want none o' them sissy gold fish in *this* fine establishment."

I shrugged and went outside where a small group of bystanders were watching Buck and Baldy wobble about on stepladders as they installed our new sign.

Bulges for Bubba, it read. "Gee, Buck," called out somebody from the crowd. "Are you sure that's such a good name for a fitness center?"

"Sure it is," he replied. "The way I figure it, if nobody signs up for the gym, we can always fall back on Plan B."

"Plan B? What's Plan B?"

"We'll turn it into a donut shop." That brought cheers and a round of applause from everyone.

Baldy finished screwing in his side of the sign. "Are we gonna let any women join?"

Buck slapped on a final piece of duct tape and climbed down. "Absolutely not. We can discriminate right along with the best of 'em." He raised his fist in the air and shouted, "No women allowed! Are you with me, men?"

All the guys raised their eyebrows and said nothing. Apparently they weren't. Buck sighed. "Okay, maybe we can hire a pretty receptionist."

Ropey slapped him a high five. "Now you're talking. Say, where do you want this candy bar dispenser?"

"Put it in the back corner," Buck said. "Next to the pop machine.

We'll keep the chips and pretzels up by the front counter."

We weren't really interested in operating a fitness gym for men – we just wanted to keep the place open until our wives got tired of working out. Even so, I questioned Buck on the high price he was charging for the snacks. "Ten bucks for a bag of chips? That's a little steep, don't you think?"

Buck laid an arm across my shoulders. "Slim, Slim…work with me, will you?" He went on to explain how the add-on sales would help pay the bills until our women came to their senses. "With any luck, these two storefronts will become vacant at the same time, and life in Slumberland can return to normal."

But until then, us guys planned to gather at Bubba's and do our own stuff.

"Are ya gonna actually deal them cards, or are ya just thinkin' about it?" Rep Tyler fed a piece of a cheese twist to the pet mouse he carried in his shirt pocket. "We're gonna fall asleep over here if ya don't hurry it up."

Ropey Lewis shuffled the deck one more time. "Just keep your shirt on, Rep. After the way you cheated on that last hand, I want to make sure they're well mixed up."

"Cheated?" Rep leaned forward in his chair. "I did no such thing! Why, if I didn't…"

"Hey, keep it down over there," I said sternly to the gang gathered around the card table. "You're making things difficult for Buck." I turned back to my friend. "Can you hear anything yet? Are they talking about us?"

Buck shifted the stethoscope to a new spot on the wall. "Nope, can't hear a word. That blasted music is too loud."

I sighed. "Buck, I'm bored." I opened another bag of corn chips and took a look around the room. "Listen guys, we've got all this weight training equipment here – maybe we should try working out ourselves. It couldn't hurt, could it?"

The glares from the rest of the group just about knocked me off my stool.

"Give yer head a shake, Slim," said Rep. "Yer talkin' 'bout a way of life here."

"Yeah," agreed Ropey. "Do you know how long it took me to get this beer belly looking the way I like it?" He cracked open another cool one. "Talk like that could ruin decades of hard work."

I went over to the front window and pushed aside the vertical blind. A steady stream of fit-looking ladies was making its way in and out of the fitness club next door. From what I could tell, there was no sign of it letting up anytime soon. By contrast, membership in Bulges for Bubba had stalled at eight and a half – we charged Baldy only half price to bring his dog, Closeshave.

Joining Buck once more at the wall, I voiced my concerns. "I think it's time to move on."

Buck looked at me. "Move on? Y'mean go to Plan B, the donut shop?"

"No, I mean move on, as in 'I'm going home.' As the head of my household, I'm going to tell Cookie where things stand, and that's that."

The fellows all stood silently as I reached for my jacket, some of them removing their hats as a sign of respect. "Been nice knowin' ya," sniffed Rep Tyler as I passed by.

Luckily for me, Cookie is a very understanding wife. "Like I said before," I announced, adding more hot water to the sink. "I'm still king of this castle, and as such, I hereby give you full permission to continue going to Contours for Chicks as long as you want...on one condition."

My wife raised an eyebrow. "And that is?"

I coughed and lowered my voice in case the kids were listening. "If you could just promise not to beat me at arm wrestling in front of the children anymore, that would be great."

She considered the idea. "I can live with that." Cookie zipped up the jacket of her new jogging outfit. "Now, when you finish those dishes, would you mind vacuuming the living room? It's getting a little dusty." She blew me a kiss and breezed out the front door for her evening run.

I sighed and rung out my dishrag. It was time to call Buck and tell him to move on to the real Plan B. With all this housework ahead of me, I was going to need a good sugar fix on a regular basis.

And Bulges for Bubba's Donuts sounds like just the right place.

CHAPTER 19

⚜ TIMING IS EVERYTHING ⚜

There was no doubt about it; Ned's pickup needed a new transmission. After hauling one too many bins of apples for his juicing business, Ned's battered old Chevy finally gave up the ghost halfway up Slumberland Hill. It arrived at our shop on the back of Dutchy's deck truck, apples and all.

"Ned's tranny is shot, ja," Dutchy informed us as he unloaded his cargo. "I told him you'd have it ready by tomorrow. You want I should call him up and tell him how much it will cost?" Dutchy loved being in control – I could just picture how big his TV remote was, back home on his coffee table.

"No, I don't!" I was fed up with my landlord's interference in our daily routines. "And why did you promise it for tomorrow? We're already backed up with work!" I shook my head in frustration. Ned's timing couldn't be have been worse.

"Bah – you can handle it." Dutchy dismissed my protests with a wave of his cigarillo. I cringed as the foul stench filled the air. "It's just a simple transmission job on a two-wheel drive pickup. I mean, ja, you got two big guys standing around doing nothing all day – you should have it done by coffee break." He tossed me the keys and drove off, and it was a good thing he did. When I turned around, Basil and Tooner were standing there practically boiling in their juices. "That Dutchy's drivin' me crazy," growled Tooner.

Basil nodded curtly in agreement. "I don't know how you put up with him, Slim. Here I'm thinking how fortunate it is that we don't work for him – and then I realize we practically do!"

I grimaced. "I hear you. But until we can find something better, we're stuck here." There weren't many buildings in Slumberland that were suitable for an automotive repair business – and the ones that were, Dutchy owned.

Replacing Ned's transmission seemed like a straightforward procedure at first. But then, doesn't everything is this business?

First we had to deal with the apples. The wooden bins in the back of Ned's truck were full to the brim, and they weighed a ton. Tooner removed his cap and scratched the back of his head. "That's a lot of apples – more weight than I'd like t' see up on that hoist. We're gonna need a forklift or somethin' t' get 'em off."

Fortunately, Slumberland is full of apple orchards, and where there's a farmer, there's a tractor. I called up Dougie Crumble, an orchardist friend of mine, and asked if we could borrow his tractor with the bin lifting attachment.

"I'd like to help you out, Slim, but your timing isn't very good. It's apple picking season and my tractor's running steady all day." He thought for a moment. "Could we do it tonight after dark?"

"Sure," I sighed. "I'll be working late anyway. Can you come by after supper?" Resigned to my fate, I broke the connection and then dialed the number for Gearbox Heaven, the transmission shop in Panicton. Fortunately, they had a rebuilt unit in stock, but they weren't too thrilled that I wanted it in a hurry. "D'ya really need it right now?" whined Gordy, the owner.

"Of course I do!" I said. "What's the matter – don't you want to make a sale?"

"Yeah," grumbled Gordy. "It's just that yer timin' is off, that's all. We just got back from deliverin' a tranny to Slumberland ten minutes ago – it's too bad ya didn't call sooner."

I hung up the phone and rubbed my aching forehead. Call sooner? Ten minutes ago I didn't even know I *needed* a transmission. *Repairing cars is one thing,* I thought. *Predicting when they're gonna break down is another.*

Next morning, Tooner got onto the job, and after a few hours of hard work, three skinned knuckles, and ten new curse words, he was ready to go for a test drive. The only problem was the truck wouldn't start.

As he cranked the engine, loud backfires erupted through the throttle body, as if the ignition timing was out. And it was – about 30 degrees.

"How did you manage to do that?" inquired Basil, as the two of them worked on getting Ned's truck running again.

"Ain't got a clue," retorted Tooner. "I never touched the blasted distributor." They reset the timing and the truck ran great – for about a week.

"What's up now, Ned?" I asked as he handed me the keys.

"I don't know, Slim, but it's driving me nuts." He sank down wearily into Basil's easy chair. "I've been processin' so much juice lately, it's startin' to come outta my pores." Tiny bits of apple peel clung to his unruly hair and rumpled clothing. "It don't help none that my truck is actin' bewitched. It's the worst time of the year for it to go haywire on me."

"Bewitched?" I said. "Can you be a little more specific? It ran like a charm when it left here last week." I handed him a cup of coffee to steady his nerves.

He took a long, grateful swallow. "Okay, here's the scoop. I think I got an electrical problem, 'cause when I start the truck in the morning, it grunts like the starter is shot. So I installed a new starter *and* a battery – no luck. I still get the same thing."

I tossed that one around in my brain while trying to look wise and pensive. "You might still have an electrical problem – maybe a dirty connection somewhere. What else?"

Ned dragged a weary hand over his face and thought some more. "Oh yeah – sometimes it starts bucking at highway speed." He drained his coffee cup. "Like I said, I think the truck's possessed."

We wondered about it ourselves as Tooner did his darndest to figure out what was ailing the old Chevy. After two days, he was no further ahead, so I went over and leaned on the fender. It was time for an update.

"Well, the first thing I did was check out th' electrical stuff," muttered

Tooner, "but that ain't it. That starter ain't drawin' heavy at all, even though it sounds like it is." He rubbed his chin. "I'm convinced it's a timin' problem again, like before – but I've tried everythin' I can think of."

"I've noticed." I looked at all the old parts piled high on the workbench. So far Tooner had replaced the pick-up coil, the ignition module, the distributor cap and rotor, and even a whole set of ignition wires. Everything connected with the distributor in any way had found its way onto Ned's truck – there wasn't much left to try. "Have any of those parts made any improvement?"

Tooner sighed heavily. "Sort of. Every time I add somethin' new, it runs better – but only for a while. The problem always comes back."

There was basically only one piece of the ignition system left. "How about a new computer?" I was grasping at straws, but we were running out of time – Ned's customers were screaming for their juice.

Tooner jerked his thumb towards a silver box on the workbench about the size of a large book – it was a used computer from the wrecking yard. "Already tried that – didn't help."

By noon, we were still no closer to an answer. "Here you go," I said to Tooner as he came into the office for lunch. "Have yourself an apple. I just picked these off my tree at home."

"Nope," he said quickly, wrinkling up his nose. "Ya picked the wrong time t' offer me one o' them. Ned's truck reeks of juice an' I been smellin' it for two days straight."

Up to this point, Basil had been pretty quiet about Ned's truck. He'd been so busy with his own share of the workload that he hadn't had time to comment on Tooner's problem. But as I looked at him peacefully eating his lunch in his easy chair, I thought I could detect a faint gleam in his eyes.

"Basil, that smug look on your face tells me you have some unlikely solution up your sleeve. What is it – an ancient ritual to exorcise demons from mechanical devices, or do you just have gas?"

He laughed. "Neither, I'm afraid."

"Too bad," grunted Tooner. "I could use an idea. Startin' to feel like

I'm wastin' my time."

Basil pursed his lips and thought for a moment. "Allow me to give you some timely advice: '*We haven't failed. We now know a thousand things that won't work, so we're that much closer to finding what will.*'"

"Who said that?" I asked.

"Thomas Edison, one of the greatest inventors of all time."

Tooner scratched his right earlobe. "So yer saying I gotta replace about 994 more things on Ned's truck before I can figure out what's wrong?"

"No," Basil chuckled, "but I do have a suggestion: try a new distributor."

Tooner's eyes popped wide open. "What for?" he exclaimed. "With all the stuff I've put in the old one, it's practically new already!"

Basil shrugged his shoulders. "Allow me to quote another wise if somewhat less eloquent person that I know: '*How things are lookin' and how they is, well, that's two different things.*'" He smiled. "You said that back when you fixed the Astro van, remember? Well, I suggest you re-examine the distributor on Ned's truck."

And that was where the problem lay. The reluctor wheel, which is pressed onto the distributor shaft, was loose, and centrifugal force caused it to rotate at random, allowing the timing to constantly change. One new distributor later, and Ned was back hauling apples for his juicer.

As for Tooner, he's still not sure how Basil knew what to look for. He's adamant that Basil can hear voices. Personally, I don't know what good that does, because I hear them all the time – they just don't seem to say anything helpful.

In this case, at least, Basil's 'fix' came from a much more down-to-earth source…like the service bulletin I found on the counter in the staff washroom, the one that described recurring problems with distributors like Ned's. The bulletin just happened to come in the mail around the same time as we were having the trouble with Ned's truck.

It's like that old saying – timing is everything.

CHAPTER 20

⊗ THE CHICKEN SAFARI ⊗

So far, it had been a perfect day.

To start with, it was the second Saturday of the month, which meant it was Basil's turn to watch the shop. Secondly, nobody had invaded my personal space to make ridiculous demands on my time. In fact, to the best of my knowledge nothing had gone wrong today – at least nothing that involved me.

But my perfect day was about to end – it was time to get out of bed.

Wandering into the kitchen in my pajamas, I found Cookie gazing wistfully at the calendar on the wall. She sighed deeply. That sent me back to the bedroom on the run to find my day-timer. I scanned it quickly to see what I'd forgotten. Her birthday? No, still six months away. Christmas? Just been there, done that.

Using every scrap of tact and diplomacy in my possession, I boldly went where no man has gone before and returned unscathed. I call it The Great Unknown, that fathomless portion of the universe where you try to discover what your wife is thinking. "Um…something on your mind, dear?" I offered her a plate of crackers and cheese. It never hurts to come bearing gifts when you head into The Great Unknown.

Cookie sighed again. "I was just thinking about our wedding anniversary." I almost dropped the plate.

"Anniversary! How did I miss that?" I grabbed the calendar off the wall in disbelief, only to discover it was still February. "Hey, our anniversary isn't for another month. Don't scare me like that!"

She laughed. "Sorry, honey. I was just reminiscing about those special things you used to do back when we were first married."

Special things? I wasn't aware that Cookie had such fond memories of those early anniversaries, especially when you consider that back then I was barely housebroken.

Not that I hadn't tried. A book I picked up at a garage sale described the proper anniversary gift types for each of the different years. For example, the first year is traditionally paper. But the book failed to mention that it also has to be the right kind of paper. "Tickets to the Monster Truck Rally? I don't think so, Slim. I don't care if they do include a pit pass; we're going to the ballet instead!"

Even by Anniversary #5 – which is wood – I still had my head in the trees. "Honest, Cookie, this Arnie Palmer 3-wood will really improve your game. Of course, I'll just borrow it until you decide to take up golf..."

Suddenly it dawned on me what special things Cookie was referring to. "You must mean that special dinner I arranged for our fourth anniversary. You know, when we were in Africa..." It was all coming back to me now.

We'd been assigned to live and work in Lokichogio, a small Turkana settlement of scattered huts and stock pens in northwestern Kenya. Loosely translated, Lokichogio meant 'the place where the giraffe died while giving birth in a dry riverbed.' It was such a remote place that people would laugh when we told them we lived there; then they'd gaze upon us with pity when they realized we weren't joking.

When we first arrived in Kenya, Lokichogio (or 'Loki' as we called it) was nothing more to us than a name on a map – provided you even had the right map. Wendell was the veteran missionary assigned to meet Cookie and me in Nairobi, and his primary objective was to get us to Lokichogio before we had a chance to get back on the plane and go home.

It was early evening and we were sitting in the study of Mayfield, the colonial-styled Nairobi guesthouse owned and operated by our mission organization. It had once been the home of some British government official during the days when Kenya was still a colony. Filled with lovely antiques, Mayfield was surrounded by lush, green gardens, and safely hidden behind high stone walls and an iron gate.

Our comfortable wicker chairs encircled a glass and bamboo coffee table that held our ornate teacups. Row upon row of bookshelves lined the walls behind us, and a chandelier hung from the ceiling in the middle of the room.

In spite of our many questions throughout the day, Wendell had been strangely quiet about our destination. But it was time to get down to business. "No, really, Wendell – what's it like?" I leaned forward in my chair. "We've heard very little about this Northern Frontier District, but you've lived there for over 15 years. Surely you can tell us something, can't you?"

Wendell considered my question carefully before answering. "Well, you could say that Lokichogio is the commercial center for the area..."

"Sort of like Nairobi?" interrupted Cookie.

Wendell paused. "Well, I suppose so, but..."

"So that means there are stores there, right?" She began to get excited.

"Stores?" Wendell frowned. "Well, *duka* is the Swahili word for shop, so yes..."

"And I hear there's an airport?" I hinted.

"Airport?" Wendell began to perspire. "I'd call it more of an airstrip...'

"And didn't you say that our house will have running water?" I queried.

"Perhaps," he cautioned. "If the water pump is working..."

I looked at my wife. "Well, dear, it sounds like Lokichogio is just like here." I gazed around the room. "I think I'm going to like living in Africa."

Wendell slumped down in his chair. "I hope so," he mumbled.

The truth be told, Lokichogio was nothing like Nairobi. Nairobi had palm trees; it had electricity; it even had rain. Loki had rocks. Just getting there meant driving north for two days until the pavement ended – then you locked in the four-wheel drive hubs and went 150 miles further. We would later joke that Lokichogio wasn't the end of the world, but you could certainly see it from there.

The 'commercial center' consisted of three mud huts in a row on a pothole-filled dirt track we called Main Street. First there was the Mogila Hotel, a one-room *hoteli* (or eatery) known locally as the Cholera Café. Next to it was the *duka*, where you could find a few canned goods, maize meal, and an odd assortment of aluminum cooking pots.

On the end of the row was the butcher shop, a foul-smelling one-room shack where you could buy meat that came from a goat, a cow, or some other mammal. We quickly discovered that meat wasn't sold by the pound, but by the piece. To sell it by the pound they would have to remove all the flies before weighing it, and that just wasn't possible.

Our introduction to African life was swift and brutal. On the initial trip upcountry, we made the mistake of sampling some local cuisine during one of our overnight stays. As a result, our third wedding anniversary was spent recuperating from a two-week bout of amoebic dysentery. So when the blessed event came around again the following year (the anniversary, not the dysentery) I decided to surprise my wife with something special: I planned a night out on the town.

A hot mid-day wind assaulted me as I left our house and set out across the yard in the direction of the Mogila Hotel. Shielding my eyes from the stinging dust and fine sand, I clamped my sweat-stained safari hat down on my head and followed the trail that led to the main road. Five minutes later I pushed open the wooden door of the *hoteli* and stepped into the cool, darkened interior.

The eatery had a good track record, meaning we had dined here on previous occasions and survived. The dim, smoky atmosphere made it difficult to see what you were eating, but sometimes that can be a good thing.

A couple of rough wooden tables filled the center of the room, flanked by plank benches on either side. In the far corner, the glowing coals of the cooking fire illuminated the face of a thin, dark-skinned man sitting on a small stool, peacefully drinking his *chai*. This man was the proprietor of the Mogila Hotel, a Somali who had moved into the area years before to eke out a living in this tough, frontier town. He was my primary objective, the person with whom I would have to negotiate for services. I prepared myself for battle.

In Africa, bartering is an art form. I learned early on that if you want a good deal, it's important not to be mistaken for a tourist. The best way to do that is to speak their language, so it was time to show off my vocabulary skills acquired through long hours spent in language study. Those lessons had cost me a fortune, since my language helper obviously knew I wasn't a local.

Clearing my throat, I rattled off the phrase I'd been practicing for weeks. "*Asaki amuji akimuj k'ekaal nakang.*" I said it confidently, and followed it up with a broad smile to show how friendly I was.

The proprietor rolled his eyes to show how ignorant I was. "Excuse me, *bwana* Slim," he replied in perfect English, "but why do you wish to have dinner with your camel?"

I made a mental note to fire my language helper. "Uh, actually I want to plan a dinner party for my wife and some friends. Can you cook us a chicken for tomorrow night?"

Sensing an opportunity for financial gain, the proprietor's face lit up with a wide toothy grin. Nodding vigorously, he exclaimed, "*Ndiyo, bwana*, yes! Welcome! My name is Assad, and I can cook for you a nice chicken stew and *chapatis*. I'll even make some *mandazis* and give you a special discount."

It turns out the special discount I received pushed Assad's monthly earnings to record numbers, but it was the old rule of supply and demand: for what I was demanding, he was the only source of supply for 150 miles in any direction. I resigned myself to my fate and turned to go. "Sounds great," I said over my shoulder. "We'll arrive tomorrow at sundown." But Assad called me back.

"Bring me the chicken early in the morning," he instructed. "I will need time to get it ready."

I stared at him. "What? I have to bring my own chicken?"

The big smile reappeared. "I only have goat meat, *bwana*. If you want chicken, you must bring a chicken. Then I will cook it and charge you money." He shrugged his shoulders. "It is the African way."

So now I had to go chicken hunting in the middle of Africa.

Upon returning to my workshop, I enlisted the help of my assistant. "Francis, I need a chicken. Where can I buy one?"

He looked up from the tire tube he was patching. "I think John Etabau has a chicken. But why do you need it?"

I tried to explain our North American custom of doing things for our wives on our anniversaries, like providing a special dinner. But Francis was having a hard time with this cultural oddity. "*Bwana* Slim," he said slowly, as if patiently instructing a child, "our women carry water and have our children. They build our huts and work in our gardens. Then they cook meals for us." He shook his head. "We don't cook for them."

"Okay, but maybe you do other things." He looked unconvinced, so I pressed on. "Sometimes at night I hear the *edonga* – the drum songs – coming from your *manyattas*. That's when the men dance and sing special songs all night long, right?" Francis nodded slowly, curious to see where I was going with this.

"Well," I persisted. "What do you sing about?"

His eyes lit up. "Oh! We sing about our camels, our goats, our cows. We sing about hunting the lion…"

I interrupted him. "Yes, but don't you also sing love songs to your women?"

His mouth dropped open. This idea had never occurred to him before. Francis laughed so hard and long that it became obvious no further help would be forthcoming. "Fine," I muttered. "I'll find this chicken myself!"

Following the well-worn path across a field of dry grass, I soon came to the *manyattas*, a large cluster of huts that contained not only the homes of the villagers, but the pens for all their animals as well. Winding my way among the closely-packed dwellings, I found the home of John Etabau and slipped through the opening in his thorn fence. When he saw me, a broad smile creased his face as he stood and greeted me in typical Turkana fashion. Tall and thin, John towered almost a full head above me.

"*Ejoka*?" (Is it good?)

I shook his outstetched hand and replied, "*Ee, ejok noi…na…*" (Yes, it is very good…but…)

He looked at me with concern. "But what, *bwana* Slim? You have a problem?"

I looked around the dusty enclosure. A skinny dog gnawed on a bone under a thorn bush while a small naked child played with a stick in the dust. Suddenly my concerns seemed insignificant. "I need a chicken, John," I admitted with some embarrassment. "Can you sell me one?"

John looked relieved and sat down on his stool. "Yes, this I can do. But why do you need it?"

Visions of Francis rolling on the ground with mirth were still fresh in my mind. "I'll tell you later," I said. "Can I have the chicken first?"

He shrugged and nodded. Turning towards his hut, he called for one of his wives to go catch us a chicken. We talked for a few minutes about his goats and the lack of rain – all the usual topics. Before long, his wife returned and I found myself holding a burlap sack with a noisy bird protesting loudly from the inside. As I paid John his money, he repeated his question. "Now tell me: why do you need this chicken?"

"It's for my wife," I said cautiously. "She would like to eat something other than goat meat for a change."

John nodded knowingly. "You are a wise man to keep your woman happy."

I looked at him in surprise. "I am? I mean, you understand this?"

He put a hand on my shoulder. "*Bwana* Slim, I used to have only one wife. But she began to complain when my herd became larger. She told me I must take a second wife to do all the work." John sighed heavily and shook his head. "Now my women fight constantly and neither of them is happy." Clenching his massive fist, he looked me straight in the eye. "When you have two wives, you have to rule with an iron fist! Take my advice: keep your first wife happy and then you won't need a second wife."

John's simple outlook on marriage intrigued me, and I gave it some serious thought on the way home. The chicken was delivered safely, and when the appointed hour arrived the following evening, everything was ready.

Cookie and I arrived at the Mogila Hotel just before sunset, accompanied by Wendell and his wife Emily. We sat down at the freshly washed wooden table as Assad hurried over to fill our battered tin cups with steaming hot *chai*. The cloying aroma of incense dominated the room, and in honor of his *wazungu* guests, Assad had gone to the trouble of changing the tape in his cassette deck. Instead of the usual East Indian tunes, we were gently serenaded by Bing Crosby singing warbley Christmas carols for the rest of the evening.

"Slim," said Cookie, gazing into my eyes. "This is so sweet. How did you ever manage to arrange all this?" She kissed me on the cheek.

Wendell and Emily grinned their approval from across the table, and I was thankful that the dim lighting hid my embarrassment. "Aw, it was nothing, really," I said, gazing back at her. "I just wanted you to be happy so I didn't have to go out and find a second wife."

I was so engrossed with my reminiscing that it took me a minute to notice the strange look on Cookie's face. "Whatever are you going on about?" she asked finally. "That meal was a disaster. As I recall, the hotel owner kept the chicken for himself and fed us goat stew instead."

"Well, you can't be sure. I mean, it was dark in there and…"

"And didn't you make some stupid remark about finding a second wife? And right in front of our friends? I was never so humiliated in all my life."

"But you know I didn't mean…"

"Besides," she interrupted, "the special things I'm talking about are

163

the times when you'd take me to that French restaurant in Panicton for romantic candlelight dinners." She sighed dreamily. "We'd order Tornédos Henry VIII for the main course, followed by Coupe Denmark for dessert…"

Now it was my turn to sigh. Reaching for the phone book, I decided that even though our anniversary was still a month away, it was time to make those reservations before I did something stupid – like forget.

I knew this meal was going to cost me a whole lot more than that quasi-chicken dinner back in Lokichogio, but Cookie deserves the best.

Perhaps if I order in French I can get a break on the price.

CHAPTER 21

❧ WASHROOM VANDAL SCANDAL ❧

Those hoodlums have been at it again!" I thundered, gripping the newspaper so tightly it threatened to revert into pulp.

Cache looked up from her homework. "Mom! I think Dad's off his medication again."

Her sister Carrie wandered into the kitchen where I sat with my evening paper. "What's up, Pops?"

I stabbed the front page of the *Slumberland Rebuttal* with my finger. "A bunch of vandals have desecrated one of our most cherished Canadian institutions."

"You mean the court house?"

"No! Our public washrooms!" I showed them the photo. "See? They've spray-painted graffiti all over it for the third time this summer."

"Oh, is that all." Carrie began opening the cupboards at random. "Why don't you do something about it? Can I have a cookie?"

According to the paper, a citizens' patrol was being formed to help curtail vandalism in Slumberland. It sounded like a good idea, so the following morning I convinced Buck to go down with me to the local RCMP office and enlist as a team. Unfortunately, we failed the physical.

Once back in the truck, Buck pulled out his rejection form and handed it to me. "What's this supposed to mean?"

I read the hastily scribbled report: *Applicant unable to maintain a non-toxic environment during stake-out sessions with other volunteer staff.* "Beats me," I replied vaguely – I knew I would need Buck's help later, so I didn't want to upset him. "I think it has something to do with sitting in a car and too much gas. But it was hard to understand the interviewer – the clothespin on his nose made his voice sound funny."

"Too much gas?" Buck reached into a brown paper bag and pulled out a bean burrito, one of his favorite snacks. "If they're worried about paying for gas, then why don't they just say so? Heck, I ain't that cheap – I'd settle for only three quarters of a tank."

"Yeah, go figure," I said, hanging a new air freshener from the rear view mirror. Suddenly I smacked the steering wheel. "I know – we'll form our own patrol!"

Buck released a long, satisfying belch. "D'ya mean we'll get to spend hours together in your truck after all, keeping a lookout for the vandals?"

I rolled down my window for some air. "Nah, I've got a better idea. Listen up…"

When I got home, I filled Cookie in on my plan. "You must be proud of me for taking such proactive steps on behalf of the community's interests!"

She just stared at me. "Sweetheart," she said finally. "For the sake of the children, please don't use the family name." Defending the public good can be a lonely road at times, but a man's gotta do what a man's gotta do. Ignoring Cookie's cynicism, I went out to buy the necessary supplies to put our plan into effect.

A few nights later, Buck and I were in position and ready for action. My walkie-talkie crackled to life as Buck checked in. "Breaker, breaker, this is Two Sheets. Come in, Longjohn, come in."

"Roger, Buck…I mean, Two Sheets," I responded. "Longjohn in position in stall number two. All's quiet here."

Slumberland has two parks with washroom facilities – Beach Park down on the shores of Hollownoggin Lake, and Mumbleton Park, just a block off Main Street. Buck was bivouacked in the lakeside biffys while I staked out the uptown beat. We were fully equipped, each of us armed with a walkie-talkie, a flash camera, and two cans of KillsAll air freshener spray. If the vandals hit, at least we wouldn't be caught with our pants down.

The evening passed slowly, with only a few false alarms to break up the monotony. At one point, someone snuck in quietly and ran water in the sink. Being hidden in the toilet stall, I had no idea who it was – I just heard the water running for a long time and figured some vandalism was happening right under my nose. With a spray can in one hand and my camera in the other, I leapt out into the open.

"Holy Moses, Slim!" hollered Rep Tyler as he rubbed his eyes frantically. "Yer gonna blind someone with that stuff! What in the world are ya doin' in here, anyway?" Apparently Rep was just getting a drink for Suzie, his large iguana. Rep kept numerous exotic animals around his house and liked to take them for walks. But he had to do it at night to avoid scaring the townsfolk.

I apologized for my mistake and explained about my mission to catch the washroom vandals red-handed.

"Vandals, eh?" he said, mopping his face with a wet paper towel. "D'ya want me to leave Suzie here fer a while? She's good at scarin' off folks."

I looked at the three-foot reptile standing guard at Rep's feet. Suzie flicked her tongue out at me threateningly – she didn't like being attacked with KillsAll, either. "Thanks, but I've pretty much got things under control here. Now if you'll just chain her up and leave, I'll climb down from these rafters and get back to my post."

After that, things got even quieter. I was just nodding off when a vehicle pulled up outside, rap music blaring loudly from its open windows. The music stopped, a car door slammed, and heavy footsteps crunched on the gravel as someone approached the building.

I mashed the send button on my walkie-talkie. "Two Sheets, this is Longjohn – possible suspect approaching. Go to radio silence and stand by. Over." I turned off the radio and lifted my feet off the floor to avoid giving away my position. The adrenalin was flowing high as I fought to control my breathing.

The outside door creaked open, and in walked one of our local no-goods, Beefus Rube. Beefus sauntered over to the urinal and whistled a cheery tune as he relieved himself. After a minute, he called over his shoulder. "That you in there, Slim Shambles?"

Baffled, I lowered my feet and stepped out of the stall. "Yeah. How did you know?"

"Saw your truck parked outside, the one with 'Slim Shambles Auto Repair' written on the door." He went over to the sink to wash his hands, which struck me as odd – Beefus wasn't known for being overly hygienic. "Whatcha up to?" he asked innocently.

Not seeing any cans of spray paint sticking out of his pants pockets, I decided to let Beefus in on my plans. "There's been a rash of vandalism at our public washrooms," I growled. "We're gonna catch the scum red-handed."

"We?" asked Beefus, drying his hands. "Oh. So that explains the walkie-talkie."

I nodded. "My partner Buck is watching the latrines down by the beach."

His right eyebrow twitched slightly. "Buck Pincher, eh?"

I'd never seen Beefus looking so thoughtful. *Perhaps it's time to reevaluate my opinions of this boy,* I thought. *Youth are so easily misunderstood these days.*

His next move settled it. Beefus reached out and shook my hand. With a big smile he said, "Best of luck, Slim. A person just can't let this kind of behavior go on unchecked. I mean, where would our town be without concerned citizens like you and Buck?"

As Beefus left, I returned to my stall, deep in thought. *Nice kid. I'll have to tell Buck about this.* Turning the radio back on, I was accosted by a wave of static and uncouth words. "Longjohn! Come in, Longjohn! Mayday, Mayday..."

"What's wrong, Two Sheets? Report, report!"

"Where in thunder have you been?" Buck broke into a fit of coughing. "Listen up – watch out for that rascal Beefus Rube. His gang threw a bucket of rotten fish into my washroom and padlocked the door. I'm all out of KillsAll...almost out of oxygen. Send help – quick!"

Suddenly I heard the outside door creak open once more, followed by a sickening thud as something wet slapped the floor and slid across the room. The rattle of a lock and chain through the door handle was followed by raucous laughter. Car doors slammed as a vehicle started up and roared away, rap music once again defiling the night air. My stomach first sank to my shoes, but then rapidly climbed back up as the malodorous aroma of rotting fish filled the room.

The only thing that saved Buck and me was the fact that Rep Tyler was returning from his walk and noticed my frantic distress call. "Good thing there's a big gap at the bottom o' that door," he said, after the fire department arrived and cut off the padlock and chain. "Otherwise I wouldn'a seen ya sending out them S.O.S. signals with yer camera flash."

A few days later, Buck and I were comparing notes over pie and coffee at Rolph's Diner. Buck was still sore at me for turning off my radio in the heat of battle. "Next time we'll take along some breathing apparatus," I said.

Buck grunted. "There ain't gonna be no next time."

Rolph came out to refill our coffees.

"Hey, Rolph, when can we sit inside again?" I asked, setting my cup down on the outdoor picnic table the staff used for their smoke breaks.

"Not for another week," he mumbled through a surgical mask. "You two smell worse than Thursday's cabbage rolls."

Through the back door of the restaurant, I could see Beefus and his buddies at the counter inside, still laughing over their latest dirty deed. "Hey, you let them in, and they're the rotten jokers who did this to us."

Rolf shrugged. "They may be rotten jokers, but they don't smell like rotten fish. Now pay up – and with coins, if you don't mind. That way I can run them through the dishwasher before taking them to the bank."

Ain't that life, I thought glumly as I dug in my pocket for some change. *You try and do your civic duty, and all you get for it is a load of carp.*

CHAPTER 22

≫ BEAN COUNTING ≪

H mm…float drop, 13/64"…" The fluorescent light fixture over my workbench was so dirty I had to squint to read the tiny numbers on the specifications chart. The light hadn't been cleaned in years, and with the way things were going lately, it wasn't going to happen anytime soon. We had neither the time nor the manpower.

The rude jangling of the shop phone threatened to break my concentration. *I'll just ignore that while I make this critical adjustment to the float setting…*

"Hey, Slim!" bellowed Tooner from across the shop. "Yer wanted on the phone – Dickie Dixon needs t' know if his car's ready."

I put down my needle nose pliers in defeat. Tiny pieces of a Quadrajet 4-barrel carburetor were scattered across the workbench, threatening to go AWOL if I so much as looked the other way. Rebuilding these complicated devices was interesting work, provided you didn't get too many interruptions.

I picked up the extension phone. "Hi Dickie – yes, your car is ready; I just haven't had time to call you yet."

"Well, it's about time, Slim," growled the owner of Dixon's Dynamite Used Cars. "I've got a deal pending on that unit and I need it back here for a test drive! We'll be right up."

I hung up the phone and looked at the clock. It was past noon, and both Basil and Tooner were already in the office having their lunch. *Might as well join them*, I thought. *I'm not making any progress out here.*

Digging my lunch bag out of the bottom desk drawer, I peeked inside. "Peanut butter and jelly again?" I closed the bag in disgust. "I thought I had that yesterday."

Basil stirred his raspberry yogurt. "You did – that's still yesterday's lunch. As you may recall, you didn't get around to eating it."

I opened the other bottom drawer and found the proper bag. "Hey, is it just me or are we getting behind in our work?"

"The answer's *yes* and *yes*." Tooner was the tactful one of the crew. "Yes, we're behind, and yes, it's yer fault." He opened a bag of corn chips and shook some into the palm of his hand. "Y'know, ya keep yakkin' about hiring an apprentice. Is that gonna happen anytime soon, or do I have t' do it for ya?"

I squirmed in my chair. "Well, let's not be hasty here. Having an apprentice around certainly has its advantages, but we have to be careful with the quality of our workmanship, with our overhead costs, and with the…

"Right," said Tooner. "So when does he start?"

Basil rummaged around in his lunch kit and pulled out some green onions. "I can appreciate your hesitancy, Slim. But if you don't mind my saying so, I would suggest that the need to add another staff member has surpassed the need for caution." He pointed out to the crowded parking lot. "Right now, we have six oil changes left to do. That's fine, but they're keeping us from the three tune-ups, a brake job, and two exhaust system repairs that are still waiting to be done."

"Yeah," added Tooner. "An' that don't even include that carb overhaul ya been dawdlin' over."

"Dawdling? Hey, back the bus up here! I'll have you know that…"

Basil raised a hand. "The point here is that our expertise is not only being stretched thin, it's being improperly allocated." He reached for the saltshaker. "When it comes to oil changes vs. brake jobs, you don't need me to tell you which one pays a better return. Those profitable jobs are where Tooner and I should be directing our full attention."

Hiring an apprentice was the logical thing to do, but secretly I was avoiding the issue. It wasn't just the extra costs. Training a young person in the trade was serious business, and I wasn't sure if we had the time to do it properly. I needed to weigh the risks: what if the person I hired turned out to be a clueless airhead; what if he damaged a customer's vehicle; what if I had to fire him; what if he lit the shop on fire; what if…

"Slim." Basil snapped his fingers to bring me back to reality. He gave me his fatherly look, the one I hate. "Slim, it's time."

"Fine!" I hate giving in when I know the other guy is right. When he's wrong, at least I can blame him for it later. "Got any suggestions?"

Basil handed me a slip of paper with a name and phone number. "As a matter of fact, I do. This young man came by this morning while you were out driving a customer home. You should give him a call – he looked promising."

I took the paper and read the name: Beanie Madison. I didn't know him from a hole in the wall, but then, what did that matter? Previous experience had already shown me that if Basil had a good feeling about something, there was little left for me to do except go along with it.

After lunch, I dialed the number and got an answering machine. A low, menacing voice began to speak:

> "Hello.
> You've reached The Bean;
> You know who I mean;
> Don't make me scream;
> Just talk to the machine."

I waited for the beep, but the message wasn't finished yet.

> "I could be outside
> Pimping up my new ride.
> Don't let me find you at night
> Parked at a red traffic light,
> 'Cause when it turns green
> I'll blow the doors off your…"

I was about to hang up in disgust when someone suddenly picked up at the other end. "Hi, B-b-beanie Madison here!" squeaked a breathless voice. "S-sorry about that message! Th-that was my kid brother D-devo again. He's always doing things like that a-a-and…"

"Hi Beanie," I interrupted. "It's Slim from Slim Shambles Auto Repair calling. I understand you're looking for an apprenticeship position?"

I could almost feel the heat of Beanie's embarrassment radiating over the telephone line. No doubt Devo was in for it once Beanie got off the phone. "Y–yes! Th-thanks for c-calling a-a-and…"

I cringed as Beanie's stutter got progressively worse the more he talked. If it wasn't for Basil's vote of confidence, I would have cancelled the whole deal right there. "Look Beanie," I interrupted, putting him out of his communication misery, "why don't you drop around the shop tomorrow morning, and we'll have a talk."

As I hung up the phone, I began having second thoughts about hiring an apprentice. There was no getting around it – hiring a staff person is almost like adopting someone into the family. You want to get it right the first time.

The next morning, a small red pickup crept cautiously into the parking lot, looking for an unobtrusive place to park. The truck looked promising – a Chevy S10 with lowered suspension and low profile tires on chrome rims. The rumble from the dual exhaust pipes gave away the fact that this rig had a V6 under the hood, and most likely had a beefed-up computer chip added to the system.

But when a geeky-looking kid with black-rimmed glasses got out and looked around nervously, I found myself thinking, *This is Beanie*? I shook my head. Coupled with his stuttering problem, it was obvious that self-confidence was a major issue.

That thought was reinforced when he knocked on the office door instead of barging right in like all of my customers did. Even little Miss Daisy Middleworth, a diminutive spinster who could barely see over the steering wheel of her Jeep Cherokee, didn't bother to knock.

"Come in," I called from behind my desk. Beanie shuffled inside, ball cap in hand, and introduced himself. "H-h-hi, I'm B-beanie Ma-ma-madison and…"

I stood up quickly and shook his hand. "Yes, I recognize the voice. Have a seat, and let's chat."

Over the course of the next fifteen minutes, I discovered that Beanie loved working on cars, was a self-admitted computer geek, and wanted in the worst way to get started on an apprenticeship program. Surprisingly, the more excited he got about his subject, the less he stuttered.

I finally brought the interview to a close. "Well, Beanie, why don't we do a trial run? Bring your tools by on Monday and we'll see how you make out."

He jumped up so quickly his chair fell over backwards. That got him all flustered again, and the stutter returned. "S-s-sorry about th-th-that, I didn't mean t-t-t…"

I reached out and shook his hand again. "Fine, Beanie. See you on Monday morning." As I watched him drive away, the butterflies in my stomach began buzzing like Spitfires in a dogfight. *Am I doing the right thing?*

It didn't help my peace of mind when Dutchy stopped by later for his daily investigation of my affairs. "An apprentice? Ja, I mean, are you nuts?" He tossed his soggy cigarillo butt into the garbage can. "Nothing but trouble, those guys are." He stabbed my shoulder with a stubby finger. "You mark my words, Shambles – you'll have nothing but comebacks from now on. They leave the lug nuts loose, they strip bolts, and they overfill the engines with oil." He shook his head. "Ja, I thought you had more sense."

I found myself agreeing with Dutchy, and suddenly that bothered me. Maybe it was I who needed an attitude adjustment about the whole thing. *Time to think positive, Shambles – you can do this!*

But suddenly Tooner, who had been so big on hiring extra help, didn't seem so sure anymore. "Dunno, boss – th' kid kin hardly talk straight. Ya gotta wonder 'bout his brain power if'n he cain't even master his own mother tongue."

Basil and I looked at each other, both of us thinking the same thing: *Look who's talking.*

When our new employee arrived for his first day of work, we were ready for him. "Come on out back, Beanie. I've got a really big job for you."

We stepped outside the back door, and Beanie stopped and stared. "B-boy, you weren't k-kidding. That thing is huge!"

We were standing in front of a Kenworth highway tractor that belonged to Long Haul Herman, one of my regular customers. We didn't work on many big rigs – none of my staff were licensed heavy-duty mechanics – but Herman lived just down the road from our shop and it was handy for him to drop the truck off between road trips when it needed something simple like an oil change.

Basil nosed the truck inside the rear bay door, and showed Beanie how to raise the engine cowling, find all the grease fittings, and do the other routine items Herman had written down. I watched Beanie from across the shop as he hustled between the truck and the used oil tank with buckets full of dirty oil. "B-boy, these trucks sure hold a lot!" he exclaimed, putting the last drain pan away. "I had s-six different drain p-pans lined up just to c-catch it all."

"The new oil is in the compressor room," Basil told him. "Be sure to get the right kind."

Watching Beanie drag over the 5-gallon pails of new oil made me realize how pleasant it was going to be having an apprentice around. *Nice to have someone else to do the grunt work for a change*, I thought.

Balancing himself up on the frame rails, Beanie tipped the first large pail over the funnel and began pouring the oil into the engine. Tooner was walking by the Kenworth on his way to the parts room, when he suddenly let out a yell. "Quit pourin', Beanie!" he hollered. "Ya got oil runnin' everywhere!"

Basil and I rushed over to see what all the excitement was about. Underneath Herman's truck, a huge oil slick was spreading rapidly and heading for the floor drains. Beanie had forgotten to put the drain plug back in the oil pan, and every drop he poured in the top was going straight out the bottom.

"I've heard of engine flushes before," I said to Basil later, "but that was ridiculous."

He chuckled. "I've spilled a little oil on the ground myself in the past, but never a whole five gallons. It took an entire bag of absorbent to soak it up."

Over the next few weeks, Beanie had his share of mishaps. But we all had them when we were apprentices, so to some degree we had to cut him some slack.

Unfortunately, Beanie was having a hard time getting on Tooner's good side. In fact, it seemed like Tooner was going out of his way to play practical jokes on the kid, almost like he was testing him. Somehow, Beanie would have to prove he could hold his own.

It was a warm mid-summer day when someone entered the office and waited silently in front of my desk. A shiver went down my spine, which was unusual considering how hot the weather had been lately. I glanced up and discovered the reason for the climate change – Dethnor Pallor, the local mortician, was standing right in front of me, his tall lanky frame swaying slightly in the morning breeze.

"Good morning, Slim," he droned in his monotone voice. "I trust you and your staff are all…well?" The way he turned the last word into a question was unsettling.

I gulped involuntarily. "We're fine, Deth," I replied. "I mean, except for Basil, who's off today with the flu…"

"Oh?" Dethnor's eyebrows shot up in anticipation.

"…but he's expected to fully recover," I quickly added.

"Oh." The disappointment was obvious. "Well, I suppose it can't be helped." He cleared his throat. "I'm having trouble with our funeral coach. There is absolutely no heat coming out of the heater. Of course, it doesn't bother my clients…" He paused for a moment of respectful silence. "…but my assistant and I get a tad chilly on rainy days, and with fall coming, we'd like it fixed."

Together we went out to the gray '96 Cadillac hearse parked in front of the shop. "I'll drive you back to the funeral parlor," I offered. Then I noticed a bulky tarp in the back of the vehicle. "Say, you're not…er… loaded right now, are you?"

"No," replied Deth. "I'm *dead empty* today." He raised a white-gloved hand to his mouth to suppress a smile at his own pun. "The tarp is there because I picked up some lumber this morning. Business has been deathly slow lately, so we're doing a few renovations at the mortuary."

I breathed a sigh of relief and took Deth back to his chapel. He was right – no matter what I did with the heating controls, only cool air came from the vents. But I also noticed that the needle on the engine temperature gauge was buried six feet under – it refused to budge off the cold side during the entire drive.

"What's up?" asked Tooner, as I pulled the funeral coach into the shop.

"No interior heat," I said. "I suspect a thermostat problem."

He grunted and opened the hood. "We'll check it out. Beanie! Put some exhaust hoses on this puppy and idle 'er up for me."

The Bean did as he was asked, but when it came time to hold the gas pedal down on fast idle, he wasn't too eager to climb inside the hearse. I could tell he was nervous – the idle speed rose and fell as it kept pace with his shaky foot on the gas pedal. That's the funny thing about a hearse: it's just a fancy station wagon with gray paint, but there's something about it that gives guys the creeps.

Tooner checked the engine temperature with his infrared thermometer. "Yep, she's runnin' cool. Time for a new t-stat." Once it was removed, we could see that the thermostat wasn't closing all the way, an obvious source of the no-heat problem. With the new part installed, the temperature came right up to spec, and the interior was as warm and cheery as an Irish wake.

To make sure he had full circulation in the cooling system, Tooner closed the hood and got ready to go out on the road. He grinned. "I've been itchin' t' test-drive one o' these things for years – ya get t' stare death in the rearview mirror."

But he wasn't smiling when he returned a few minutes later. "Hey, what's with all the steam?" asked Beanie.

Tooner got out and opened the hood with a snarl. "Now the dang thing is overheatin'! As long as it just idles, it's fine. But the moment ya get up t' cruisin' speed…"

He checked for air locks, blown head gaskets, anything that would explain the problem. But he came up blank every time, and soon Tooner was more steamed than the Caddy.

Beanie had a suggestion. "It's j-just a thought, but m-maybe that thermostat you put in isn't w-working properly."

Tooner glared at him. "And yer the expert on coolin' systems now, are ya? That thermostat's workin' fine – at least at idle. Ya can see the temperature gauge fluctuatin' like normal when the t-stat opens and closes."

Beanie blushed, but held his ground. "Yes, but maybe something quits working when the engine is running faster. Maybe the increased water flow is messing it up or something."

"He's got a point, Tooner," I said in Beanie's defense. "The thermostat is the only thing you've changed since the car came in. It's certainly worth taking it out again for inspection."

Tooner grudgingly threw the drain bucket under the car and began to empty the coolant. I could tell he wasn't thrilled about following the advice of an apprentice – in his mind, Beanie's main function around the shop was to do the oil changes and stay out of his way. But at the moment Tooner didn't have any other options.

Sure enough, when he compared the new thermostat with the old one, Tooner discovered that the new one had been packaged wrong. The internal opening was far too small, and as a result, it was restricting the coolant flow at highway speed. After we located a proper thermostat and installed it, our heating problems were over.

As Tooner and I sat in the front seat testing the heater one last time, he finally began to relax. "Yep, I should get me one o' these," he said, patting the dashboard. "Luxurious, low mileage, only driven on weekends. Why, I'd be the envy of all…"

Just then, a cold, pale hand reached out from under the tarp behind us and grabbed Tooner by the back of neck. Screeching like a banshee, Tooner leapt out of the car like a bat out of…well, you know where.

Behind me, Beanie collapsed in a fit of laughter. "Whoa! Did you see the look on his face?" He pulled the white latex work glove from his hand. "I thought this would be a cool prank, but I never guessed it would work this good. I've never seen Tooner move so fast!"

I stared at Beanie in wonder. His stutter had completely disappeared. It was as if being right about the cooling problem had completely restored his confidence. I glanced across the shop at Tooner, who had just figured out who was behind the practical joke.

"Well, he might be fast, but I hope you're faster," I said. "Once Toon gets down off his tool box, you'll be running for your life."

And so began the love/hate relationship between our seasoned veteran and our young apprentice. Occasionally they would get on each other's nerves, or pull some stupid stunt as a joke, but that happens in every family. What mattered most was the satisfying feeling that this 'adoption' was going to work out just fine.

CHAPTER 23

❧ SNEAKY WATERS RUN DEEP ❧

I've always disliked sneakiness; it's so underhanded. Give me straight up, in your face, brutal truth every time – at least then a guy knows what he's dealing with. But things that sneak up on you when you're not looking? Well, they're just…sneaky.

Spousal birthdays are in this category, right up there with wedding anniversaries, the last day of vacation, and most of all, the credit card bill. Sneaky, sneaky, sneaky. I detest it.

One particularly annoying form of sneakiness is the kind that accompanies household chores. When we were newlyweds, I told Cookie that I would be the *Director of Outside Jobs*, meaning that I would handle all building and yard maintenance if she would take care of the housework. So what's so sneaky about that? Just the fact that she agreed to it without any argument, for starters. What I took to be a good idea on my part really meant that I didn't know what I was getting myself into. Cookie did, but she chose not to tell me. I call that sneaky.

What I failed to take into account was Cookie's exceptional delegation skills. Over the years she has trained me to unload the dishwasher, brush the tangles from Buddy's fur, and reheat my supper in the microwave while she watches the figure skating championships on TV. I also have to put the garbage out on Wednesdays.

At first, I wasn't sure that these jobs belonged in my area of responsibility. I protested about the garbage, but she convinced me it was an outside job, since that's where the curb is. The dog issue was easier to swallow – it's common knowledge that Buddy spends most of his time outside digging up my flowerbeds. But when it came to the figure skating, I felt her explanation was riding on thin ice: "But everybody knows you can't ice skate in the house, dear." And as far as unloading the dishwasher is concerned, well, there *is* no rationale – I just have to do it and that's that.

Now at the shop, I'm a great delegator. I can keep three techs working seamlessly, arrange for parts to be delivered right on time, and keep the majority of my customers happy – provided Buck Pincher doesn't show up.

But around the home, my delegation skills are abysmal. I can't even teach my dog where to do his business, much less get him to handle a shovel or a lawnmower. Mostly Buddy just lays around in the shade giving bad advice.

The latest sneakiness to invade my private world came disguised as *The Birthday Present*. Camouflaged with colorful paper and lavish ribbons, it should have been a new power tool or a piece of fishing gear – even a set of keys for a new 4x4 would have been nice. Instead, it was a water pump for a garden pond. We're talking sneakiness in its lowest form.

"What am I supposed to do with this?" I complained. "We don't even *have* a pond."

Cookie patted my hand. "As Director of Outside Jobs, I'm sure you'll figure it out. And take Buddy with you; he'll help you dig."

By the time I got out to the minivan, Buddy was already inside, sitting in the driver's seat. He looked at me with his big brown eyes. *Can I drive?*

"In your dreams," I muttered. "Now shove over." I was fairly certain he had something to do with the pond idea, a suspicion that later proved to be true. Once we got to the building supply center, Buddy led me straight to the aisle where they kept the plastic pool liners. I could tell he'd been there before.

"How much are your plastic pre-formed garden pools?" I asked.

The gum-chewing sales clerk rolled her eyes. "If you have to ask, you can't afford it," she replied. "Sheesh, haven't you ever done landscaping before?"

A knot of forlorn-looking Directors of Outside Jobs was clustered around the stack of plastic pools. "Let me guess," I said to the nearest one. "You got a pump for your birthday?"

He nodded glumly. "Have you seen the price of these pools?" he asked. "It'll suck up all my golfing money."

The fellow in front of us turned around. "Forget your golf game, mac. Once you start, these projects never end." He held up a box. "I'm on my third birthday pump – this year they want multi-level cataracts complete with thundering mist and screeching tropical birds."

I became faint when they showed me the total cost of my pond project, especially once we added in the filters, hose, lighting, and pink flamingoes. But the sales clerk was very accommodating. Grabbing a wheelchair from behind the counter, she took time to personally wheel me into the office of their in-store financial agent. After arranging for a second mortgage, I managed to stuff everything into the back of the minivan and drive home.

True to Cookie's word, Buddy does enjoy digging. He chose a lovely spot just off to the left of my front steps and dug furiously – for about two minutes. Then he stopped and looked at me with his tongue hanging out. *That's enough; you can take it from here.* He padded over to my burning bush. *I'll just lay under this* euonymus alatus *and have a little snooze.*

I hate it when Buddy speaks Latin – the arrogant sneak only does it to show off.

Mumbling terms of endearment just loud enough for my lazy dog to hear, I stepped into the hole and swung my pick. It took about five minutes for the feeling to return to my wrists, but when it did I was able to scrape aside the thin layer of dirt covering the large rock pit I was standing on. Sneaky rocks – I hate them too.

But I would need some big rocks for the waterfall anyway, so I decided to be grateful that I didn't have to go far to find them. Two hours of prying and digging finally left me with a hole large enough to bury the expensive plastic pool.

Buddy watched this whole process from under the bush. The sneaky fiend chose to wait until I had the pool in place and the waterfall built before he dragged over the thick plastic liner that was supposed to go *under* the pool. He sat down and cocked his head to one side. *You'll need this to protect the bottom of the pool.*

"Thanks," I snarled. "Is there anything else you'd care to tell me?" He yawned and went back to his bush. I knew that dog had something else up his sleeve, but he wasn't about to tell me what it was.

"Honey, that's a great looking waterfall!" exclaimed Cookie a couple of hours later.

"It better be," I puffed, heaving the last rock into place. "It's the sixth time I've rebuilt it."

She frowned. "How come?"

"Watch," I said, plugging in the pump. A steady stream of water gurgled out of the small black hose at the top of the rock pile, and then promptly disappeared among all the lower rocks. "See? I can't get a single drop of water to fall into the pool."

As Buddy rolled on his back, snickering shamelessly, it finally dawned on me that you can't build a waterfall out of round rocks – you need flat ones if you want the water to drop down off the edge. Obviously, my dog had watered enough rocks in his day to have figured this out. "Thanks a lot, pal. You could have told me sooner."

Refusing to pay big money for rocks from the gardening store, I instead wasted an entire day and a whole tank of gas cruising country roads until I found what I wanted – a nice pile of thick, sharp-edged shale.

"Hey, give me a hand with these." I staggered under the weight of the stones. "They're heavy!"

Buddy didn't answer. He was too busy sniffing at the wooden sign posted off to one side. He looked at me sternly. *It says* Slumberland Ornamental Community Gardens. *Should you really be taking those*?

I ignored him – if he thinks I'm going to believe that he can actually read, he'd better think again. We were soon headed home with the minivan listing badly to port, and for the seventh time the waterfall was rebuilt. The pond was finally functional.

Of course, it didn't end there. I installed a park bench, planted some groundcover, and set up a monthly schedule to clean the muck out of the filter. But in the end it was worth it just to listen to the sound of trickling water on a warm summer night.

On one such evening my wife and I were sitting on our bench, my work finished and my blisters healed. Life was good. Then Cookie spoke up. "Wouldn't it be nice to have a multi-level fountain in the *back* yard?" she hinted.

"Sure it would." I chuckled to myself. I knew I was safe – my next birthday was almost a year away.

"Well," she cooed sweetly, "we have an anniversary coming up, so I bought you a little present." She whistled sharply. "Here, Buddy!"

My traitorous sidekick trotted up to our bench, wagging his tail shamelessly. The small envelope tied to his collar contained a gift certificate for yet another water pump. He raised his ears and blinked at me innocently. *Hey, big guy, does this mean we get to go for another ride in the van?*

I groaned in defeat. *Doggone sneaky mutts – I can't stand them.*

CHAPTER 24

WARNING: SEVERE SERVICE CONDITIONS

Most business managers believe in the concept of *Service with a Smile,* and make a point of drumming it into the mindset of their noble and talented employees. But a few select Slumberland businesses operate on a different premise: it's called *Service with a Smirk.*

"Hey Ray, have you got any of those French Vanilla coffee whiteners around?" I poked through the creamer bin on Ray's coffee counter with a stir stick, but all I could find was plain milk, and 2% at that.

The owner of Got Gas & Groceries didn't even look up from his newspaper. "Nope. Don't see the need to keep all that fancy stuff around; people just use it up."

Slumberland has a number of service stations scattered around town, but I'd been using Ray's for some time because it was handy to my shop. But my increasing love for flavored coffee was starting to influence my decision-making process.

"You know," I hinted subtly, "I like to buy a coffee whenever I fill up my truck with fuel, and I *really* like French Vanilla flavoring."

Ray turned the page of his paper. "Yeah," he said. "I get lots of folks askin' for that one – seems to be a favorite." He bit off a piece of jerky and chewed contentedly while the rest of the world passed him by.

I rolled my eyes and made one final attempt. "Did you know that the other gas stations offer three different kinds of creamers? In fact, getting French Vanilla flavoring in my coffee could *greatly influence* where I buy my gas from now on…" I left the end of my sentence dangling right out in the open, hoping Ray would take a swing at it, or at least acknowledge its presence.

"That's a buck fifty for the coffee, Slim. And which pump are ya at?"

And it isn't just the sellers of high octane fuel: the lack of customer service has hit the world of high finance as well.

Armed with her first paycheck from a part-time job, my wife went into Slumberland Savings and Loan to open up a second savings account. She wanted to put the money aside for our next vacation.

The teller gave her a questioning look. "Open a new account? You mean, right now?" She frowned at Cookie's audacity. "You do realize that you need an appointment, don't you?"

Cookie looked around. She was the only other person in the bank. "All I want is a simple savings account," she explained. "Why do I need an appointment?"

"Why?" The woman rolled her eyes, aghast at my wife's naïveté. "Because our financial planner needs time to discuss your options and assess your long-term goals." She smiled condescendingly. "We don't want to be reckless with our hard-earned money, now do we?"

Cookie sighed. "And how long will that take?"

"About 30 minutes," came the smirky reply, "and you'll need to bring your bank statements from the past three months." The teller opened up an appointment book. "Now, when would you like to come in?"

Cookie's blue eyes began to smolder. If I'd been there, I would have warned the woman it was time to start running, or at least backpedal in a big hurry.

"I'm here now," Cookie growled through clenched teeth. "Can't I just sign some forms or something?"

But the teller wasn't backing down. She glared over the top of her eyeglasses. "That's not how it's done these days, ma'am." She paused and took a deep cleansing breath. "However, we sometimes make an exception, *provided* we feel confident that our client possesses a good understanding of certain financial matters." She cleared her throat. "Now, can you tell me exactly *why* you want a savings account?"

Cookie stared at her in disbelief. "To put my savings in!" she cried.

"Hah! It's just as I thought!" The woman slammed her appointment book closed triumphantly. "You obviously don't have a clear grasp on your financial goals." She stuck her nose in the air. "Now please step aside – I have another customer."

When I came home for lunch, Cookie was on the couch with an ice pack on her head. "What happened to you?" I asked.

"Bank teller intimidation," she moaned. "It was awful."

"Hmm," I replied absently. Pulling a bundle of letters out of my coat pocket, I went through the day's mail. "Hey, honey, speaking of banks, there's a letter here from the Savings and Loan." I ripped open the envelope and read the note inside. "Listen to this – it says we have a dormant savings account that we haven't used in a while. Heh, heh, I'd forgotten about that one." I shook my head as I went to tear up the letter. "I'll just tell them to cancel the account and..."

A few seconds later, I was lying on the floor, staring up at the ceiling as I pondered the huge impact financial institutions have upon our daily lives. At the mere mention of the existing bank account, Cookie underwent a complete transformation. She lept off the couch, practically dislocating my shoulder as she tore the letter from my hands and lit out for town in the minivan, leaving a cloud of smoke and the smell of burning rubber hanging in the air.

Banks can certainly be a pain, I thought, rubbing my shoulder as I searched for Cookie's ice pack. *I wonder if this means I'll have to make my own lunch now?*

To be fair, lackluster service is not confined to Slumberland; Panicton has its share of woes as well. We discovered this when our children were still quite small.

I was calmly reading the newspaper in my living room, enjoying a few moments of peace, when a faint noise caught my attention. Removing my earplugs, I heard my wife conversing with our two-year-old in the kitchen.

"ARRRRRRGH!!"

With a sigh, I put down the paper and went to investigate. Cookie was standing in front of Tipper's high chair with a stream of *Spaghetti-O's* dripping from her hair. Tipper was wearing his now-empty bowl upside down on his head while he splashed merrily in the mess on his tray. As far as I could tell, not one O had made it into his mouth.

"So…everything all right in here?" I asked brightly.

Cookie glared at me. "I've had it! I'm not cooking another thing today. Pack up the kids, 'cause we're going out for dinner."

My mouth dropped open. "G-going out? Don't you remember what happened the last time we took Tipper to a restaurant? They told us not to come back until he was older – that they weren't set up to handle young children."

"Yeah, well, McDonnell's isn't the only place in town." Cookie wiped her face with a towel. "Besides, I've got a plan."

Plan or not, I was more than a little apprehensive about unleashing our toddler on a bunch of unsuspecting diners. It reminded me of a sign I saw when we were on vacation the summer before. It read: *CAFE DURANGO – Casual fine family dining and spirits in a south-western atmosphere.*

As any parent of young children can tell you, using the words *casual* and *fine* in the same sentence as *family dining* is the mother of all oxymorons, not to mention being downright false advertising. *Spirits* might be acceptable, since taking a pre-schooler anywhere at all is definitely a spirited event. But for the average family, fine dining just doesn't happen between the birth of their first child and the graduation of the last.

So as soon as my wife was able to clean herself up, we all packed into the van and headed for Panicton. Once we were on the highway, Cookie put her plan into action. She took my cell phone and dialed the number for Piece O' Pizza Parlour. "Kids, we're having pizza at Triple P tonight."

Cache and Carrie bounced up and down with excitement. "Hooray!"

cried Cache. "We haven't been to a restaurant since forever."

"Yeah," echoed Carrie. "Not since Tipper set fire to that menu."

"That was the restaurant's fault," I said in defence of my son. "Anybody who leaves lighted candles at the same table as a toddler has brain damage." Tip screeched in agreement – he could tell that exciting events were in store for the evening.

"Hello?" said Cookie into the phone. "Yes, we're coming to town for dinner, a family of five with young children, and I'd like to order two pizzas." She listened for a moment. "No, this is not take-out. We want to eat in, and I'd like to have supper ready when we arrive." She glanced over her shoulder at Tipper, who was taking aim at his sister with his juice bottle. "Why? Well, let's just say my son can be a little impatient."

The waiter on the other end of the line was unsure. "I'm sorry, ma'am. We need a table number for our computer before we can place an order, and until you get here, we won't know which table you'll be seated at."

"Then assign us a table number now," suggested Cookie. "We'll be there in less than ten minutes."

Apparently that wasn't standard procedure, so there was a pause while the waiter called for the assistant manager. Cookie winked at me. "Keep driving – I'm sure the assistant manager will understand."

"Dad," called Cache from the back seat. "Are we there yet? Tipper's getting restless and I'm running out of jelly beans."

The assistant manager came on the line and listened while Cookie once again explained what we wanted. "Believe me," she warned. "You don't want to listen to my son's screaming while he waits for his food."

"I'm sorry," said the assistant manager. "This really is against procedure. I'll have to let the manager decide." He called for the manager, who listened as Cookie went through her spiel for the third time.

"Very sorry, ma'am," he said finally, "but we're not set up for such a request. You'll just have to order when you get here. Goodbye."

My wife turned to me in amazement. "He hung up on me. Now what?"

By this time Tipper was beating the back of my headrest with his teddy bear, so I grabbed the cell phone. "Here, let me try." Punching redial, I got Triple P back on the line. "Hi, my name is Slim Shambles, and I'd like to order two medium pizzas to go." I gave them the necessary particulars, such as toppings, home address, social insurance number, and my mother's maiden name. "Pick them up in 15 minutes? Great! I'll be there."

Since we were almost to the restaurant by then, we killed time by driving up and down back alleys. Dodging dumpsters and bouncing through potholes proved to be the perfect entertainment for Tipper, who squealed with delight at every sudden swerve or jarring bump. When the allotted time had passed, we pulled into the parking lot of Piece O' Pizza Parlour, where the sign read *At Triple P, we aim to please*! We got out of the minivan and trooped into the restaurant, hungry as bears.

"A table for five?" asked the friendly waitress. She looked at Tipper. "Will you need a high chair as well?"

"Yes," I said. "One with extra restraints…and no candles, please."

Once we were seated, she began to hand out menus. I glanced around and lowered my voice. "Uh, we don't really need menus. There should be a take-out order ready for the Shambles family." I slid a five-dollar bill in her direction. "Could you just bring it to our table?"

The waitress winked and slid the five back. "You bet." She leaned over and whispered, "Got two pre-schoolers of my own."

The food arrived, hot and tasty, and it was the best take-out pizza we'd ever eaten. Tipper was so engrossed in painting his tray with tomato sauce that he didn't utter a single screech over 80 decibels. It was relaxing to be out in public as a family again.

The manager walked by once or twice with a frown on his face, trying to figure out how our food had arrived so quickly. I nodded and smiled pleasantly. "Great staff you have here. Your cooks are just amazing!"

Cookie leaned over to kiss my cheek. "Thanks, sweetie; I really needed this break. And you even ordered all my favourite toppings."

I chuckled. "The topping *I* like best is the one you can't see."

She looked surprised. "Oh? What's that?"

"The tastiest part of all," I said. "The topping called *Gotcha*."

Of course, as a business person myself, I take customer service very seriously, and I remind my staff about it on a regular basis.

"Okay, guys, rule number four: *Treat a customer's questions with respect, and offer polite, informative answers to the best of your ability.*"

Beanie scribbled copious notes in the margin of his employee handbook. "Wow, there are a lot of rules in here. How am I ever going to remember them all?"

Basil licked some icing sugar off his fingers and reached for his coffee mug. "Relax, Beanie. Customer service is more of an art form than a science. It will become natural as you engage in it more and more."

"Exactly," I agreed, taking a peek at the donut box. If I didn't act fast they'd all be gone. "Even if you work on just one rule per week, you'll have this down in no time..." Our training session was suddenly interrupted by a loud backfire as Buck Pincher's battered car pulled into the parking lot. Even from where we were sitting, we could see his muffler dragging on the ground.

Tooner gave a grunt. "Told ol' Pincher last week that he needed a new exhaust system. I'll bet he just wants us t' patch it up again."

I sighed. "Buck should fix that exhaust properly, but you know how cheap he is."

Tooner got up and headed for the door. "Let me handle 'im. Be right back."

The rest of us watched with interest as Tooner and Buck debated the merits of spending money on a muffler. Beanie snuck over and opened the door a crack so we could hear better.

"...an' I'm tellin' ya, Buck, we're puttin' on a new system from front t' back. Now I don't wanna hear no more whinin' outta ya – understand?"

Buck was sweating profusely, his right hand clutching his wallet pocket as if he was afraid his money would jump out and spend itself. "But...but...I mean, couldn't we..."

"NO!" roared Tooner. "Now, gimme yer credit card and skedaddle. We'll call ya when it's done."

Beanie's mouth dropped open as he watched Buck scurry off down the street on foot, leaving his car and his charge card behind. Beanie looked at me in confusion. "But I thought we were supposed to treat a customer's questions with respect, and offer polite, informative answers."

I looked at Basil. "I keep forgetting that Beanie is still new around here – we forgot to tell him about rule number five."

Beanie looked at the handbook he was holding. "Number five?"

"Yes." I opened my copy and read it to him. "Rule number five: *When Buck Pincher arrives, forget about rule number four and send out Tooner.*"

I closed the book. "The secret of success, Beanie, is knowing your customers."

"Yep," agreed Tooner as he came back into the office. "An' then adjust yer services accordingly."

Poor Beanie was bewildered. "But I thought rule number 1 was *Service with a Smile*, and yet Tooner here just gave Mr. Pincher a royal chewing out."

"You bet I did," snickered Tooner. "An' if you'll notice, I'm grinnin' from ear to ear!"

CHAPTER 25

✺ TOTALLY TEA ✺

"Cookie, will you please do something about these children? You'd think they have no table manners at all!"

My wife looked up from the morning paper and glanced around the breakfast table. "What seems to be the problem?"

I was astounded. "Can't you see it? Here we are, trying to have a quiet family meal and they're jumping all over the place." Cache and Carrie were bouncing up and down on their chairs like jumping jacks, while Tipper was being especially irritating, imitating a jackhammer as he vibrated from side to side on his booster seat. How they could eat their cold cereal without making a huge mess was beyond me.

Cookie gazed calmly back at me. "Slim, the kids are fine – it's your eyeballs that are jumping up and down. I think it's time to cut back on your coffee intake."

"Yeah, Pops," piped up Carrie. "That's your third cup and you haven't even finished your first piece of toast."

"How can he finish it when he can't even hold it?" said Cache. "That's the fourth time he's dropped it already."

Sometimes my children's powers of observation are downright irritating. "But I can't quit," I protested. "I'm a mechanic and mechanics drink coffee. It's…it's part of the code." Just the thought of forgoing my favorite beverage was so unsettling that I reached for the pot one more time.

Cookie laid her hand on my twitching arm. "Why don't you try something with a little less caffeine, like tea? You'd probably feel better." She glanced at the kids. "I know we would."

Tea. Tea? So I'm supposed to drink tea now, like the Queen? I shuddered to think what the crew back at the shop would say when

I hauled out my little bags of Earl Grey at coffee time. Besides, I've been the tea route before and, well…let's just say I have some rather unpleasant memories in that department. Even thinking about it now leaves a peculiar taste in my mouth…

East Africa is where I really learned that tea (or *chai*, as it's commonly known) is simply a medium to which you attach local culture. Anything goes and anything does. Although the tea leaves all come from the same plantations near Lake Victoria, the individual tribes insist on adding their own local flavor.

When my wife and I began our two-year stint working overseas – me as a mechanic and Cookie as a bookkeeper – we were met at the Nairobi airport by a staff person who whisked us and all our worldly goods through customs without having to pay a single bribe. We were very impressed.

After careening through traffic in a mini-van crammed full of our gear, she deposited us on the doorstep of Mayfield, the mission guesthouse situated on the outskirts of Nairobi. It was our opportunity to become acclimatized to the local culture, buy some necessary supplies, and most importantly, say our fond goodbyes to indoor plumbing before heading upcountry to our assignment.

As I sat down for breakfast the next morning, a server came by with a large teapot in each hand. "*Nataka chai?*" he asked politely (would you like some tea?).

"*Ndiyo,*" I replied affirmatively, exhausting half my Swahili vocabulary in one fell swoop. I leaned over to my new friend Wendell, who had come to escort us to our post upcountry. "What's with the dual teapots?" I whispered.

"One's tea, the other's hot water." He squeezed some lime juice onto his papaya. "They make the tea so strong here you could clean your carburetor with it." He glanced at the waiter and said, "*Nusu nusu.*" Turning back to me, he explained. "That means half and half. Dilute the tea with hot water and it becomes palatable."

"*Nusu nusu.*" I committed the phrase to memory, figuring it might come in handy in the months ahead.

We soon headed upcountry to begin our work and it wasn't long before I was able to observe one of the local villagers making tea.

"Francis," I said to my shop assistant, "don't you use a teapot?"

He carefully placed a small aluminum cooking pot over the fire, using pieces of cardboard as potholders. "No, *bwana* Slim, we make *chai* like this." He added a couple spoonfuls of raw tea leaves to the water, brought it to a boil, and then poured the tea through a strainer into plastic cups, finally adding goats milk and lots of sugar. In his own cup, he sprinkled a few extra tea leaves on top as a garnish.

"Of course," he admitted, "this milk is not the way we really like it." I wasn't so keen on goats milk either, especially when it was warm and curdled.

"What's wrong with it?" I asked, looking inside my cup suspiciously.

Francis waved a hand in disgust. "It's too weak. We like to give it strength. We do that by bleeding our animals and mixing the blood with the milk."

"Ah, the old *nusu nusu* routine." I stole a glance at the bottle of milk I'd bought from a local woman that morning, checking it for any trace of color. There was a smattering of floating debris, but thankfully no blood. "Francis, I stopped in Kakuma last month and had *chai* at Mahmud's *duka*. It had a burnt taste. Why was that?"

He nodded knowingly. "Because we don't have refrigerators like you *wazungu*, we must ferment our milk to keep it from going bad. Our tribe burns charcoal inside the milk gourds first, and that makes the milk last longer."

Nusu nusu and smoky gourds – I was quite proud of my growing knowledge about African tea. But there was more to learn.

A month later I discovered the unofficial government version of *chai*. Driving through the Marich Pass, my progress was halted by a large steel spike belt spread across the road. It was my first encounter with a police checkpoint.

A scary looking man wearing a uniform and carrying a rifle approached my driver's window. Dark sunglasses hid his eyes. "Where are you going, *bwana*?" he asked, the tip of his rifle carelessly pointing just past the end of my nose.

I gulped. "T-to Nairobi for supplies." I glanced over at Wendell, who was taking a nap in the passenger seat. Obviously, he'd been through this before and didn't consider it worth waking up for.

The police officer grunted and made a show of checking out my Land Rover from front to back. Then he returned to my open window. Resting his gun over one shoulder he held out his other palm and asked nonchalantly, "*Wapi chai, bwana*?"

Wapi chai? He was asking me for tea! When a man with a gun asks for tea, there's only one thing you can do – so I did it.

Wendell was still shaking his head in disbelief 20 minutes later as we continued on down the road. "I can't believe what just happened," he said in admiration. "When the police say *wapi chai*, they're not asking for tea – they're really asking for a bribe. Those check points can sometimes cost us 100 shillings."

My ears burned at my apparent failure to understand the local culture. "I dunno – he seemed to appreciate what I offered him."

Wendell rubbed the back of his neck. "No doubt that's the first time anybody has pulled out their camping supplies and made him a real cup of tea, right on the side of the road." He shook his head in disbelief. "Well done, Slim!"

But my most memorable brew came a few months later from a small *hoteli* just south of Nairobi. I was traveling with a young Irish lad named Fergus. We were driving around the city buying supplies when we noticed that our Land Cruiser pickup was hitting the bumps a little harder than usual. "Hate to say it, mate," declared Fergus, "but I think we've got a wee bit of a suspension problem."

We pulled over to the curb and got out for a look. I wasn't pleased with what we found. All four leaf springs had flattened out, leaving the axles riding hard up against the rubber suspension snubbers. It was obvious we couldn't drive much farther like this, especially with the load of supplies we needed to buy. If we did, we'd end up with a broken frame. "Rats," I said. "And I just had those springs replaced two months ago. You'd think they'd last longer that this!"

Fergus surveyed the sagging pickup thoughtfully. "Well, they did a bodge job of it, that's for sure. Let's go out to the factory where they make the springs – maybe they'll replace 'em under warranty."

Fortunately, the factory was easy to find. It was on the main road, just a few miles south of Nairobi, and we managed to make the trip without causing any further damage to our vehicle. After a brief but animated discussion with the plant supervisor, our Land Cruiser was grudgingly pulled into their shop where a low-level helper was assigned the job of replacing the springs. The only problem was, we had a lot to do on this trip and the helper was moving slower than a sleepy lion after a good feeding.

"At this rate," I muttered, "we'll be here all afternoon. Maybe I should go find his boss and see if we can hurry things up."

"It'll be a blooming waste of your time, Slim," replied Fergus, running his fingers through his red curly hair. "I don't think your man knows the meaning of haste. This is Africa: you might as well be whistling jigs to a milestone." He put his hat back on his head and shaded his eyes. "Tell you what – I remember passing a small *duka* just down the road. I'm feeling a mite peckish, so why don't we find us a wee cuppa tea while we're waiting?"

So off we went, trudging along on foot under the hot mid-day sun. Arriving at the local hangout, we stepped inside the dingy mud-walled building that served as both a café and dry goods shop. I was grateful to get out of the heat. A few suspicious-looking characters lounged in the dark corners, smoking cigarettes and watching us closely as we sat down at a rickety wooden table. I got the distinct impression that not too many *wazungu* darkened the door of this establishment on a regular basis.

A tall dark-skinned man brought over a pot of *chai* and a couple of cups, and roughly set them down on the table. He didn't look particularly happy to see us. From his scars and features, I figured him to be of the Maasai tribe. I filled both of the chipped porcelain cups with *chai* and pushed one over to my companion before taking a sip from my own. "Fergus," I said, flicking away some flies. "Does this tea taste strange to you?"

He shrugged philosophically. "Aye, but there's nothing so bad that it couldn't be worse. If the locals can drink it, then so can I."

The thought crossed my mind of asking the waiter for *nusu nusu*, but from the look of our surroundings, I wasn't sure what the other half would be. We had a lot of time to kill, so when the waiter came back we ordered *mandazis* and went for seconds on the *chai*. *Hmm*, I thought, *the taste of this chai isn't so bad after all. A guy could get used to it.*

However, when we headed back into the city later with our repaired vehicle, I found myself wishing for a piece of gum or a mint – anything to rid my mouth of the peculiar aftertaste.

We pulled into the Mayfield, parked out back, and then went inside to wash up for dinner. Having some free time before dinner, I wandered out on the veranda to take in the beautiful gardens surrounding the grand old building. It was like a small English oasis in this distant land I now called home. That's were I found Donald, our gracious guesthouse host, having a cup of tea before dinner. "Sit down, old boy," effused the elderly Brit. "Let's have a chin wag, shall we? Tell me how your day's been going."

"It's been fine, except for a little vehicle trouble." I explained about the leaf springs.

Donald arched his bushy eyebrows and stroked his goatee. "Cor! Sounds to me like you were diddled on that purchase." His eyes narrowed. "You were fortunate that they went good on it in the end."

I agreed with him. "Say, got any tea left in that pot?"

Donald surged forward in his chair. "Right-o! Where are my manners? Have a spot, lad, and tell me what you think – it's some of my own private stock." He gave me a wink. "I think it's the real bees knees, you know.

Bought the tea leaves myself, right from a plantation near Kisumu."

I swallowed a mouthful of the hot liquid. "I don't know about the bees part, but it certainly clears the palate." I returned my cup to its saucer. "Say, I'll bet you know a thing or two about African tea."

Donald smiled modestly. "Well, now that you mention it, I do consider myself a bit of an expert. Why, I've sampled *chai* from the south of Tanzania to the western border of Uganda." He sat back in his wicker chair and placed his fingertips together. "As a matter of fact, just the other day I was down in Maasai country and…"

"Uh, the Maasai…they're just to the south of Nairobi, right?"

Donald frowned at the interruption. "Quite right, old chap. Now, as I was saying, I was down in Maasai country, and they were preparing some new milk gourds…"

"Milk gourds? Hey, I know about those," I said, cutting him off again. "The Turkana prepare them with charcoal. It kind of makes the milk taste smoky."

"Blimey, would you let me finish?" Donald shook his head in exasperation. "You blokes from across the pond are always in such a blooming hurry!" He smoothed out his cravat and continued with his tale. "Now, these Maasai blokes, they're just bonkers about their cattle. Practically worship the silly bovines, don't you know. So when they want to sour their milk, they take the milk gourds, go to the cows and…"

I waved my hand frantically in the air. "I know, I know – they nick the cow's neck vein and bleed them into the gourds first!"

Donald glared at me. "Blast it, Shambles, will you hold your tongue? Now, where was I?" He took another sip of tea to calm his nerves. "Oh yes. I was *going* to say that the Maasai take these long, decorated gourds and wash them out with pure cow's urine…" He paused and smiled smugly at my shocked expression, satisfied that he'd finally gotten my attention. "Believe it or not," he continued, lowering his voice conspiratorially, "despite our western preconceptions, urine is totally sterile when fresh. Did you know that it actually operates as a mild antiseptic and..."

Just then, a server came by with his dual teapots. "*Nusu nusu*?" he asked politely.

I grabbed my cup and thrust it in his direction. "No – give it to me straight!" I'd had enough mixed drinks lately; what I needed now was a good carb cleaning to wash out my system.

All things considered, Cookie was probably right – too much coffee can't be good for you. So when Monday morning coffee break came around, I reached into my lunch kit and pulled out the tea bag my wife had given me. Basil looked up in surprise. "My, my – this is a radical departure from the norm."

"Yeah," I replied glumly. I went over and plugged in the electric kettle. "Cookie wants me to cut down on my coffee intake."

"Been there, done that," said Tooner from his chair in the corner. "Mabel tried t' do the same thing t' me a couple of years back. But I showed her."

I was all ears. "Really? What did you do?"

Tooner chuckled. "I told her, if'n I had t' drink tea, I was gonna do it my way – half tea and half whiskey!"

I raised my eyebrows. Apparently, every tribe on earth has its own version of *nusu nusu* – even Tooner's.

The kettle came to a boil, so I filled my mug with hot water and watched the teabag slowly disperse its feeble stain. To be honest, it didn't look very appealing. Something was missing – some essential element that would give it body and substance. I considered my alternatives: Charcoal, blood, urine, and now whiskey. *I wonder what it would taste like with just a couple drops of engine oil?*

In the end, I came up with the perfect solution – the Shambles Tribe version of *nusu nusu*. I stirred in two spoonfuls of instant coffee.

CHAPTER 26

❧ THERE'S NO PLACE LIKE HOME ❧

I f a man's home is his castle, then how come I *get stuck with cleaning out the moat*? Dark thoughts filled my mind as slime and muck dripped off my elbows. It was my monthly battle with the fishpond filter, and as usual, the filter was winning.

Buddy yawned and wandered over from where he'd been lying in the shade of my burning bush, his favorite shrub. He sniffed the pump and filter assembly spread out on the front lawn and began to raise a hind leg. *Want some help with this?*

"Don't you dare," I snarled menacingly. "One drop out of you, and I'll put you up for adoption."

Sticking his nose in the air, Buddy turned and trotted over to the pond where a couple of my bigger goldfish were swimming near the surface. *Fine!* He licked his snout. *I'll just see what's for lunch.*

Before I could respond, a couple of loud backfires shook the neighborhood as a familiar pile of rusty blue metal rumbled to a stop in front of my gate. Steam hissed out from under the hood as the engine vibrated at a fast idle.

"Hop in, Slim!" shouted Buck Pincher above the noise. "We're doing some estate planning, and you should come along."

Giving my dog one last warning glare, I washed my hands off with the garden hose before climbing into the back of Buck's old car. Baldy, our town barber, was up front riding shotgun. "Estate planning?" I asked. "You mean we're going to some kind of financial seminar?"

"Nope," replied Baldy. "We're gonna tour one of those new seniors' strata developments. To Buck, that's *estate planning*."

"Yeah," said Buck. "I wanna see which estate I'm planning to retire into." He threw Old Betsy into gear and floored the gas pedal. "Another ten years and I'll be eligible to move in."

I shook my head at the thought of Buck retiring. He didn't do much of anything as it was, so what was he going to retire from?

A few minutes later, we pulled through the security gate of Prune Bush Manor, a fancy strata development built on what once was a productive apple orchard. But instead of apples, the large acreage now grew pink stucco houses with pointy roofs. Each immaculate bungalow was an exact replica of the one next door, right down to the pink flamingo in the corner of each lawn.

I stared at the copycat homes as we ground to a halt. "It's a good thing they've got house numbers on them or you'd never know which one was yours."

"Ain't that the point?" asked Baldy. "From what I've been hearing, these strata places ain't really yours to begin with. Even after you buy it, you still gotta pay rent."

I looked at Buck incredulously. "Is that true?"

Buck kicked his door a couple of times until it opened. "That's what we're here to find out. Upward and onward, men – the tour is about to begin."

Francine Gusher met us at the front door of the clubhouse in a cloud of perfume and overbearing enthusiasm. "Come in, boys!" she cooed, taking Buck's arm to coax him inside. "Looking ahead to our future, are we?"

"Nope, I'm already married," Buck stated flatly as he shook his arm free. "But I would like to see inside one of your houses."

Francine was a true professional – it only took her 23 seconds to recover from Buck's twisted sense of humor. Pasting a smile back on her face, she said coolly, "Of course. Allow me to provide you with a small brochure about our lovely facility before I take you through the show home." We followed her into the clubhouse where we discovered a large billiards table in the center of the room. But there were no balls on it – only a stack of promotional materials and a plate of cookies. A coffee pot gurgled merrily over on the counter to one side.

Buck's eyes lit up. "Hey, this looks nice! Can I have a coffee to go with three sugars and lots of cream?"

Francine allowed a thin smile. "Perhaps later," she said. "First I'll give you one of these." She loaded each of us up with a thick booklet, crammed with tight, single-spaced typing. "This contains a few rules and guidelines for those who choose to make Prune Bush Manor their home," she explained.

I began looking through the booklet as Baldy eyed the billiards table. "Is that for the residents to use?" he asked hopefully.

Ms. Gusher flashed her perfect teeth again. "Eventually, yes – once we don't need the clubhouse for a sales office. Then the residents will have full use of all our facilities, provided they book well enough in advance."

I just happened to be reading that portion of the rulebook. "Yeah – three months in advance, according to this."

"Three months?" Buck's eyebrows shot skyward. "That kind of makes it hard to have an impromptu time of beer and billiards with your buddies."

Francine laughed lightly and shook her head. "I'm afraid I've given you the wrong impression." Her voice went hard. "*No* alcohol and *no* buddies – the clubhouse is for residents *only*."

Buck stared at her in bewilderment, wondering what other things weren't allowed. "Well, what about…"

"No, it's against the rules," she said.

"Yeah, but every Friday I…"

"Not anymore you won't."

"But on my birthday my wife and I like to…"

She glared at him. "We especially don't allow *that* here!"

Before Buck could recover his lower lip from the carpet, she turned on her heel and headed for the door. "Now, if you'll come with me, we can begin our tour."

"Sheesh," Buck whispered to me as we prepared to follow her single file. "Ms. Gush-bucket is stricter than a kindergarten teacher. I get the feeling she's a bit of a control freak."

"You're overreacting," I whispered back. "Now hurry up – the line's moving. And don't let go of that rope or you'll get lost."

Once outside, Francine had us stop for a session of show and tell. "Gentlemen, you'll note how clean and spotless we like to keep our driveways."

"Yeah, Buck," I said, showing him page 22. "According to this, if your car leaks oil, you have to fix it or replace it. I like this place already."

Buck glared at me. "Old Betsy don't leak that bad, Slim. And I ain't replacing my car just to move into a new house."

"Hmm, wouldn't bet on it," spoke up Baldy, his nose deep in his own rulebook. "Says here, '*You must not accumulate or keep scrap metal or old car parts*.' If that don't describe your car, then I don't know what does."

After much tugging, Francine got the line moving again. She led us through the front door of the show home into a tastefully decorated living room. Buck looked at the drapes. "First thing my wife would do is change those to green. It's her favorite color."

Another cool smile. "Um, no, she won't. All window coverings must be approved by the strata council, and green isn't in our color scheme for the foreseeable future." Walking over to the living room window, she pulled back the offending drapes and changed the subject. "Gentlemen, you'll notice the beautiful marble bird bath situated in the commonly-shared green space. We are quite proud of it!"

Baldy squinted through the glass. "I see the bath, but I don't see no birds. Where's the bird feeder to attract them with?"

"Sorry, no bird feeders. We find that having animals around is too messy."

We looked at each other. "You mean you don't allow any pets?" ventured Baldy nervously, thinking about his old hound, Closeshave.

"No cats, birds, or goldfish – page 24," came the reply. "They may cause allergies."

I turned to page 24. "But it *does* say here that dogs are allowed, right?"

Francine sniffed. "We do make exceptions for small canines, but no higher than twelve inches at the shoulder."

Buck nudged Baldy. "You're in luck," he whispered. "That means you can bring Closeshave after all. He's under twelve inches lying down, and that's the only position I ever seen him in." Baldy nodded, greatly relieved.

I sat down on a designer couch to read some more, which earned me a disapproving glare from Miss Manners. "Look here, guys. It says you can't hang your laundry outside where others can see it. And no garden structures, either." I looked up. "Dolly isn't going to like that, Buck."

He rubbed his chin. "Yeah, but then I won't have to build any more stuff for her flowerbeds. What else does it say?"

I read on. "*You may not use any instrument or device which causes a disturbance…*"

"Hey, Buck," broke in Baldy, "now Dolly can't chase you around the yard with a broom no more."

Buck grinned gleefully. "This is sounding better all the time. What else, Slim?"

I turned the page. "Whoops – you're not gonna like this. *No satellite dishes…*"

He cringed. "I guess I could pay for cable…"

"*…and no hot tubs.*"

"No hot tub?!" hollered Buck. "That's where I plan to spend half my time when I retire!" He turned to Ms. Gusher, who was not smiling by this time, not even coolly. "Why not?" he demanded.

She adjusted her designer glasses. "They're too noisy. It disturbs the neighbours next door."

"What about computers?" I asked, thinking of Buck's passion for playing computer games into the wee hours of the morning.

She frowned. "No loud noises after 9:00 p.m., and if you're going to type letters, I'd suggest a blanket over the keyboard."

Buck was dumbfounded. "Who decides all this stuff?" he growled.

"The strata council, of course," replied Francine. "Residents may bring their suggestions, and the council will vote on them." She pointed out the front window. "In fact, there's our council president right now, over beside your junk...ahem, *car*."

The three of us crowded around the window and peeked out. A portly man wearing a starched shirt and a bow tie was walking around Buck's car, clucking his tongue and scribbling furiously on a clipboard. He wore a flattop haircut, military style, and his black shoes shone like polished ebony. A white glove dangled out of the back pocket of his trousers.

"That's the Major," Francine informed us proudly. "He was the first one to move in here, and he's been on the strata council ever since. I'm pleased to say he runs a very tight ship."

By contrast, Buck's dream of a happy retirement home was sinking faster than the *Titanic*. He looked over at the common green space again. "So, is that where I can put my tool shed?" he asked. "It's where I like to keep my tools for my hobbies."

Ms. Gusher sighed. "We don't allow tool sheds, and if we did, we certainly wouldn't allow them in the green space. However, we do permit *Attached Conforming Containment Annexes*."

Buck looked at me for the translation. "She means it has to be built onto the house by an expensive contractor, with pink stucco on the outside and covered with a pointy roof." I closed the booklet. "Page 46."

"Anything else I should know?" Buck asked weakly.

Francine thought for a moment, and then mentioned the strata fees. After we got Buck's heart pumping again, she continued. "And, as you already know, all residents must be over 50 years of age: anyone younger can only visit for a maximum of three days." She grinned gleefully. "And I'll warn you that the Major likes to do spot checks for proper ID."

"Well," said Baldy, "that takes care of the grandkids, but it don't keep out the in-laws. Pretty obvious flaw in your rules, if you ask me."

"Just hold it a minute!" cried Buck. "You mean my daughter can't stay in my house if I go on vacation for two weeks?"

"She can when she's 50," sniffed Ms. Gusher.

"When she's 50," growled Buck angrily, "I won't need a vacation: I'll need cremation!" He headed for the door. "Let's go, boys. I can tell this estate planning ain't for me."

Before we could get into the car, we had to stand at attention while the Major inspected the troops.

"A dishonorable discharge?" Baldy studied the scribbled note the Major had thrown at us as we pulled away. "This ain't gonna look good on my record, you know."

As Buck's car struggled to get over a speed bump, I looked in the front window of a duplex unit close to the drive. I could see an elderly woman inside holding a glass tumbler up to the wall as she tried to eavesdrop on the neighbors. *Hmm, maybe it's somebody's birthday next door – I hope they don't get reported for non-permitted behavior.*

Two houses down we came across a man pouring some oil into his engine. Buck stopped the car and I rolled down my window. "Do you live here?" I asked, staring at the dark sunglasses and fake beard he was wearing.

The older gentleman put his finger to his lips. "Quiet – they'll hear you." He looked around furtively. "Actually, I live on the other side of the complex." He lowered his voice to a whisper. "I'm using someone else's driveway to add oil to my car." He winked at me. "Just in case I spill any."

I was shocked. "Is it that strict around here?"

He stared at me. "Are you kidding? One guy had to remove all the doors from his kitchen cupboards because his neighbor complained that they made too much noise when he closed them!" He shook his head sadly. "Take my advice – if you have to move in here, be afraid… be very afraid."

"That settles it," said Buck. "I'm outta here!" He punched the gas pedal, and as we passed through the security gate, I gave Prune Bush Manor one last look out the back window. I liked it better when it was all apple trees.

"So what are you going to do about your retirement home, Buck?"

asked Baldy. "Should we check out the rules at Memory Banks Haven over by the highway? They might not be so strict."

"Nothing doing," muttered our friend. "I'm going home and staying home. At least there I can make up my own rules."

"Ahem," interjected Baldy. "Aren't you forgetting something?"

"Oh, alright," admitted Buck. "So it's Dolly who makes the rules around my place – but at least I'm used to them."

Buck and Baldy dropped me off at my house and I waved goodbye as they drove away – although I don't know why I bothered – Buck couldn't see anything out the back window because of all the blue smoke.

Coming up the sidewalk, I caught sight of Buddy effectively blocking my front steps with his prostrate body. "Do you plan on moving anytime soon?" I asked.

The lazy mutt opened one eye and stared at me for a moment. *Last time I checked, Sunshine, this house had a back door. If I were you, I'd use it.* And with that he promptly went back to sleep.

I sighed and headed around the side of the house. When it comes to making the rules around my place, I can't tell who has more pull – Buddy or my wife. But compared to what I'd just seen, it really wasn't worth worrying about.

Old familiar sayings like *A man's home is his castle* and *A dog is a man's best friend* are nothing more than bald-faced lies, but I do know one altruism that isn't. There really is no place like home.

CHAPTER 27

❧ A BATCH OF TROUBLE ❧

angez, Monsieur Slim, *mangez*! Eat! You are wasting away to nothing." Madame Pichette's eyes twinkled as she piled more French pastries onto my office desk. Basil and Tooner were already reaching for their fourth helping, while Beanie sagged on a stool in the corner, looking green around the gills. "No more for me," he mumbled. "I think I overdosed on the creampuffs."

I held up my hands in self-defense. "Really, Collette, I couldn't eat another bite!"

This ritual of pastry stuffing had become a regular occurrence. That was because once a week, almost to the day, Madame Pichette's Volkswagen Jetta would suddenly stall. "*Oui*, I am driving along and *voilà*! *Ma petite voiture*, she just stops." Fortunately, it would restart immediately. Collette would then drive straight home, bake a batch of goodies and come right over to visit her favorite mechanics.

As much as I enjoyed her baking, I was starting to feel guilty – this was her fourth visit this month and we hadn't been able to discover the cause of her car's irregularities. It ran perfectly when we drove it, and all of our testing on the fuel and ignition systems had failed to even replicate the problem, much less offer a solution.

Part of me wondered if the Jetta was really acting up, or if Collette just had a secret fondness for overweight techs.

"About your car…" I began, brushing the crumbs off my coveralls.

"*Ah, oui*! I was just going to tell you." Collette started packing away the empty plates into her large wicker basket. "I'm going away for a month to the south of France, so I've decided to leave my Jetta for you to drive. Then when it quits, *bon* – you can fix it!" She looked very pleased with herself.

Basil started choking on his éclair, while Tooner gasped. "What!" he cried. "Y'mean there'll be no home baked goods for a whole month?"

She laughed and patted his shoulder. "You are a rascal, Monsieur Tooner. I am thinking you don't fix my *voiture* because you like my baked treats too much, *n'est-ce pas*?" She handed me the keys. "*Au revoir.*"

A sense of gloom descended over the shop as Beanie left to give Collette a ride home. Her bakery treats were a vast improvement over the day-old donuts we were used to. "Well," sighed Basil, "I suppose we'll just have to get serious about fixing that car. I, for one, want to remain on the good side of Madame Pichette."

I didn't like the sound of that. "Are you telling me that we haven't made a serious effort to fix this stalling problem?"

"Of course we have!" declared Tooner. "But imports ain't really our specialty, y'know." He rubbed the stubble on his chin. "Maybe we'll have t' go next door t' Dieter's import shop and pick his brain."

I was wondering why we hadn't done that sooner...until I remembered the flaky croissants, the Napoleon bars, the fruit tarts. Quite frankly, we were loathe to share these delicacies with anyone outside our shop.

Basil was thinking the same thing. With a grunt he hauled himself out of his easy chair. "Fine. But don't breathe a word about Collette's pastries – we don't want Dieter stealing our baker...ah, I mean our customer." With Basil, as with the French, food was not just food: it was a way of life.

In the days that followed, two significant events took place. First, the Jetta never skipped a beat, no matter how much we drove it. As a result, we never did go over and talk with Dieter. After all, what could we tell him? That we had a nice clean Jetta that ran perfectly?

The second event was that Beanie made cupcakes in the microwave oven we kept on top of the filing cabinet.

"Beanie!" bellowed Tooner as he ran for the bathroom. "What'd ya put in these things?!" Basil took one sniff and threw his cupcake in the garbage. I was glad I'd waited for the others to do the taste testing.

Our young apprentice gulped. "We didn't have any bowls to mix up the ingredients, so I emptied out one of those old coffee cans we use for storing bolts. I thought I'd cleaned it out pretty good."

"What did you use?" I asked facetiously. "Cleaning solvent?"

Beanie looked down. "Well, I…"

As the time drew near for Madame Pichette's return from France, the atmosphere around Slim Shambles Auto Repair grew so heavy you could cut it with a pastry knife. And our work was suffering for it. The guys wandered around the shop like zombies, taking twice as long to finish even the simplest repair job.

But the flour really hit the fan when I came out of the office one morning to find the lube bay floor flooded with used engine oil. "Beanie!" I yelled. "Watch what you're doing! You're missing the oil drain bucket by a mile!"

Startled out of his reverie, Beanie sheepishly jammed the drain plug back into the oil pan. "Sorry, Slim. I guess I was thinking about that Jetta out there…"

I'd had enough of this. "Alright everyone, it's time for a staff meeting – now!"

It was a sorry looking bunch that shuffled into my office. "Look guys, I know it's frustrating when a difficult repair job comes along, but you're letting this one small import car ruin your concentration. We've got other work to do, and I need you at your best." I pointed out the window at Madame Pichette's Jetta. "I repeat – it's just one car."

Basil sighed and shook his head. "I beg to differ. That car is not just a car, Slim. That car and its owner represent everything that's decent in the world of culinary art." The other two stooges nodded glumly in agreement. Basil began to get agitated, something he rarely did. Pacing back and forth, he raised a forefinger in the air and declared, "I submit that my colleagues and I have been ruined by the domestic oven of one tiny French lady! Three grown men, brought to their knees in submission by her seemingly innocent acts of kindness." Basil shook his fist, his voice rising. "Oh, but there's devilry at work here. These small tokens of appreciation have become an addiction to us, our taste buds now refusing to be satisfied by anything less. We are men being driven to despair by the deft turn of the hand at the mixing bowl!" Basil stopped pacing and stared at me, a wild look contorting his face. "And how did this all begin, you ask? With *that*!" His body shook as he pointed at Collette's car. "That *menace* is ruining our lives!"

With great reluctance, I realized that our options had run out. *Tarte aux framboises* or not, it was time call up Dieter. He listened while I explained our problem. "Cutting out at odd times, eh?" He thought for a moment. "Well, we *have* had lots of relay problems on those models. I'd suggest replacing the main ones and see what happens. They're not very expensive."

We had little to lose, so Tooner went over and picked up the new relays, one for the on-board computer and another for the fuel pump. He showed me the boxes they were packaged in – the language on the outside was Spanish, not German. "Dieter didn't have any OEM relays," he explained, "but he figures these white box specials will work."

"OEM?" questioned Beanie. "What does that stand for?"

"*Original Equipment Manufacturer*," I explained. "It means parts made by the same company that supplied them to the factory when the car was new." The aftermarket brand Dieter had given us was what we in the industry referred to as *white box* parts, because they were made by offshore companies and came in white boxes with very little information on them. We installed the relays, and when Madame Pichette returned a few days later, I explained what we had done.

"So...*ma petite voiture*, she is fixed?"

I crossed my fingers behind my back. "It should be good now, Collette," I said more confidently than I felt. "Here are your keys, and if you have any questions, don't hesitate to drop by." *And coffee breaks are at 10 and 3!* I could tell by the facial twitches on the three faces peering around the corner of the shop door that they were all thinking the same thing.

A week later, Madame Pichette did return, but she wasn't wearing her apron and she was noticeably empty-handed. The Jetta had quit again. "Monsieur Slim, I'm losing my patience, *non*? There will be no more French pastries until *ma petite voiture* runs properly!"

Beanie watched her storm out of the shop. "Do you want me to try my hand at baking again?"

"No! I want you to figure out how to fix that car." I stomped off to my office to drown my sorrows in a cup of specially brewed coffee. I kept a selection of flavorings in my bottom desk drawer for days like this, days when things got really bad. I chose Swiss Mocha. My favorite was usually French Vanilla, but at the moment I was fed up with anything *en français*.

A few minutes later Beanie cautiously poked his head in through the door. "Uh, Slim, I might have an idea…"

"Out with it, Bean – right now I'll consider anything!"

"Well," he began nervously. "I thought I might try surfing around on the Internet. My friend told me about a forum where mechanics from around the world chat and share ideas. What do you think?"

We didn't have the Internet at our shop – very few shops did in those days. The 'Net' was still new and had yet to prove itself in the commercial world. Although I had my doubts, I sent Beanie down to the public library to use their computer. I didn't expect him to find anything useful, but I didn't know what else to do.

A couple of hours later, Beanie's little pickup careened into the parking lot, spraying gravel in all directions. Jumping out of his truck, he waved a piece of paper and shouted, "Hey guys, look at this – I think I found something!"

We all gathered round, curious to see what he had. "I found that mechanics' forum," explained The Bean. "I posted a message about our problem, and some technician in Missouri wrote back – apparently he ran into the exact same trouble last month." According to Beanie's printout, there was a bad batch of aftermarket relays floating around and the technician recommended using only OEM relays from the Volkswagen dealer.

"Well, don't that frost yer cookies," exclaimed Tooner. He looked at

Beanie with renewed appreciation. "From a bad batch of cupcakes to a bad batch of relays. I guess ya redeemed yerself, Bean."

With the OEM relays installed, the Jetta never quit again, and out of gratitude Madame Pichette began sending over regular installments of her fancy pastries. However, Beanie had been bitten with the baking bug himself, and he showed up one morning with a box of instant brownie mix. "How about I take another stab at whipping up some goodies for coffee break?" he suggested hopefully.

"Sorry, Bean," said Basil as he buttered his third croissant. "We have a new shop policy – we only use OEM baked goods around here."

Chapter 28

SOMETHING ROTTEN IN SLUMBERLAND

Hmm, I smell something rotten here," I said, putting down the morning edition of the *Slumberland Rebuttal*.

"Sorry." Buck sheepishly licked his fingers as he worked on his fourth three-bean taco. It was *Mexican Madness Saturday* at Rolph's Diner, a favorite time for Buck to get his money's worth of food. "I can't help myself – they're just so good!"

"No, not you – I mean this story in the paper." I pushed my bowl of cold chili off to one side. "It says here that town council is going to spend almost $14,000 on a study called *The Sanitary Landfill Expansion and Closure Proposal.*

Buck stopped chewing and looked at me. "Well, are they going to expand the landfill or close it?"

I shrugged. "I don't know, but I think it's our civic duty to find out. Let's drive out there and see what's going on." A stack of dirty dishes and half-eaten food littered the table between us. "Are you almost done here?"

He wiped his greasy chin with a napkin. "Finished with the tacos, but I still got this plate of burritos." When it's an *All You Can Eat* special, Buck has a simple rule: 'No food gets left behind.'

I signaled to the restaurant owner. "Hey, Rolph, we want to take these burritos to the dump. Can we get a doggy bag?"

As we sped away down Main Street a few minutes later, Buck took another look in his rear view mirror. "Wonder what got into Rolph? He doesn't usually chase us out of the diner with a broom."

"Beats me," I said, turning around to look out the rear window of Buck's rattletrap. "But you can slow down now – I think we've lost him."

For Buck and me to go to such lengths over a newspaper article was unusual. As a rule, I don't pay much attention to what Mayor Dewgood and his ragtag band of council members do on a daily basis. The way I figured it, I had my business to run and they had theirs. After all, that's what we voted them in for.

But lately there'd been a few things coming out of town hall that had me wondering. Like six months ago, when they tried to turn Slumberland into a city...

A Saturday morning stroll around Main Street seemed like a good idea, and that was where I found Buck. He was leaning in a doorway beside one of his favorite spots – the used book table outside the second hand store. And he was doing one of his favorite things – getting something for free.

"Hey, Buck, give your eyes a rest. You can't read the whole book standing here on the sidewalk. Just buy it and take it home – it's only 50 cents."

My tightwad friend put down the pulp novel and rubbed his bleary eyes. "And at that price, it's still an outrage. To charge anything for this trash is unconscionable."

I smirked at him. "If it's so trashy, then why are you reading it?" The only things thinner than Buck's generous streak are his excuses. "Come on, you cheapskate – I'll buy you a coffee at The Bean Dust Café."

"Aw, I don't know, Slim," grumbled Buck. "That fancy coffee they serve in there ain't like the brew they make over at Rolph's."

"Exactly," I replied. "It's encouraging to see that some things are improving around this town."

Buck shrugged. "Well, I guess if you're buying..."

We entered the coffee shop to find the normally subdued crowd caught up in animated discussions as they buzzed noisily around one of the tables.

"What's all the ruckus?" I called over to Rep Tyler, who seemed to be in the center of the action.

Rep was laughing so hard that tears were streaming down his face.

The parakeet perched on his shoulder was chuckling right along with him. "Lookit this, Slim!" He smacked the newspaper he was holding. "Slumberland is goin' t' become a city!"

I grabbed the latest issue of the *Slumberland Rebuttal* and scanned the article in question. Sure enough, there was a proposal before Council to change the name of our little burg from its current and long-winded official title, *The District of the Corporation of the Municipality of Slumberland*, into something you could say in one breath: they wanted to call it *The City of Slumberland*.

Soapbox Henson, our local activist, sighed deeply. "If that happens, it'll be the only city in Canada to have the *Entering City Limits* sign and the *Leaving City Limits* sign mounted on the same post." He drained his espresso in one gulp – the potent mixture helped fuel his frequent crusades. "I think we should organize a citizens' group and fight this thing!"

"But ya can't fight city hall," said Rep to Soapbox.

"I know," he replied. "But you *can* fight town hall – that's why we don't want the name to change."

Rover Dangerphrase was also worried. "Gee, fellas, I don't know – it's hard enough reporting the town news all by myself. I don't think I can cover a whole city beat. I'll have to ask the Chief for extra staff."

Buck was deep in thought, a painful experience from the look of it. "Does that mean Main Street is gonna get a traffic light?"

Rep shrugged. "Dunno." His eyes lit up. "Hey, d'ya think we'll get our own public transit system? I always wanted t' ride a subway…"

Just then the owner of the café passed by. "Hey, Dusty," I said. "How about a couple of lattes for me and my friend?"

Dusty stopped and scrutinized Buck. "Are you sure he won't just spit it out? I've seen his kind in here before; if it isn't black and toxic, they don't know what it is."

I assured him that Buck would behave himself, but I received a shock when he brought the two cups of frothy mixture to our table.

"That'll be sixteen dollars, Slim," stated Dusty.

"What?! They were half that yesterday. How come the price increase?"

He shrugged. "We're a big city now, so I need to charge big city prices."

It was time to put a stop to this nonsense.

We caught up with our town planner half way down Main Street. Hank Brink looked nervous as Buck and I fell into step on either side of him.

"Congratulations, Hank," I said, slapping him on the back. "I understand this idea to call Slumberland a city is your brainchild. Well, it's brilliant! I must say I'm impressed."

"You are?" asked Hank, not sure whether to believe me or not. His eyes darted from side to side. "Gee, a lot of other folks seem to be upset…"

"Forget 'em," advised Buck heartily. "The prospects are endless."

"Uh, the prospects?"

"We'll start with the overpasses," he said. "One at each end of town."

"Overpasses? But why?" Hank was thoroughly confused.

Buck's eyebrows shot skyward. "Why? Because every city deserves an off ramp from the nearest major highway. It's only fair!"

Before Hank could reply, I whispered conspiratorially into his left ear. "And when you start building the public transit system, could I convince you to put a stop out by my automotive shop? It would really help my business."

Buck jumped right back in. "Now, if you need a place to put up one of them high-rise hotels on the highway, I'll gladly let my motel property go." He nudged Hank in the ribs. "Of course, I'll need to be properly compensated. We're not just talking small town real estate anymore."

"High-rises? Public transit?" Hank exclaimed. "What are you guys talking about? All I suggested was a name change to simplify my paperwork!"

"Hank, don't be so modest," I chuckled. "Perception – that's the name of the game. Slumberland's image is on the line here. Obviously you're a man with vision, looking ahead to our future, and we're downright fortunate to have you." I turned serious. "But tell me, where will the international airport go? I haven't quite figured that one out yet."

Hank clenched his fists in frustration. "There's not going to be any…!"

I cut him off. "I'm also a little concerned about the potential traffic problems. With everybody commuting into the city every morning, do you think we'll have enough parking?" I frowned. "Maybe we need to consider paving Mumbleton Park."

"Look," said Hank in exasperation, "all we're talking about is a simple name change. It'll be the same town it always was."

Buck and I were speechless…almost. "What?" I cried in astonishment. "A city that's not a city? Then just call it *The Town of Slumberland*. That's how we refer to it anyway, so why not make it official?"

Hank sighed. "Because with an actual *town* designation, you're only allowed to have three councilors instead of six, like we have now."

"Hmm," said Buck, thoughtfully scratching his chin. "Now there's an improvement."

"*A village*?" I suggested.

"Got to have less than 5,500 people," replied Hank. He'd certainly done his homework.

"Well," I sighed. "I guess *City* it is. But you'll have to tear down our tiny town hall and build a new, bigger City Hall. Of course, people won't appreciate the tax increases you'll need to pay for all of this. Better lock your doors at night." I shook his hand gravely. "You're a brave man, Hank. It's a tough job, but somebody's gotta do it."

"Aw, he'll be okay," put in Buck. "Our new City Police force will keep an eye on him." He paused. "At least, I hope they can…Redneck Rube and his son Beefus can be hard to control at times, especially when they start dragging out their shotguns." He looked at me. "Did you know that they got this grudge against city slickers? Why, twenty years ago some guys went canoeing out in the bush and never returned…"

That's when Hank excused himself and hurried off, mumbling something about redoing some paperwork back at the office. I think he got the message, because the name change issue never came up around the council table again.

Tall stands of jack pines flew past my side window as we made our way out into the hills behind town – that's where Slumberland likes to hide its garbage. I wasn't sure what we were going to find when we got there, but it seemed like the logical place to start.

We were accosted at the landfill gate by the guard, Heave Brightly. Wearing an old cooking pot on his head for a helmet and brandishing a fire poker, he approached Buck's car. "Halt, who goes there?" he cried. Meanwhile, Tri-Pawed, his lame German Shepherd, played dead on the road behind us in order to block our escape.

"It's just me and Slim," said Buck, cautiously eyeing the poker aimed at his nose.

"Whatcha bringin' in?" asked Heave suspiciously.

"Nothing," I replied. "We just want to look around."

That threw Heave into a frenzy. "That's what they all say," he screeched, knocking off Buck's side view mirror with one stroke. "This ain't no place for looky-loos." He pulled out a crumpled pamphlet. "Says right here, rule number four – I weigh ya's when ya go in, and I weigh ya's when ya come out. Then I charge's ya so much a pound." He aimed the poker at us threateningly. "And ya's better be lighter comin' out."

Buck squirmed in his seat. "But what if we find some neat stuff in there to take home? If we weigh more coming out than going in, will you pay us instead?"

Heave had a fit and started pounding on the hood of the car with his poker. "No, no, no, no…you ain't gonna steal none o' my good junk!"

"Don't worry, Heave," I interjected. "We won't touch anything." The ground was so rough inside the dump area that I knew something was bound to fall off Buck's old Topaz. "I promise we'll be lighter coming out."

After a few more dents for good measure, Heave finally calmed down and let us proceed.

As we rattled our way into the dumping area, we could see numerous vehicles in various stages of loading and unloading. One inventive soul had brought in a trunk full of tree stumps and left with a load of old toasters, bent bicycles, and some used carpet. Another fellow off-loaded a pile of rocks, then filled up his truck with broken lawn chairs and washing machine parts. "As long as I'm lighter when I leave, old Heave won't know the difference," he chortled when I came over to see what he was doing.

"What are you going to do with all that stuff?" I asked him.

"Why, sell it in a yard sale, of course." He straightened up and took in the mound of cast-off items with a grand sweep of his arm. "Every day people throw out all kinds of good stuff. But they have these stupid rules saying you can't take anything out of the landfill."

Buck mournfully surveyed the dents in the hood of his car. "Yeah, I heard about them rules."

Our new friend picked up some used shelves from an old refrigerator and put them in his truck. "And now I hear they're complaining about the landfill getting too full." He shook his head. "They wanna do some kind of study to figure out whether to close it or make it bigger."

Suddenly the lights went on. "That's it!" I cried, turning to Buck. "Let's go back and ask Council to call off the Garbage Police. Instead, let people take whatever they want – that way, the landfill will never get full."

"Yeah," he said, "and us taxpayers won't have to spend all that money for a study." Buck paused. "But then Heave might lose his job." He shuddered at the thought. "He'd be even scarier with nothing to do all day."

After careful consideration, we finally found something to remove from Buck's car to make it lighter. We paid Heave our five dollar tipping fee, while Tri-Pawed washed one of the back tires as a farewell gesture. Then we motored back into town with our proposal for Mayor Dewgood and team. But Buck wasn't very happy.

"First time in my life that I ever paid twice for a bag of burritos and didn't get to eat 'em," he muttered morosely.

"You should be glad," I said. "Everybody, including your stomach, will thank me for it later." I took a tentative sniff. "By the way, would you mind winding your window down all the way?"

CHAPTER 29

❧ EARTH TO DAD ❧

I woke up early one Sunday morning in June with great anticipation – everything was quiet at the moment, but I was sure there were going to be presents. I'd heard all the whispering over the last couple of days – that and the subtle hint from my kids: "Dad, do you like fishing rods?" Oh yes, there would be presents.

Ah, I'll probably get breakfast in bed as well, I thought. *Or maybe the morning paper brought to me* before *the dog anoints it.* But twenty minutes later, when nothing and no one appeared at the bedroom door, I had to be content with cold cereal. I even had to prepare it myself. "The least they could have done was buy me a new box of Crispy Puffys," I muttered under my breath. The only thing my half-hearted search through the pantry revealed was an old bag of bran flake dust.

Cookie ignored me as usual and breezed by with an "I don't know why you stayed in bed so long this morning, dear, but you'd better hurry up or we'll be late for church." With a sigh, I resigned myself to higher things and tried to forget about my troubles for a while.

A couple of hours later, I made a few hopeful suggestions as we left the church parking lot. "So, what'll it be for lunch? The Burger Bucket? Pizza Pit? Chez Roberto's?" Heck, I would have settled for Rolf's Diner – anything to commemorate my special day.

"Nope," said Cookie, reading the church bulletin. "I think there's some macaroni dinner in the fridge from yesterday. We'll warm that up." My stomach sank, but my hopes rose – after all, the new aluminum fishing boat I wanted would have been difficult to fit into a restaurant. *Maybe they've hidden it somewhere around the house!*

But after scouting out the backyard and the garage on the pretext of bringing in the trash cans, I discovered no watercraft – not even a belly boat. Undeterred, I went over in my head a mental list of all the gift possibilities – things I'd been blatantly hinting at since the last time I didn't get what I wanted. *Maybe they bought me that new putter. I'll bet it's waiting in the living room right now.* I sauntered into the house humming a tune. "Hi, I'm in the house now. Sure looks like a lovely day for golfing."

With a puzzled expression, Cache looked up from the couch where she and her sister were reading their comic books. "Everything okay, Dad? You've been acting awfully strange this morning." It's amazing how even young children can be so good at hiding surprises. To look at them you'd think there was nothing going on.

"Oh, I'm just great," I replied cheerfully, looking around for bits of ribbon or colored paper – any clue that would give away a secret hiding place. "Anything I should know about, girls?"

Carrie looked up quickly. "Uh, something you should know about?" She glanced at Cache. "Gee, I don't know how you found out, Dad, but honest, we didn't know your fishing rod would break so easily…"

"What! You broke my fishing rod?" I was in shock. "How did you…?"

"But it's okay!" Cache interjected quickly. "You can hardly see the scratch in the hood of the van."

I gasped. "There's a scratch on the hood of the van?! How did that…?"

"I'm just glad the windshield didn't break when the hammer slipped," Carrie said to her sister. "Then Dad would really be choked."

Fortunately for the kids, Cookie came out from the kitchen and called us for lunch – the macaroni dinner lunch. At least it took my mind off the broken fishing rod and scratched hood.

All through the meal I kept looking for any indication that a big surprise was about to appear. By this point I would have taken almost anything: a bag of golf tees, a bookmark for the novel I would buy later with my own money, or even a coupon for a free coffee at The Bean

Dust Café. But nothing came – not even a hand-scribbled card from Tipper. I was crushed.

But not for long. Being the emotional giant that I was, I quickly moved beyond crushed and became ticked off. Sitting down at the desk in our bedroom, I made a list of all the nice things I'd done for everybody else on their special days. It was a short list, so I added some things I had planned to do, but never got around to.

By evening, I had worked up a fair head of steam and decided to give somebody a piece of my mind. Trouble was, I couldn't decide who to give it to. The kids ignored my outbursts at the best of times, and at worst, they'd roll on the floor laughing. And Cookie…well, let's just say I've learned not to push my luck. So I did the next best thing – I took it out on the dog.

Buddy just rolled over and begged to have his tummy rubbed. "There's no respect anymore, Buddy," I said, scratching him under the chin. Raising my voice a little, I continued, "If *you* were a father, I'd give *you* a present." He glowered back at me with his beady brown eyes and growled menacingly. *If I was a father? Yeah, and who took care of that, Mr. Friend of the Vet?*

Cookie looked up from the crossword puzzle she was working on. "Did you say something, dear?"

"Oh, nothing." Suddenly I decided I might as well get it out and be done with it. "Of course, on MOTHER'S DAY I always bring you breakfast in bed."

She frowned. "Mother's Day?"

Buddy flashed me a warning look, but I was past caring. "But that's okay," I continued a little more loudly, and to no one in particular. "I know that FATHER'S DAY GIFTS must come from the heart, so I'll just have to WORK A LITTLE HARDER at being a better FATHER. Maybe next year I'll even DESERVE A PRESENT."

The four 'no ones in particular' looked at each other mystified. Finally Cache spoke up. "Is that why you've been so grumpy all day, Dad? Because we haven't given you a Father's Day present?"

Finally, we're getting somewhere, I thought to myself, winking at Buddy. *Maybe they did just forget after all.*

Cookie got up and came over to kiss the top of my head. "Slim, your sense of humor is one of the reasons I married you in the first place." She chuckled. "How you come up with these outlandish jokes is beyond me."

The kids joined in laughing, and Tipper wiped the tears of mirth from his eyes. "Yeah, Daddy, you almost had us believing you really didn't know that Father's Day was *next* week!"

I stared at them blankly. "Uh…next week?" I swallowed quickly as my neck began to turn red. "Heh, heh…well, I guess there's no fooling you guys…" Fortunately, the family moved on to other things, leaving me alone with the dog.

Buddy looked up at me with a smirk. *Yeah, right, Bozo – and you ain't fooling me either.* He scrambled to his feet and trotted away. Then he paused at the hallway door and looked back over his shoulder. *Hey Pops, don't forget the big juicy bone next Sunday – you owe me.*

CHAPTER 30

❧ COMING UP SHORT ❧

Just for the record, Jimmy Lee Rupert isn't short; he's just vertically challenged. And the pillow on the front bucket seat of his Ford Mustang is for comfort, not to help him see over the steering wheel. And finally, he most definitely doesn't drive a 'muscle car' to make up for his personal lack of the same – he just likes the color blue and the convertible top.

I know all this to be true because Jimmy Lee points it out on a regular basis whenever he brings his vehicle in for service. Lately, however, his pony car has been relying on Dutchy's tow truck to make it back to the corral.

"Is that fusible link blown again?" I asked incredulously as Jimmy Lee came into the office. The errant electrical device I was referring to was a specially designed section of wiring near the battery that acted like a fuse – if too much electrical power tried to flow through the fusible link, it would melt. Annoying, yes, but it keeps the rest of the wiring harness from burning up if there is a dead short in the circuit. We tend to look upon it as the lesser of two evils.

Outside, I could see Dutchy backing up to the bay door, ready to put Jimmy Lee's Mustang inside our shop for the third time in as many weeks.

"Yep," confirmed Jimmy dejectedly. "Look, Slim, I'm not blaming you guys, because I know you can't duplicate the problem when my car is in your shop. But it's starting to cut into my social life. I'm supposed to take Veronica Sweetly to the beach today, and now I'm late." He hopped up into Basil's easy chair – it seemed to be a favorite with our customers – and sank back into its cushioned comfort, his short legs dangling a few inches above the floor.

"We could do a quick patch job," I offered, "and then ride along with you to see if it happens again."

But the thought of Tooner or Basil chaperoning from the back seat didn't appeal to my customer. "Naw, I'll take a taxi instead." He frowned pensively. "I suppose I *could* borrow a car from one of my friends, but I don't like picking up my date in someone else's ride. You know how it is – their seats just don't have the same ergonomic feel as my 'Stang." What he really meant was, they didn't adjust up high enough.

"Well, you could take your pillow with you," I offered. Jimmy Lee glanced up at me suspiciously. "Er… I mean, we wouldn't want to dirty it up with our coveralls, so it'd be better off with you than…"

He snapped his fingers. "Good point, Slim. I'll do that." He slid off the chair and came over to my desk. Standing on his tiptoes, he reached for the phone. "Mind if I make a few calls?"

I left Jimmy Lee to reorganize his day while I went into the shop to find the crew. Tooner, Beanie, and Basil already had the hood open and the offending piece of fusible link removed. Tooner held up the burnt scrap of wire. "Sure didn't take Jimmy Lee long t' make *short work* o' this," he chuckled.

Beanie grinned. "Yeah, I guess it was a *tall order* to think that our previous repair would last more than a week…"

Even Basil couldn't resist. "If you're asking me, I'd say it's the *height of audacity* to expect…"

"Knock it off, you three – he might hear you." I glanced towards the office door. "At least wait until he's left the building."

"Sorry, Boss." Basil tried to regain his composure. "Jimmy does have a legitimate problem. It's just that the sight of him and that pillow…"

At that moment Jimmy Lee scampered into the shop, his short legs churning frantically. "Hey Slim, toss me my pillow – the taxi's here already and Veronica is waiting!" In a flash he was gone, but it was too late – the gang had already collapsed with laughter.

"Okay, enough of that," I growled. "Let's get to work." I reviewed the symptoms one more time while the other three pulled themselves together. Basil got out his wire crimpers and installed a new fusible link.

According to our records, the problem always occurred whenever Jimmy used the convertible top – that's when the electrical system would overload and blow the link. The problem was, we could never duplicate the condition in the shop. We ran the top up and down a dozen times while monitoring how much electrical current went through the wiring harness, but it never became excessive. No matter what we did, we couldn't get the wire to melt, let alone heat up.

"Maybe Jimmy Lee's not telling us everything," Basil reasoned. "Maybe there's some small detail he's leaving out that would give us a clue."

"What?" broke in Tooner. "Ya mean he's only givin' us the *shortened version* of the story?"

That set everyone off into hysterics again, including me. "Alright, alright," I gasped. "We really have to get serious here. All joking aside, this Mustang has an obvious problem, and if we can't fix it, then who can?"

"You're right, Slim," said Basil, wiping the tears from his eyes. "Beanie, get in the car and pretend you're Jimmy."

The Bean obliged and climbed into the driver's seat. He slouched down until his head was at the same height as Jimmy's would be if he were in the car. "Wow!" he exclaimed. "It's a whole new world down here."

Tooner snorted. "I didn't know Jimmy Lee drove one o' them '*low-riders*.'"

"Save it," I warned them. "Okay, Beanie…now put the convertible top down."

Beanie started the car, and then sat up straight to unlock the right-and left-hand roof latches at the windshield frame. "Hold it right there!" I shouted, as a crazy idea slid into my brain. "Slouch back down again, and try to unlock the roof."

Beanie looked at me like I'd lost my senses. "There's no way," he replied, pointing out the obvious. "If I slouch down, I'd be too low to reach the latches."

"Exactly," I said. "But if you were Jimmy Lee, how would you reach them without getting out of the car?"

That caught everyone's attention. "Hmm, I never thought 'bout that," said Tooner. "Maybe he's uses a stick or somethin'." But a thorough search of the interior revealed no such device.

Beanie had a suggestion. "Well, if I were Jimmy Lee, I'd probably grab the steering wheel and pull myself up higher…like this." As soon as he put his weight on the steering column, the Mustang sputtered and died.

"Well, look at that," said Basil in amazement, as a small puff of smoke rose from the wiring near the battery. Finally, we had duplicated the problem.

Beanie removed the lower dash cowling underneath the steering column, and that's when we discovered that the main ignition feed wire was being pinched between the steering column and the sharp metal edges of the dash bracing. Every time Jimmy Lee pulled down on the steering wheel, it put pressure on the wire, until it had finally cut through the insulation and shorted the wire to ground. And that's what was blowing the fusible link.

Basil taped up the wire and moved it to a new location, and after a few more test runs by Beanie, we called the case closed. I went on a donut run and the gang settled into their office chairs for a celebration, confident that Jimmy Lee's problems – at least with his car – were finally over.

But Tooner couldn't resist one last pun. "Hey, d'ya realize we just pulled off a medical miracle?" He reached for his first donut. "We should sell this repair solution t' them scientific types who do all that genetic research stuff."

Beanie looked at him blankly. "What are you talking about, Toon?"

He grinned broadly. "Why, with a little bit of electrical tape and a couple of zip straps, we've just solved Jimmy Lee's *short* problem!"

Beanie and I groaned, while Basil shook his head and chuckled. "You forget, Tooner – Jimmy Lee doesn't even think he *has* a shortness issue."

Tooner nodded slowly. "Ya got a point there. I guess it's like the feller once said: 'There's none so blind as he who won't see'...over the dashboard, that is."

CHAPTER 31

⊰ A MODEST PROPOSAL ⊱

I've had it," barked Tooner, coming through the shop door. "That Dutchman is drivin' me crazy!" He tossed his ratchet into the top drawer of his tool cabinet. "I'm walkin' across the parkin' lot, mindin' my own business, and he has the gall t' holler at me from his office window – wants t' know what's takin' me so long t' finish the brake job on ….

His grumbling was drowned out by the loud rapping of Basil's air gun from behind me. Suddenly the rusty wheel stud snapped clean off, eliciting a loud and verbose response from my head technician.

But I didn't have time to worry about Basil's broken bolts or Tooner's tender sensibilities; I had troubles of my own. "Beanie, where's that Honda that needs a new headlight?" Our shop was so over-crowded, we weren't just losing tools – we were starting to misplace entire cars.

Beanie blinked the sweat out of his eyes as he struggled to lift a large truck tire onto the wheel balancer. "Over there, behind those boxes of antifreeze," he gasped, pointing with his nose. "Good luck getting near it!"

By now Basil had calmed down and was assessing the situation in front of him. "Slim," he called. "I require your presence when you get a free moment." A free moment? I hadn't seen one of those for six months. There *were* some living out back under a stack of old batteries, but I think a stray cat finally got them.

If I'd had any doubts in the past about hiring new staff and keeping them busy, I didn't anymore. For reasons beyond my comprehension, our shop was getting busier by the month. The lot was so full we had to park at Dieter's Imports down the street just to come to work.

As if I didn't have enough on my mind, Buck Pincher got bored and came by to harass me and the boys. "A fellow could starve around here, you know," he said loudly, draping his gut over the fender of the Honda. "I come by for a nice friendly visit and there ain't a donut in sight."

"That's because you forgot to bring them," I retorted, squinting in the dim light as I fought with the tiny screws that held the broken headlight. "Here's novel idea: go down to Tommy's Donuts and buy two dozen fresh ones with your own money."

"What!" Buck was shocked. "Me – buy donuts?" He suddenly had difficulty breathing. "I've never heard of anything so…so inconceivable!" He staggered back outside towards his car. "Ow, my head hurts…I need to lie down…."

Just then a 5-ton freight truck pulled into the parking lot and backed up to the bay door. A smartly dressed driver in a uniform jumped down from the cab and practically saluted me as he held out some weigh bills. "Morning, Mr. Shambles! I've got your winter tires on board – all 150 of them. Where would you like me to unload?"

Now *I* was in shock. I'd forgotten that Zeke the tire guy had bamboozled me into placing an order for tires the month before. There was simply no place to put them – the shop was too full of broken-down vehicles and stressed-out mechanics.

Dutchy sauntered over, eager to offer a solution. "Ja, I mean I can rent you some more space in my other building down the street. I'll just double your rent and you can unload those tires right away."

In the end we managed to find space for all the tires, although it took the three of us plus the driver to put them into place. "Hey, cool view," called Beanie from his perch up on the roof of the office. He grabbed another tire from Tooner, who was clinging precariously by one hand to the top rung of the ladder. "How many more we got to go?"

"That's it for the roof," I yelled up at him. "The rest will go inside – somewhere."

My blood pressure was heading for nosebleed territory. The situation was not good and getting not-gooder by the day. I made a mental list of some of the issues we faced: an overbearing landlord; a shop that was too small by half; only one vehicle lift; an overbearing landlord; a metal building that was hot in the summer and cold in the winter…and did I mention the overbearing landlord? Suddenly it felt like today would be a fine day for a drive…for me.

"Take over, Basil," I said. "I've got some thinking to do. If you need me, you can try my home number."

Basil reached over the stack of tires surrounding my office desk and grabbed a pad of paper. "So you're going home for a while?" he asked, preparing to write down my number.

"Nope," I said, putting on my jacket.

His pencil hovered over the notepad. "Then why am I writing this down?"

I shrugged. "I said you could *try* my home number; I didn't say I'd be there."

Half an hour later I was standing at the lookout on Hunchback Mountain, a surprising thing given my fear of heights. But somewhere in the past year and a half, the mountain and I had come to an understanding: if the mountain promised not to fall down on my shop, then I would reciprocate and not fall off the mountain. It wasn't my favorite place to be, but it was quiet, and the hike up from the parking lot gave me time to think.

Fall was upon us. Up on Hunchback I was surrounded by green pine trees, but the farms and orchards spreading out below me created a rich tapestry in warm hues of red, orange, and yellow. A smoky haze hung over the Hollownoggin Valley as orchardists burned their piles of prunings. Winter was on its way and I shivered in the chilly air.

It was almost two years since I had opened Slim Shambles Auto Repair, and a lot of things had changed. My business was thriving and growing by the month. Judging from their waistlines, my staff was doing the same. I made a note to cut back on the donut intake.

On the financial side, we weren't doing too badly. Basil's equipment loan was paid off, and I now had a proper line of credit with the bank.

There was even a little bit of money hidden in the savings account that only my wife knew about – Cookie did our books, and very wisely kept me in the dark about a few things. If there was money around when the tool truck came into sight, she knew what would happen.

But for the past couple of months I'd been plagued with thoughts that there was something more I needed to do. Looking down on my shop far below, I could see the frantic activity buzzing around it: the customers driving in and out; young Rodney roaring up to the back door with a delivery; my staff working on vehicles outside because there was no room in the shop. I especially noticed Dutchy's tow truck pulling out from his own shop across the road, and driving slowly past mine as he made sure we didn't slough off and fall short on our monthly rent. That's when the realization hit me – that wasn't my shop down there; it was Dutchy's.

Oh sure, it was my business and they were my customers. It was my staff and they were using my equipment. But it had a strange feel to it all, a feeling of transition, of something 'in between'. Suddenly I knew what was bothering me. It was time to take a risk and move on to the next level.

It was the same sort of feeling I had when I asked Cookie to marry me…

"And here you go, Mr. Shambles." Crystal Jangles smiled sweetly as she slid the sales invoice across the top of the glass display case. "Will that be cash or credit card?"

"Credit card," I said, holding out the thin piece of plastic as I took one last look at the invoice total. Suddenly I froze.

"Uh, Mr. Shambles," said Crystal, as she tugged on my card. "You're going to have to let go first…" But I couldn't let go; my fingers were locked tight. Not because of the price – outrageous as it was – but because of what it meant. It had just dawned on me that I was taking the biggest gamble of my life.

This was an engagement ring I was buying, and I was about to offer it to Cookie McDream, a girl I'd been dating for only six months. It occurred to me that I might be rushing things.

What if Cookie said no? What if she laughed in my face, thinking it was just another one of my silly jokes? What if I had to return the ring and ask for my money back? I'd never be able to show my face in the mall again. I'd be a marked man, skulking from pillar to post to avoid the jewelry store staff, who would surely point me out as 'the guy who got turned down.'

By now Crystal had her letter opener out and was prying my fingers loose from my credit card, one paralyzed digit at a time. She forced a tight smile. "I'll be right back with your receipt."

I had trouble walking in a straight line when I left the mall; the small ring case in my pocket had me drifting to the left. It was heavier than it looked – or was that just how it felt to me? I briefly thought about taking it back, but I knew that was hopeless. There was no way around it: I was hooked on Cookie McDream, and there would be no rest until I asked her to marry me. With a determined *crack*, I straightened my spine and picked up my step. *Alright, Slim-bo – let's get 'er done.*

Cookie and I had a date arranged for that night. Her parents were out of town, so once again I was being treated to another wonderful homemade meal at Cookie's house. We'd be alone for the evening, the perfect opportunity to pop the question.

"How is your dinner, Slim?" asked Cookie with concern.

"Huh, what?" She had startled me out of my reverie. "Oh, the food's great...just marvelous!"

"Really?" she said doubtfully. "You seem distracted."

I tried to focus on what she was saying. "Distracted? Uh, why do you say that?"

"Because you're chewing your napkin," she replied. "Was the meat really that tough?"

As we washed up the dishes later, it only got worse. "Slim, tell you what...after you've dried the dishes, just leave them on the table. I'll put them away later."

"It's no problem," I protested. "I really don't mind."

"I know," said Cookie. "But mom will never find her silverware if you keep putting it in the microwave."

Finally the dishes were done and we found ourselves in the living room, where I pulled out my guitar and played a couple of songs to set the mood. Hidden in my guitar case was a small hand-carved wooden ring box, one that I'd picked up during my travels in Europe the year before. I had bought it in anticipation of such a time as this, although back then I didn't even have a girlfriend.

Drawing a deep breath, I put away my guitar and took the ring box out of its hiding place. I knelt down before Cookie as she sat on the couch. "Here," I said simply. "This is for you."

Cookie was speechless as she took the small box and opened it. She drew in her breath as the diamond ring sparkled in the light. "Oh Slim, it's beautiful," she said softly. "I…I don't know what to say…"

"Well, I thought that might be a problem," I replied, reaching quickly into my back pocket. "So I wrote down a few appropriate responses. Feel free to use whichever one best…"

The sudden ringing of the telephone interrupted the moment…and the moment was lost. We sat in awkward silence as it rang a few more times, and then Cookie excused herself to go answer it. The ring box stayed behind on the coffee table.

I could hear her side of the conversation from where I sat, and it didn't sound good. "Oh, hello Woody…yes, it's nice to hear from you, too." She paused. "What's that…? Go out with you for lunch… tomorrow? Well, I don't know…yes, it has been a long time and…" I quit listening at that point. Woody was an old friend from high school, someone Cookie had known long before I came along. Now he was back in town. I hadn't met the creep…er, the guy, but I was pretty sure I didn't like him.

After an eternity, Cookie came back into the living room. She seemed distracted. "Um, that was…"

"I know…I could hear…"

"Yeah…well, he was wondering if…"

"You probably should…it's been a long…"

"Well, a few years, yes…and so I hope you…"

"No problem…have a wonderful…"

"You, too." Cookie looked up at me, and then away. It was time to leave.

I slowly walked out to my truck and angrily tossed my guitar case in the back. What was I thinking? Of course Cookie wouldn't want someone like me. Sure, I could make her laugh, though most of that was unintentional. But she deserved more than that.

When I thought about it rationally, how could I compete with old boyfriends, and with people she'd grown up around and gone to school with? Heck, I was still unsure of where I even stood with her parents, and it was obvious I didn't fit the family mold. Slim Shambles was a goof, a lark, someone to have a good time with – not someone to grow old with.

Climbing into the cab, I took the ring box out of my pocket and looked at it. "Let's face it, Shambles – you don't belong here." It was a long drive home to Narymatter.

For the next couple of days I stayed as far away from Cookie as possible, especially in my mind. I worked on my truck, helped Pa with chores around the orchard, and basically threw myself at anything that prevented me from having to think.

I even put in some extra hours at work, but when I came home late Monday night, Ma was waiting up for me. "Cookie called," she said, studying me closely. Ma didn't know what was going on exactly, but she could guess. "She'd like you to call back."

I opened the refrigerator and took out the milk container. "Sure," I said, pouring myself a glass. "I'll take care of it."

But I didn't. Three days had passed since I'd laid my heart out on my sleeve and the bloodstains were still fresh. I was tired, and not in the mood to hear about Cookie's lunch with Mr. Blockhead, or to hear her explain why she didn't want to marry me, nice guy that I was, yadda yadda yadda. So I went to bed instead.

But driving to work the next morning, it was impossible to keep Cookie out of my mind. Inside, I knew she'd done nothing wrong, and that it wasn't fair to blame her for being honest about her feelings. Entering the town limits of Slumberland, I realized that it was important for Cookie to have closure on the whole thing – I owed her that much – and so on a sudden impulse I hit the brakes and turned off the highway. I shifted into low gear and rumbled quietly down the street and around the corner to where she lived. There was a light on in the kitchen, indicating that Cookie was up and would soon be leaving for work. With a sigh, I turned off the ignition and got out. I was halfway up the sidewalk when the front door opened. Cookie stood in the doorway, her eyes searching my face as she watched me approach.

"Thanks for coming," she said, looking up at me with a nervous smile. "I…I didn't know if you would."

I shuffled my feet and looked at my watch. "Yeah, well…figured I should at least stop by…you did call the other night and…"

Cookie stopped me. "Slim, there's something I need to say." *Oh boy,* I thought – *here it comes.*

She looked down for a moment. "I was…" She paused and looked up. "I was wondering if I could still have that ring?"

From what Cookie told me later, I'd been stewing and fretting needlessly all weekend, that choosing me over Stickbrain had been…well, a no-brainer.

"I *was* a little concerned that we'd only been going together for six months," she began thoughtfully.

"Okay," I said. "I can understand that. People are complicated, and it takes time to get to know someone…"

"Exactly what I was thinking," continued Cookie. "But then I remembered that you are not like other guys – I had you all figured out by our second date. So really, what was I waiting for?" She smiled at me. "Feel better?"

I gulped. "I think so."

What was I waiting for? That was the question Cookie had struggled with back then, and now I was struggling with it too. It was time to take my business to another level, and for me that meant one thing: it was time to build my own shop. But where? And how?

I looked down from my rocky perch and noticed something I hadn't noticed before. There in the distance, somebody was moving dirt on a vacant lot. *Hmm, and a pretty big lot at that.* Having received my epiphany, it was time to descend from the mountain.

Twenty minutes later I pulled over to the side of the road at a spot halfway between my shop and the town center. Digger Dan was manipulating his excavator around the large muddy construction site as he leveled out the high spots and filled in the lower marshy areas with rock and gravel. I got out and went up to the fence. "Hey, Dan!" I called, waving my hands over my head. "What's going on here?"

Dan climbed down out of his machine and squelched his way through the mud. "Spriggs and Portly are putting up a mini-storage," he said. "I'm supposed to turn this mess into something they can build on."

I looked at the size of the lot. It was huge. "Are they gonna use all the land?"

Dan wiped some dirt off his hands. "Funny you should ask. I heard 'em saying just yesterday that they wanna sell off a corner lot. Give 'em a call."

It didn't take me long to find out that, yes, Spriggs and Portly Contractors would sell me a half acre corner lot, and for a reasonable price at that. The more difficult trick was finding the money to buy it with.

I sat at our kitchen table the following morning, dejected and deflated. I'd tried to squeeze some funds out of Lewis Change, my banker, but Old Lewis doesn't squeeze well. Cookie sat down and looked at me. "You really need to do this, don't you?"

I pushed my cold porridge around with a spoon. "If I don't, I'll always regret it." I sighed. "But I just don't know where we're going to find the money."

Cookie chuckled. "Okay, Shambles, you win. We've got enough money put aside to pay for the lot, though I don't know how we'll be able to build anything." She patted my hand reassuringly. "But I'm sure you'll figure that out."

Cookie sat there for a moment longer, looking at me thoughtfully. Finally she said, "Slim, you knew I'd go along with spending all of our savings on an empty lot, didn't you?"

I tried to look surprised. "What? I don't know what you're talking about, honey."

She gazed into my eyes, a humorous twinkle in her own. "It reminds me of the day I said I would marry you. You had the ring with you, right in your coat pocket. In fact, I'll bet you carried that ring with you all weekend."

I looked away. "Um…and why would I have done that?"

Cookie grinned mischievously. "Because in spite of how you act, I think you know me better than you let on. I'll bet you even knew back then that I'd agree to marry you eventually."

I looked into her bright blue eyes…and just smiled.